RED GAMBIT

BOOK ONE OF THE HARVESTERS SERIES

LUKE MITCHELL

Cover design by Yocla Designs

Cover illustration by Hokunin

Editing by Lisa Poisso

Thank you for reading.

CHAPTER ONE

The Rath was a real charmer, Rachel decided as she drew up beside the sputtering neon sign. Every bit the kind of establishment she'd been expecting.

Somehow, the air outside the dingy pub felt even muggier than everywhere else in the dilapidated town. But maybe that was simply her imagination—a manifestation of her disdain for the sickly green tint of grimy alley lights and the mixture of muffled voices, bad music, and pungent odors wafting out of the pub.

"A real charmer," she confirmed to the empty alleyway, running her thumb along one of the glyphs etched into the light gray surface of her staff.

A hint of a breeze ruffled a few wavy strands of her dirty-blond hair, but she hardly noticed as she closed her eyes and sank into a deep focus. Time to see what she was about to walk into.

She directed her thoughts toward the sounds and the smells of The Rath, guiding nebulous tendrils of her mind outward as she had a million times before.

The inside of the pub took shape under her extended senses. A greasy haze of smoke permeated the place, accentuated by the clinking of glass mugs on wooden tabletops and drunken slurs that she felt more than heard. The smoke poured most heavily from one table in particular, where six men sat awash in a sea of cigars and drinks, playing cards.

"C'mon, Jim," one of them, a hulking gorilla of a man, was saying. She focused in.

The big guy scratched at his head and tapped the excess ash of his cigar into an empty mug. "If you're gonna play with yourself between hands, at least have the decency to leave the table and let us have on with it."

"Piss off, ya wanker," another—Jim, she supposed—replied in a bad imitation of the big guy's thick English accent. "Have someplace to be tonight, do ya?"

"Give us a minute to call your wife, and I'll let ya know at that."

A low rumble of laughter made its way around the table as Jim shook his head and began dealing out cards. The men carried on, verbally deprecating one another between swigs from their heavy mugs.

She swept on with her extended senses.

Near the card game, two men nursed drinks at a smaller table. Across the room, a man tapped his greasy fingers at the touchscreen of an ancient jukebox, which proceeded to wheeze out an unfortunate tune from the early 2000s.

"Christ, Darrel," someone called, "can'tcha pick something from this half of the century?"

Another round of chuckles filled the pub. There hadn't exactly been an outpouring of contemporary music since the Catastrophe.

Two more men at the bar, not counting the bartender behind the thick wooden counter. A dozen men inside, assuming no one was cloaked from her senses. Another quick sweep told her that every single one of them was packing, save for the bartender, whose sawed-off double-barrel shotgun was stowed under the bar and technically not on his person.

Shit.

She drew the tendrils of her mind back home and opened her eyes, her senses shifting back to her own sweaty palms and dry mouth. It wasn't as if she'd been expecting to find a roomful of well-mannered gentlemen sharing an evening of lively debate, but that didn't make her any happier about walking into a den of armed assholes.

Michael had been missing for nearly a week now, and if that punk from earlier had been right (which was, admittedly, highly debatable), this dive was her best bet of finding out why.

Cursing her brother for having run off in the first place, she pushed open the door of The Rath.

Inside, the big guy must have been faring poorly at cards. His thick voice was the first thing she heard. "Son of a—"

He paused as she stepped through the doorway, presumably to turn along with every other head in the bar and get a look at the tiny blond chick who'd just walked in. She didn't need to gauge their expressions to know that very few outsiders, small blondes or otherwise, casually walked into this place. Especially not outsiders carrying glyph-covered staves.

Her eyes settled on the gorilla in the cheap suit she took to be the closest thing to a boss in the room. Focusing on one man instead of a dozen was a hell of a lot less daunting, and if she ended up needing to make a point, starting with the biggest and baddest was probably her best bet.

The big guy stared right back, a hint of amusement creeping onto his round face. "My heart alive. Whatever brings you to this side a town, little sweetling? Do you know where you are?"

Her throat initiated a dry swallow without her leave. She bit down, steeling herself. "I'm looking for someone. I think you boys might be able to help me."

The tension in the room was palpable as the men exchanged looks, then eased as they reached the unspoken agreement that a lone girl couldn't possibly pose a threat. Shoulders relaxed, and hands shifted away from the weapons they'd gravitated toward upon her unexpected entrance. A few men went back to their drinks. She started to hope, and then—

"I'll help you here, sweetie."

The asshole at the bar leaned back and patted his lap. "Why don't you come tell ol' Darrel what it is you want?"

Why did they always have to go there? She wrinkled her nose, glancing around to take in the dozen stares that bored at her from all around, waiting to see what kind of prey she was.

"Why don't you fuck off, Darrel?" She shifted her gaze back to the suited gorilla at the table and hoped that would be the end of it.

It wasn't.

Wood creaked, and the faces in front of her took on hungry expressions as they watched ol' Darrel rise from his barstool behind her.

"Well look at the pretty little mouth on this one," Darrel said, loud enough that the room could hear and share in his stupid chuckle.

So it was going to be like that, then. He'd staked his claim, and now he couldn't let it drop.

With slow deliberation, she shifted her staff toward the giant dick resembling a man named Darrel and reached out with her mind to form a channel between the battery packs on her belt and the fist-shaped glyph on her staff.

Darrel took a step toward her.

She unleashed her gathered energy, and he flew backward as if he'd been struck in the chest by an invisible battering ram. He toppled messily over the bar, colliding with the bartender on the other side. Both men went down in a tangle of limbs and undignified noises.

The others were off their barstools in an instant, digging for their weapons. From behind, there was an ensemble of rustling fabric, sliding chairs, and mechanical cocking sounds. She didn't need to extend her senses to know she would find the rest of the weapons in the pub pointing at her.

A long, tense silence stretched out as the pub's denizens took her in with fresh eyes. She turned back, commanding her suddenly wobbly legs to get their shit together and resisting the urge to look everywhere at once. More by nerves than design, some of the energy she held ready bled out around her, rustling her hair in the still air.

The men scarcely moved—a tighter grip on a weapon here, an uncertain glance at a neighbor there.

"Tom . . ." One of the men at the card table eyed the suited gorilla from behind his raised pistol.

The big guy—Tom, apparently—silenced his man with a raised hand, his beady eyes studying her all the while. "Who the hell might you be then, love?" All traces of amusement were gone.

She met his stare. "Someone who's looking for Michael Carver. And in case it was unclear, when I said I thought you might be able to help"—she tilted her staff toward him—"what I meant is that you're going to help me."

Tom considered the staff for a long moment. Then he began to chuckle, low and steady, and looked around at his fellow thugs. "Right then, gents. I reckon the King'll be wanting a word with this one."

Her stomach fell at his words, and then it plunged through the floor when he pointed at her, his eyes taking on an eager glint.

"Take her."

She squeezed her eyes shut and clamped her free hand over them, then raised her staff and channeled energy to two of its glyphs. Pins and needles crackled through her body, and the room exploded with a blinding flash of white light and a deafening bang.

Everyone staggered back in disoriented confusion—everyone except Rachel. She pushed through a wave of channeling fatigue, past the ringing in her ears, and struck while she had the chance.

She shifted her grip and brought the staff down on the head of the closer of the two at the bar. The staff kicked in her hands, a dull thunk of bone and sinew she felt more than heard. She spun and cracked a heavy blow over the other man. Through her boots, she felt the thump of bodies hitting the floorboards.

The men by the card table were regaining their senses.

"Shoot the bitch!" Tom roared. He pointed a shiny, oversized pistol at her.

She jabbed her staff toward them and focused her will once again. A low thrum rushed through the air, and a wave of unseen force plowed into Tom and two of his companions. They sprawled to the ground, upsetting the table and taking two more men down in a mess of limbs, broken glass, and spilled beer.

She trained her staff on the three men still standing with sawed-off shotguns and a revolver all raised her way. They hesitated, looking around uncertainly at their battered colleagues.

She turned back to Tom, resisting the urge to shake her head clear. That last telekinetic blast had left dark spots in her vision, but now wasn't the time to let them see her vulnerability. She raised a hand, fixed her mind on the big gorilla, and pulled.

Tom sailed through the air and slammed heavily against the solid wood of the bar, sending two bar stools crashing to the floor.

She strode over to him, trying not to stumble from exhaustion. "Where is he?"

Tom tried to lunge for her, and she drew the necessary energy to slam him back to the bar. He snarled a curse and spit at her. She punched him in the groin. He bucked and gave a furious yowl, but when he tried to move again, she kept him pinned to the bar with her mind.

"Where is he, asshole?" she said, her face only inches from his.

A gunshot roared from the direction of the overturned card table, shockingly loud in the enclosed space of the pub. She whipped around in time to see the dull bullet that had snapped to a halt in midair a few feet from her head. It dropped impotently to the ground.

She extended an open hand toward the shooter. The man's revolver drove back into his face hard enough to send him toppling onto the table behind with a pained grunt. The two guys beside him recoiled at a look from her.

Tom's eyes were wide with disbelief—or maybe terror—as she turned back to face him. She suppressed a shiver at the sudden coolness of the air around her and faced him as calmly as her adrenaline-soaked brain would allow.

So the bullet catcher worked. But now wasn't the time to celebrate.

She made a show of carefully holding the end of her staff over Tom's right foot as if preparing to drive it down. "Where is he?"

He tried to raise his hands and found them secured by invisible bindings. "All right, Jesus, all right. Word is, a week or two ago, Carver and his mate managed to get their mitts on somethin' that wasn't theirs to trot off with. Somethin' big—a shipment from the Red King straight to the Overlord, word is."

"And?" She glanced around to check that the room's stunned obedience was holding.

"Well, the King wanted it back, didn't he? He went after them two. Nabbed Carver and killed Huxley trying to do the same to him, I heard . . ." He frowned as if he'd only just realized he was still talking. "That's all you're gonna get here, love. That's as much as any of these lummoxes know."

This sounded bad. Beyond bad. What the hell had Michael gotten himself into?

"Where do I find this Red King?"

His brow furrowed and his mouth opened and closed a couple of times. Then he glanced around the pub, apparently looking for a partner to share in his disbelief. "Christ, love, you're not from around here, are ya?"

She scowled and punched him in the groin again. "Clearly I'm on holiday, asshole. Now where do I find him?"

Once he got past his indignant yowl of pain and colorful stream of curses, he began to chuckle, shaking his head. "You'll find him at the Red Fortress, you crazy bitch. Across the river—old industrial area. Be my guest and hop on over."

She gave him a long, measuring glare and turned to leave. No one said a word.

When she reached the door, she released her hold on Tom. He snarled a curse and rushed for her back, yelling something about her having the balls to walk into his joint and disrespect his authority.

She spun on her heel and, with one last effort of will, hurled Tom back to join the men on the floor behind the bar. Then she walked out of the pin-drop silence of The Rath and into the muggy Newark night.

CHAPTER TWO

The first thing Jarek noticed when he woke to the vibration of his comm was the deep ache behind his eye sockets, throbbing in time with his pulse. The second thing he noticed, squinting with bleary eyes through the familiar soft red lighting of the ship cabin, was the dark shape of the rectangular bottle on the nearby dresser.

"Come to papa," he mumbled, leaning over the edge of his cot to reach for the whiskey.

"Isn't it a bit early for a drink, sir?" The smooth voice with a light English accent came from the cabin speakers.

"Aren't you a bit nosy for a robot?"

And wasn't it nighttime anyway? A glance up to the cockpit windshield confirmed as much. He managed to snag the bottle without falling off the cot and flopped back down to tip the remainder of the fiery liquid into his dry, sleep-stained mouth.

"Would that I could look away, sir."

"Pshhh. You'd miss me in a heartbeat. Or, you know, a CPU pulse. Or whatever."

"An immaculate comparison, sir."

"Yeah." Jarek frowned as he raised his left wrist to glance at the comm that had buzzed him awake. "Remind me again where we landed on dialing down that sarcasm setting of yours?"

The message from Pryce was simple enough, but it set his heart beating faster: "Possible lead on our girl. Stop by."

Could this be it? Would they finally find Fela?

"I believe it was right at the conclusion that I don't have a sarcasm setting, sir," Al said.

He snapped his fingers in mock letdown. "Clearly those computer jockeys had no idea what they were unleashing on the world."

Al sniffed, an affectation that was completely unnecessary for a digital construct. "Some called me the crowning achievement of the twenty-first century, you know."

"Oh, I remember." He slid off the cot and pulled on a dark, long-sleeved Henley and a pair of brown cargo pants. "And then all those pesky nukes had to come rocketing down to steal your thunder."

He added a pair of socks and boots, ran a hand through his dark, disheveled hair, and blew out a long sigh. "What if it's just another dead end?"

"Then we'll keep looking, sir. We'll find Fela. And if we don't, life will go on nonetheless."

"Not for long, if I keep running around in squishy meat suit form. And besides, how can you say that, man? Fela's our home—yours even more than mine."

"Much as I would delight at being whole again, sir, I feel compelled to point out that an armored exosuit doesn't do us much good if you die retrieving it."

Jarek closed his eyes and rubbed at his temples. "What the hell else am I supposed to do?"

"Live," Al said without hesitation. "Farm, hunt, find a special friend. Settle down. You know, the human thing."

Jarek snorted and went to buckle on his gun belt and sling his sword over his right shoulder. "Yeah, how's that working out for the rest of the world?" He slapped the ship's rear hatch release. "Besides," he added, slipping in an earpiece as the boarding ramp lowered with an electronic hum, "what do I need friends for when I have you, buddy?"

Al sighed in his ear. "I'll inform Pryce you're on your way, sir."

Pistols within easy reach at mid-thigh and sword securely strapped at his back, Jarek descended from the ship and into the muggy night.

Pryce's shop—or his emporium, or whatever the hell the old madman happened to be calling it—was located in the old West Ward, part of the area most Newarkers simply called the 'Skirts these days. It wasn't that far of a walk to the sparse little community. Given the muggy warmth of the night, Jarek was glad for its proximity.

He only passed two people along the way. Both of them rushed indoors when they saw him, one into a crappy apartment building and the other into a crude shanty.

The shanties that had sprung up in the aftermath of the Catastrophe fifteen years past had slowly grown into more permanent structures as their inhabitants came to the realization that things were not simply going to snap back to the way they'd been anytime soon. Granted, most of the buildings in Newark weren't in much better shape. Some shining souls had banded together and done their best to repair what they could with what resources they could scrounge together, but between the lack of any real government and the persistent threat of roaming marauders, the drive to restore society to its pre-Catastrophe splendor had been a slow one at best.

They probably had the vamps (or the raknoth, as Pryce insisted on calling them) to thank for that. He shook his head, wondering what sick twist of cosmic fate had brought those vicious things to Earth, as he turned a dark street corner and approached his destination.

"Young master Slater," Pryce said as Jarek stepped into the shop.

The small front room was relatively empty aside from the counter that Pryce was fiddling behind and the bulletin board that hung on the wall. The board displayed a mixture of odd jobs, bounties, and resumes of all shapes and sizes. As much of a hodgepodge as the board was, Jarek knew it was nothing compared to the smorgasbord of supplies in the back room where Pryce kept his proper shop.

"Got your message," he said, pulling the metal door closed behind him. "What did you hear?"

A knowing smile crinkled the older man's forehead underneath the ludicrous set of round goggles strapped there. Above all else, Jay Pryce was a scholar and a tinkerer. He never liked to wander too far without his goggles, just in case he should need to make use of a power tool or a welding torch or any other ocularly unfriendly device. Coupled with the greasy, tool-stuffed shop apron he so often wore, the thin, bushy wisps of white hair exploding from under the bands of his goggles left Pryce looking every bit the mad scientist he actually was.

"It seems," Pryce said, "that the Resistance may be involved—to your delight, I'm sure."

"This is my 'jumping for joy' face," Jarek said, carefully setting his dark eyes and strong jaw in a flat expression. "Can't you tell?"

Pryce grinned and stepped around the counter to offer him a battered canteen of water, then paused, sniffed at the air, and wrinkled his nose. "Or perhaps something a bit stronger?"

"That's a pretty astute schnoz you got there, old-timer."

"A congested anosmic could smell the booze on you from across the room."

Rather than ask what the hell an anosmic was, Jarek swiped the canteen from Pryce's hand and took a long pull of cool, clean water. "I'm going to choose to take that as a compliment. So who do I need to talk to, then? Huxley? Johnson? Please say Huxley. He's the only one of those Resistance a-holes I can almost stand." He smacked the canteen onto the counter in a flurry of droplets. "And what do you mean, they may be involved? What did you hear exactly?"

Pryce studied him with a mild frown. "How old are you now, son? Twenty-five?"

"Twenty-six. So about a quarter your age, if my calculations are in line."

Pryce rolled his eyes at that. "I know you've been through the shit and there and back again more times than I can count, and with no one but Al beside you, but—"

Here they went again. "Ah Christ, man. Look, forgive me if I decide to have a drink or two while I wait around for something to pop up. How else am I supposed to tolerate being stuck in the ship with Al?"

Al directed his indignant sniff through the comm speaker so Pryce could hear as well. "It's technically me who's stuck there with you, sir."

"Yeah, yeah," Jarek said, flapping his fingers and shaking his head for Pryce to see. A smile warred with the frown on Pryce's face. "Come on, Pryce. Give me a break and tell me what's up. Just don't tell me the freaking Resistance has her."

"Not as far as I know. To answer your previous question, though, I hear Johnson hung up his hat, and Huxley . . ." A shadow crossed over his face. "Huxley is dead, allegedly by the Reds' doing."

"Shit. Sorry to hear that."

"At any rate, it's probably Huxley's understudy you need to talk to. Michael Carver, I believe it is."

"Double shit," Jarek said, wrinkling his nose. "That boy scout? You think he knows where Fela's at?"

"Maybe," Pryce said. "Maybe not. Someone was in here a few days ago saying that Carver and Huxley intercepted something of prodigious value bound for the Overlord himself. No one seems to know much beyond that."

Jarek absentmindedly picked up the device Pryce had been working on. He wasn't sure exactly what it was, but that wasn't uncommon in Pryce's shop. "You think it was Fela?"

"Could be. I'm guessing the guys who nabbed Fela when you were —what was it again?"

Jarek narrowed his eyes at the device. "Decompressing."

"Ah yes, decompressing. Well, it stands to reason that they were either Reds themselves or in league with them, and we know who's at the top of that booty chain. If Fela was headed anywhere, it feasibly could've been on that shipment."

And yet Pryce was only thinking to tell him this now, days after he'd heard the news?

"Something else happen tonight?"

"You bet your pasty ass it did!" Pryce said, putting on his unreasonably excited scholar face. "This is where it gets good. According to the gents I just talked to, a little blond woman blew through The Rath earlier tonight looking for Carver. Cute too, they said."

That was interesting. The Rath was a real shithole, typically full of uninspired but dangerous thugs. As delightful as it would've been to watch a cute blonde kick The Rath's ass, though, he didn't really see why this mattered.

"I think we have an arcanist on our hands!" Pryce said.

Jarek looked up from the device in his hands. "An arcanist? Seriously?"

Pryce nodded, looking like he might simply burst with excitement. "No one at The Rath had the fuzziest about what the hell they'd really seen, of course, but judging from the descriptions . . ." He shrugged.

"And so the plot thickens," Jarek said. "Wait, why would this chick be looking for Carver there?"

"Oh, right. I may have forgot to mention that Carver was allegedly captured by the Reds earlier this week."

"Well, triple shit, old man!" Jarek cried, throwing his hands up. "You couldn't have started with the bit where the guy with the info is locked up in the damn Red Fortress?"

"In hindsight, I do see where that seems problematic. And it sounds like the clock's ticking on this one."

He tossed the electrical whatever back to the countertop, much to Pryce's irritation. "Jesus. Even if I could figure out a way to get to him before they kill him, assuming they haven't already, it's not much to go on."

"You're right. Better go follow all those other leads of yours. Maybe you can stroll right into the big city and ask nicely."

"Please don't encourage him," Al said.

Jarek smiled as a strategy crystallized, and he began to unfasten his gun belt. "Yeah, about that—you mind holding my hardware for a day or two, old-timer?"

Pryce frowned. "Why do I suddenly feel an ominous sense of déjà vu?"

"Sir," Al added, "if you're thinking what I think you're thinking, I really must protest."

"Imagine my shock," Jarek said.

"You should try listening to Alfred for a change," Pryce said. "You'd live a lot longer—probably still have Fela too."

"Guys," Jarek said. He turned his hands palm up with the gun belt still hanging from the one. "It's totally different this time. I'm older, wiser. All that bullshit."

"We could find another way, sir," Al said. "Perhaps the Resistance would be willing to—"

"I'd rather have a round of fisticuffs with the Red King in my birthday suit than work with those idealistic idiots." He removed his sword and offered it to Pryce with the guns.

Pryce scowled but took the weapons. "Guess I won't waste my breath trying." His expression darkened as Jarek removed his earpiece and comm and handed those over as well. "You're sure about this?"

Jarek shrugged. "It'll all just end up in some asshole's hands when they take me in."

"I wasn't talking about the damn comm. This is ballsy, son. Even for you."

He raised a hand as if to say *What's one to do?*

"It's only an exosuit, sir," Al said quietly. "It's not worth dying for."

"That's our home, Al. Of course it's worth it. Christ, you're still in there, man—the real you. Did you forget?"

The heat in his own voice almost surprised him. Almost.

"Of course not," Al said. "Just . . . Don't leave me alone here, sir. I don't want to be a ship forever."

"Just keep her warm for me, buddy. I'll be back."

"Be careful," Pryce said as Jarek grabbed the door handle.

"Don't ask me to start now, man," he said, pausing to look back. "You'll just get me all confused."

THE WALK THIS TIME WAS considerably further, which was unfortunate. Deciding to pull a risky move was one thing. Deciding and then having to walk a few miles toward the impending unpleasantness—that was something more. As much as he liked to play it cool, Jarek couldn't deny the anxious fear dancing in the pit of his stomach. He was walking into the belly of the beast, essentially naked. Ballsy he might be, but he wasn't crazy enough to do it without breaking a bit of a sweat.

But what choice did he have?

He needed to get Fela back. If there was a chance Michael Carver could help him do that, then he needed to get to Carver. Al could insist all he wanted that Fela was only an exosuit and they could survive without her, but Jarek wasn't buying it. Fela had been their shelter for fifteen years now. She'd seen them through thick and thin. Fela was more than an exosuit. She was a part of him, and more than a part of Al. More than anything, she was theirs, dammit, and he was going to take her back.

After half an hour's trek through the summer night, he arrived at The Rath. Perspiration ran down his forehead and soaked through his shirt. A light breeze breathed over him, and he delighted in the cool relief as he stopped at the mouth of the alley to focus up. The smell in the alleyway implored his nose to wrinkle, but he forced himself into practiced composure as he approached the pub's entrance.

He wasn't the same frightened kid he'd been the last time he'd walked into this shithole. And he was going to get Fela back.

Grumbling voices carried through the door, along with the subtler sound of broken glass being swept across a wooden floor.

He pushed open the door, and an amused smile spread over his face at the overturned furniture and the clearly disgruntled denizens. "I'll be damned," he mumbled.

He'd heard stories about arcanists—their alleged existence happened to be one of Pryce's favorite topics—but he'd never taken them for more than that. They were stories, legends. The scene before him didn't prove anything mystical was at work, but it was certainly interesting.

Every eye in the room turned his way as he stepped through the doorway. He wasn't surprised to see half the men's weapons follow a second later.

"Gentlemen." He nodded amicably to the room at large, doing his best to ignore the guns and keep the grin on his face wide and easy. "I'm looking for a friend of mine. I hear he's a hot topic here tonight." His gaze fell on the big guy sitting at the bar in a cheap, worn-out suit. Distant, unpleasant memories scratched at the edges of his mind. "It's Tom, right? Care to help a brother out?"

Big Tom had been the only one in the pub who hadn't turned to look when he walked in, but the glare he shot Jarek now more than made up for the initial neglect.

"You," he said, clearly taking his own walk down memory lane. "Jarek Fucking Slater."

At the sound of his name, several men tensed and eyed him with renewed wariness, their weapons shifting from his general direction to his chest and head.

He couldn't help but smile at the reaction. "Long time, big guy. Care to help an old pal find Michael Carver?"

"Right, then." Tom looked around the room. "Tie the fucker up, lads."

CHAPTER THREE

J arek was no stranger to tight spaces. Having spent most of his teenage and adult life in a full-body exosuit, he might even be considered the world's leading expert. Somehow, that expertise didn't make riding between the two beefy thugs in the back seat of a cramped SUV any more comfortable. It didn't help that his hands were tied behind his back—or that both men stank, but he probably wasn't in a place to point fingers at the moment.

Luckily, they didn't have far to go, and after a brief holdup at the gate, they were permitted into the Red Fortress.

Beefy Thug Number One slid out of the SUV to the left. Jarek waited for Tom to turn his beady-eyed gaze into the back seat and tell him to move. No reason to waste energy riling up this crew when it would probably buy him nothing but a sucker punch or a nice little backhand. Tom and his gang would likely turn him over to the Reds inside, and then it would be time to start the head games.

He slid out of the SUV and stood waiting as Tom and the rest of his goons piled out and moved into formation around him.

"Right," Tom said. "Stick with us, then, and keep those hands where we can see 'em."

Jarek clenched his jaw and bit down on his wiseass reply. Apparently, his amusement still bled through to his expression.

Tom frowned. His eyes flicked down to Jarek's bound hands, then back up to his face.

"Smart-ass prick." He let loose with a backhand.

Jarek leaned back just enough that the blow whooshed past. Beefy Thugs One and Two grabbed him by the arms and shoulders and held him still as a frustrated Tom gathered himself and clocked him right between the eyes.

His vision exploded in a kaleidoscope of whites and reds, coalescing and fading into black spots as concussive disorientation began to resolve into deep, throbbing pain along his nose. He shook his head, knowing it would do little to clear his vision, and allowed a small grin to spread over his mouth. So much for avoiding the backhand and the sucker punch.

"Called it," he said quietly.

"What?" Tom said, half-raising his fist again.

"I said good hit." He stared pointedly past his throbbing nose to the enormous building beyond, hoping the gorilla would remember why they were here and drop it.

Tom gave a satisfied nod and waved his thugs on. In the pre-Catastrophe era, the Red Fortress must have been a massive factory of some sort, but it had since been heavily added to and fortified until it loomed over Newark, threatening and formidable from across the Passaic River.

They were admitted through the heavy front doors without too much of a fuss, then shuttled promptly down a sprawling network of drab, harshly lit concrete hallways.

No wonder the Reds were such a gloomy bunch. And a well-armed gloomy bunch at that. It had been years since he'd seen so much modern firepower in one place. When the smokeless powder had started getting scarce, most of the thugs like the ones at The Rath had fallen back to black powder and manual action firearms. Of course, the scarcity of the good stuff was largely thanks to the hoarding efforts of groups like the Reds, so where Tom's thugs carried shotguns and old revolvers, most of the Reds they passed were armed to the teeth with automatic weapons.

The mundane halls didn't offer much in the way of landmarks, but that was okay. Keeping track of turns and distances was easy enough, and it wasn't like he was planning on trying to make any hasty getaways through the front entrance anyway.

Five or six minutes into their doomy-gloomy march, they came to the brig. It wasn't enormous: twenty steel-barred cells in total, arranged in four clusters of four at the front and middle of the room and a pair of doubles toward the back. A central path divided the room into left and right clusters, which were further divided by two paths that ran perpendicular to the central one.

The cells all seemed to be empty, aside from one in the middle-left cluster. A short, bald guy stood in front of the cell, talking to a prisoner Jarek couldn't see.

A pang of excitement coursed through his chest. This could be it. He'd gotten himself into a pretty significant pickle just for the chance to see what Michael Carver knew about his suit. If that was Carver up ahead, he'd better be freaking ready to capitalize on the opportunity.

"See ya soon, sweetheart," the bald guy was saying as they drew up to him. "Be thinking about ya."

Baldy turned to face them with light brown eyes that weren't quite right. It was a look Jarek had seen too many times before, the look of the kind of person who'd swung cats by their tails and picked the wings off of flies as a kid. The cold smile Baldy turned on him was the final push that set off the internal alarm.

This guy liked hurting people.

The Reds escorted the group to the next cell down. Baldy watched Jarek like a hungry hyena.

"Got a fresh one for you, ya sick bastard," said one of the escorts.

Jarek paid them little mind. Behind Baldy, in the dirty cell, Michael Carver huddled against the concrete wall like a beaten dog.

Jarek had only interacted with Huxley's protégé in passing, but it wasn't hard to see that he looked like hell. The big dude was curled into an impressively tight ball, and when he looked up, his dark face was ashen and bruised, his lips visibly cracked and caked with bits of dried blood. His eyes were a little wild and disoriented, but they seemed lucid enough as they locked onto him in sudden recognition.

"Yo, Mikey!" Jarek said. "Fancy seeing you here, man. Long time."

Michael ran a hand over his short, bushy crop of dark hair, his movements cautious and twitchy, which wasn't so surprising given the way Baldy was staring at him.

"Yeah, man, been a little tied up."

"Ha!" Jarek turned a wide smile on Baldy. "Tied up . . . See what he did there?"

Baldy stared at him as if he were questioning Jarek's mental stability. Which was probably kind of rich, coming from him. Finally, he shook his head. "Someone lock this idiot up."

"Oh, oh!" Jarek shuffled in place and jutted his head toward the cell opposite Michael's. "Can I have that one?"

Tom let out an irritated growl and stepped toward Jarek, but he froze as a voice called from the brig's entrance, calm and authoritative.

"Calm yourself, Tom."

An athletic-looking guy with a buzzed head and cold eyes strode confidently toward them. In a base full of armed, armored men, his cargo pants and form-fitting T-shirt stood out. Jarek pegged him as Seth Mosen, the Overlord's right-hand man (or at least the closest thing to one who wasn't a raknoth). He'd never had the displeasure of meeting Mosen, but he'd heard a few stories—the kind that elicited dubious frowns and sent chills up spines.

"Jarek Slater," Mosen said, eyeing him with a keener version of Baldy's creepy stare. If the things he'd heard about Mosen were half true, it was more than sadism that was off behind those pale eyes. "The Soldier of Charity himself," he added, splaying his hands in mock awe. "They didn't tell me we had a celebrity on our hands."

"Oh don't sell yourself short, Mosen," Jarek said. "You've got quite the reputation yourself." In a mutter that was still audible, he added, "As a creepy psychopath."

Tom inched closer to Mosen with the air of a dog looking for a treat. "I thought I best let you lot decide how to handle him, what with him being the second one tonight and all."

"And the second-best-looking one at that, from what I've heard," Jarek said, wiggling his eyebrows. "How many of your asses did that little blond girl kick, again?"

Muscles tensed on Tom's neck and jaws, but he bowed his head deferentially as Mosen opened his mouth to speak.

"Normally, I'd say you should use a gag with world-class wiseasses like Slater here, but he raises a fair point. The girl. What happened?"

Tom proceeded to sputter out a story about a young blond woman bursting into The Rath, waving around some kind of pre-Catastrophe tech that let her stop bullets and throw full-grown men around like rag dolls. It sure sounded like the explanation of a baffled guy who'd seen some mind-boggling shit and either knew nothing about arcanists or firmly disbelieved they existed. Pryce was going to do backflips if this panned out.

Jarek didn't miss the way Michael's eyes widened at Tom's story. It stood to reason he might know the chick who was willing to kick an entire bar's ass to track him down, but the fact that she'd decided to even hit The Rath for that information (not to mention the worried recognition in Michael's expression) . . . Something didn't quite add up.

But now wasn't the time to worry about it. Right now, he needed to find a way to talk to Michael before these a-holes pulled one or both of them off for a nice, private torture session.

Mosen's expression was unreadable as Tom concluded his tale.

"Crazy shit, huh?" Jarek sidled up closer to Mosen and leaned into his personal space with a conspiratorial air. "You wanna know what I think, man?"

Mosen looked at him as if he were a particularly stubborn clump of scum caught at the bottom of a drain. "No."

"Because I'll tell you what I think. I'd say that Tommy-boy here—"

Mosen pivoted and drove an open palm into Jarek's chest. The attack was viciously fast and strong, and in the split second leading up to it, Jarek could have sworn Mosen's eyes flashed light red.

Jarek crashed back into the bars of Michael's cell. He managed to keep his chin tucked tightly enough to avoid slamming the back of his head into the bars, but there wasn't much else to be done. He slumped to the floor, back against the bars, as a wave of pain enveloped him, resolving into specific areas across his back and bound arms.

The worst of it was the elbow that had caught a bar full on. "Argh! Why do they call them funny bones? How is this funny?"

"You're an annoying little shit, you know that?" Mosen said. "Without that damn suit, that's all you are."

"Speaking of which," Jarek said, "you haven't seen a stolen exo lying around somewhere, have you?"

For a second, Jarek thought he'd poked too hard and that Mosen might kill him then and there.

Mosen turned on his heel. "Tom. Cutter. A word."

"Ah, come on, guy!" Jarek called after him.

Mosen stopped Tom and Baldy by the next cluster of cells and began speaking in a low tone. Tom's three beefy thugs and the two Reds who'd escorted them to the brig were talking among themselves and trying to eavesdrop on the bosses.

Now or never.

"Yo, Mikey." Jarek spoke quietly over his shoulder without turning around. "How ya holdin' up?"

"Fantastic, obviously," came Michael's voice, equally quiet. "You still in one piece?"

"Got 'em right where I want 'em."

"What?"

"Never mind. I'm looking for my suit. Heard you might know something."

"Wait, did you—"

Shuffling from inside the cell.

"Did you get captured on purpose to ask me about your exosuit, dude?" Michael's voice was closer now.

"Let's just say it's gonna be an embarrassing story if you don't know anything."

Silence. Then, "I might know something."

He froze, pain forgotten. "Tell me."

"Get me out of here."

One of the Reds looked over from the thug huddle. Jarek shot the guy his iciest grin, and the guard turned back to the huddle, uninterested.

"Tell me where to find Fela, and I'll bring back the artillery," he said quietly.

"No, now," Michael said, a hint of frantic desperation in his tone. "Get us out now, or no deal. You're going to need me with you anyways."

Jarek clenched his jaw. The fact that he would have done the same thing in Michael's position didn't make the demand any less infuriating. "Prove you're not fucking with me, and we can move on to how the shit you propose I do that."

"Huxley hid your suit in his safe with the rest of our score. I don't know where it is, but I know how to find it."

Jarek turned that over, watching Tom waving his hands as if deflecting blame. It wasn't exactly hard proof, but it might have to do. Besides, if he could trust anyone in the room (or in the Resistance), it was probably Michael Carver. From what little he'd seen and heard, the kid was a boy scout through and through.

"Fine. I get us out, you take me to Fela. Deal?"

"Just like that? You're going to trust me?"

"Hell no. Trust is for sissies. But we don't have time—and if you're lying to me, I can always kick your ass later. Win-win."

"Uh, okay then. What's the plan?"

That was the question, wasn't it? He'd always been a let's-see-what-happens kind of guy. He'd played out a few scenarios and escape routes in his head earlier, but those were more fluid possibilities than actual plans, and they sure as shit hadn't involved springing a buddy.

"Well . . ."

"You don't have a plan, do you?"

"Please. What kind of guy walks into an enemy base without a plan?"

A heavy, whooshing sigh from the cell.

The sound of his name drew Jarek's attention to Mosen's private huddle.

"He was asking about Carver, sir," Tom was saying.

Shit. The big idiot.

"What?" Mosen snapped, glancing back toward Michael and Jarek. "And you didn't think to tell me that before you brought him straight to Carver? You!" He pointed at the two Reds standing with Tom's men. "Bring Slater here." He shot Baldy a meaningful look. "We're going to get to the bottom of this right now."

Double shit. Jarek's stomach tightened. Looked like their time was up.

The one upside of having his hands bound behind his back was that he was supremely prepared to shoot Michael a discreet thumbs-up as he said quietly, "Operation Save the Boy Scout commencing. Phase One."

Now all he had to do was figure out what the hell that operation entailed. No big deal.

CHAPTER FOUR

Rachel leaned back from the concrete barrier at the outer edge of the freeway to consider everything she'd observed of the so-called Red Fortress in the past hour.

The place hadn't been hard to find. Between the ten-foot perimeter wall and the small armada of armed men making the rounds within, it was pretty clear the complex was hosting a serious operation. Of course, it wasn't like there was a sign hanging out front. It was still possible she'd stumbled upon the wrong hive of armed goons, but she didn't see any other super-bases in the area.

Had the situation been different, she would have taken her time and done due diligence before engaging in this kind of madness. Actually, scratch that. She would have passed on sticking her neck onto the chopping block and gone home instead, back to Unity, the closest thing to safe one could hope to find these days.

But if Michael was truly in there, that wasn't an option. At least, not until she had him by her side. Once that happened, they would return to Unity even if she had to drag her brother there by his spongy locks.

She tried his comm for what had to be the millionth time in the past week. The call went straight to voice mail like it had every other time. She ended the call with a curse.

How much could she really trust the word of that big gorilla-man Tom? Enough to try slinking into a heavily guarded fortress in the hopes that Michael was really in there? Maybe she could snag one of the patrolmen and pick his brain before she was past the point of no return. Of course, that would introduce a whole new set of risks.

The thought of descending from her perch, of standing and willingly moving into that den of danger, made her want nothing more than to be home, to be in her own bed, safe and secure and content under a pile of blankets. As proud (and surprised) as she was that she'd kept it together back at the pub, this shit was not her cup of tea—not even close. Sure, she'd dealt with her fair share of ornery and sometimes violent assholes during her years helping keep the peace in Unity. She'd trained to handle herself. She'd helped scare off marauders with flashes of light and fire on occasion. But going it alone, surrounded by a roomful of hard men looking to hurt her as she had been back at The Rath . . .

It had taken a good fifteen minutes for her breathing and heart rate to even begin to slow after the fight and the better part of an hour to get her hands to stop shaking.

And here she was, about to wade into worse than that.

At least the catcher had worked—that was something. She'd tested it before, of course, but it was a new creation, and given the complexity of the enchantments she'd laid on the device, she'd been more than a little skeptical about whether the thing would successfully stop bullets when it really mattered. Relying on the catcher probably still wasn't the best idea, but as long as no one got too close to her, she feasibly shouldn't have to worry about getting shot. She'd have to deal with the cold as the thing drew the energy it required from the air around her, but that was a small price to pay.

But enough. She'd been watching the Red Fortress long enough to know she wasn't going to gain any additional insight sitting here. She was only wasting time because she was afraid. If Michael was in there, he could well be running out of time.

She needed to move, and that meant breaching the Red Fortress.

In reality, the place looked like more of a fortified factory complex than an honest-to-god fortress. Still, whether or not the place would stand up to heavy artillery wasn't exactly important right now. It was only her, after all, and the sheer number of armed men in there was more than enough to make the prospect of storming the place sound like suicide.

Of course, just because she couldn't walk away didn't mean she had to go in staff blazing. With a little luck, she might be able to find Michael and slip out before anyone noticed a thing. The perimeter wall would be easy enough to hop. It was the question of what she'd do from there that was twisting her stomach into knots.

She checked over her gear one last time. Her bullet catcher was ready to go, as was the cloaking pendant hanging from the thin chain at her neck and the twin batteries clipped at the back of her belt. When she was ready to go, she hefted her staff, a much more versatile tool than the rest. It had evolved along with her skills as an arcanist, beginning as little more than a kind of telekinetic battering ram and growing steadily in function and precision alongside her creativity with the arts of channeling and enchanting. It also made a handy whacking stick when the need arose.

She killed her comm holo and closed her eyes for a long moment, trying to dissipate some of the anxious energy. As if that were going to happen.

She stood, took one last look, and leapt over the concrete barrier at the edge of the freeway. As the ground rose up to meet her, she focused her mind and channeled the energy of her falling body, redirecting it into telekinetic force applied at an upward angle to slow her fall. A familiar crackling buzz rushed through her head and body as the energy flowed through her, but it was nothing she couldn't handle.

Despite having jumped from a height of twenty feet, she touched down as if she'd simply hopped from a small stepladder, no worse for the wear aside from the small expenditure of effort.

As she stared up at the looming Red Fortress, worried scraps of plans swirling through her mind, only one thing seemed certain: if and when she got Michael out of this whole mess, she owed him one solid kick in the ass.

SHE COVERED THE DARK STRETCH between the highway and the Fortress wall at a light run, keeping as low and quiet as possible. A few yards from the perimeter wall, she gathered herself and jumped, drawing energy from her surroundings to telekinetically amplify her leap to something well beyond what would be humanly possible. The ten-foot wall passed beneath her, and for a brief second, a small trill of panic rose at the sight of the ground rushing up to meet her on the other side. Then she took another pull of energy, applied another effort of will, and settled safely to the grass inside the perimeter of the Red Fortress.

She remained frozen for a second.

No shouts, no shots.

The only guy in her immediate sight was thirty yards away, headed toward the far end of the complex with his back to her. For the moment, she seemed to be in the clear.

The yard between the perimeter wall and the Red Fortress itself was lit along its considerable length by several large floodlights. Ample patches of shadow remained beside the stacks of supply crates and lines of transport trucks that populated the space.

She was moving to take cover behind a line of trucks to wait out the lone patrolman when the sounds of voices and crunching gravel from the direction of the front gate made her stop in her tracks.

She forced herself to breathe again. With a base this size, people were probably coming and going at all hours. It had nothing to do with her. She was still good.

That didn't stop her from flinching when the front gate gave a pair of sharp clicks and began to pull open with a low hum. She covered the last few feet to the nearest truck in a panicked shuffle and hunkered down by its front grill, gripping her staff as if it were the only thing keeping her from plunging to certain death.

Yeah, she was still good. Definitely.

Get it together.

She peered around the front of the truck. A dark SUV pulled through the front gate and headed for the building entrance. She glanced over her shoulder to ensure she was still alone. Ahead, the rear left door of the SUV popped open, and a big guy slid out.

He only looked around for a second before turning back to the vehicle, but she recognized him. She was sure about that. It would take more than a couple of hours to forget the face of the guy who'd tried to shoot her dead in that awful pub.

More men began to emerge from the SUV, five in total. She sucked in a breath when she spotted gorilla-man Tom. What the hell were these guys doing here?

They must have come to track her down for revenge, or at least to tip the Red Fortress off to her. But wait—one of the guys from the back seat had his hands bound behind his back. The possibilities expanded.

The maybe-prisoner was on the tall side, with dark hair and a lean build. He was the only one of the five she didn't recognize from earlier. He stood out. As she watched, he had some kind of exchange with Tom, who stepped forward to backhand him. The guy leaned out of harm's way on the first strike, but the other men immobilized him and Tom threw a sharp jab into his handsome face. The guy shook off the punch, and by the time the five of them turned to head into the Fortress, he actually wore an amused grin.

She was ready to bolt just observing the interaction. She watched them go, wondering what the guy had done to land himself here, and maybe admiring the view of his retreating backside just a little bit, despite everything else.

It didn't matter what he'd done, she reminded herself. She was here for one thing, and the sooner she got Michael, the sooner she'd be able to get out of here. All she had to do was—

Click.

Gun. That was a gun.

She slowly began raising her hands in surrender.

"Stop. Drop the stick."

She did, wondering if the guy could hear the sonorous pounding of her heart. He wasn't crying for backup yet, at least. That was good.

There was a rustling sound, then a hand grabbed her shoulder and pulled, turning her around and pressing her back into the truck's grill. The tense but controlled-looking patrolman kept his pistol trained on her and out of her reach as he extended his other hand with a long length of zip tie.

"Hands." He waved the gun to urge her to get to it. "Make 'em tight."

He looked like he was about to say it again when she finally got over her initial shock. She slowly took the zip tie and made a show of beginning to pull it closed around her wrist.

She paused, arriving at a plan. "You're not gonna shoot me."

Before he could say anything (and before she could talk herself out of it), she sprang forward and reached for the patrolman's face.

He pulled the trigger. Nothing happened. She'd already locked the pistol's hammer back in a telekinetic vise grip. The patrolman glanced in surprise at his weapon and then up at her.

She closed the last step between them and clamped her hands to the sides of his head. He went slack as she rode their physical contact like a shortcut into his mind and subdued him. She struggled to keep his bulk from collapsing too noisily, then used a combination of telekinesis and old-fashioned dragging to get him into the shadows between two trucks.

She poked her head back out. They were alone.

Normally, she made a point of avoiding that kind of use of her telepathic abilities. Diving into another's mind, manipulating them like that—it felt perverse and wrong. But she wasn't in any position to be above that right now. She'd wanted a stray patrolman, and here he was.

She scanned their surroundings more thoroughly with her extended senses and settled down to deliberate on what she was about to do. Once she'd convinced herself there was no other way, she turned her focus to the patrolman and slid into his quiet, vulnerable mind. Her body shuddered at the sensation, but she allowed herself to sink deeper into his head, sifting for thoughts and memories pertaining to Michael.

It only took a few seconds to begin finding what she was looking for. Once she was this far into someone's head, searching their memories was nearly as instinctive as recalling her own. Images flashed in her mind's eye, accompanied by sporadic bursts of sounds and smells and other sensations. She saw Michael arriving in a large transport truck like the one she was currently hiding beside. He'd looked rough and scared, but he'd been okay.

That was about all this guy had happened to see. But it wouldn't be all he knew.

He'd know where Michael was being held.

The brig, came the dreamlike response.

He would also know how to get there from here—discreetly. At that thought, a new series of images flashed through her mind, rapid and disjointed in places but coherent enough to paint a picture of an out-of-the-way side door and the way to the brig. From there, she'd have to figure out how to get them out, a thought that conjured a much more confused jumble of thoughts and images from the patrolman's mind. But she'd gotten what she needed for now.

She pushed the patrolman into deep unconsciousness and returned her senses in full to her physical body. She was getting ready to move when the patrolman's comm crackled to life, sending a jolt through her as violently as if it'd been a gunshot.

A tinny voice asked for a status update.

Shit.

She snatched up her staff with sweaty palms, options playing through her head, none of which sounded particularly good.

Trying to feign a passable response seemed like the worst of them. Running for the hills to formulate a more organized plan with what she'd learned was probably the smartest option.

But no . . . If she ran now, they'd only beef up their watch when this guy woke up and reported the breach. And that wasn't to mention Tom's presence. Even if he was only dropping off a prisoner, all it would take was one mention of the crazy chick who'd attacked the pub looking for Michael Carver, and they'd probably double Michael's security or maybe even move him.

No, she couldn't run. It was now or never.

Halfway to the door, it occurred to her that she could have dived back into the patrolman's head and used him like a human puppet to respond to the call. It was too late now, and the thought made her shudder anyway.

She could still do this. She had to do this.

She repeated the affirmation to herself over and over as she crept through the compound to her destination. She repeated it when she saw three patrolmen jogging back in the direction she'd come from, their comms alight with chatter. She repeated it again as she drew up to the target door and placed her hand to its surface, extending her senses to probe at the lock.

She could do this. She *had* to do th—

"Hey!" a voice cried from off to her left, yanking her attention away from the delicate task of turning the door lock. "Hold it!"

Two men jogged toward her from further down the building, one with his weapon raised, the other busy with his comm.

She turned back to the door, planted the tip of her staff against the lock, and drew in the energy she'd need to blow it out by force.

So much for the stealthy route.

CHAPTER FIVE

D espite whatever airs he'd put on for Michael, Jarek had to admit he was in a tight spot.

When Mosen had left with Tom and his men, Jarek had thought he might have a chance at getting a drop on Baldy and the other two Reds outside the brig. It turned out Mosen had three more men waiting outside the brig, though, and he'd sent them all to stick with Baldy.

Jarek was good—damn good, even—but a one-on-six fight against armed, lightly armored opponents? Not exactly a sure thing. Especially not with his hands still tied behind his back.

So he waited, hoping one or two guards might split off from the group or at least post themselves outside of wherever they were headed. Who knew? If they tried to transfer him to another set of restraints (say, a nice torture rack), he might even get a freebie. When it came to worming his way out of hairy situations, Jarek fell firmly into the school of thought that revolved around flying by the seat of one's pants, and it hadn't failed him. Yet.

He kept up his steady chatter as his chaperones marched him down one dull, dreary hallway after another, asking names and cracking jokes. Talking made him feel better as much as it annoyed the crap out of his guards—a win-win in his mind.

Inside 120 seconds, Baldy called a halt, shoved a balled-up bandanna into Jarek's mouth, and covered it with tape. But that was okay. Reactions were good. Upset people made more mistakes, and mistakes just might get Jarek somewhere.

The next small victory came when Baldy stopped at a door that looked just like the other dozen or so they'd passed, posted two of the six men outside, and funneled Jarek inside. He couldn't exactly say that was two down, but at least it might momentarily improve the odds.

His spirits didn't stay so high for long.

The small room was as dull and lifeless as the hallways outside, but for the few toys contained within.

His gaze went straight to the old dentist's chair in the center of the room. It was fitted with leather wrist and ankle straps well-suited for use in any number of unpleasant activities, and the bloodstains on its tan polymer cover gave clear evidence that many such acts had occurred in its plastic embrace. The rolling surgical cart next to the chair didn't help matters, topped with a metal tray of blades, pliers, and other cruel tools Jarek had no desire to be on the working end of.

Baldy was watching him with a cold grin. It looked like his window for action was going to be closing sooner than later.

Most likely, they'd undo his wrist restraints to strap him into the chair, but if they were even half intelligent, they'd only do that after his ankles were already secured. At that point, he might be able to take down anyone within arm's reach, but then he'd be stuck until he could undo his restraints. They'd placed the tray of tools out of easy reach of the chair, so buying time with projectiles probably wasn't a viable option either.

It was just as well; he'd take mobility over the use of his hands most times, anyway.

He ran through a rough sequence in his head. Implausible, but it'd have to do.

Any second now.

Baldy gestured toward the chair and turned to a set of shelves in the back of the room with an almost bored expression. "You know the drill. Feet first, and—"

Jarek jumped, planted a foot into the back of the guard in front of him, and kicked off hard enough to twist around and slam his foot into the face of the guard behind him. The first guard cleared the dentist's chair and came down with a crash of falling tools. The second toppled to the ground beside Jarek as he narrowly avoided falling over himself.

Cries of surprise joined grunts of pain as he recovered his balance and darted toward the next guard. The guard swept a rifle butt at his head, but he easily dropped underneath the blow and slammed the guard into the wall with a hard hip check. From there, he exploded upward to slam the top of his head into the bottom of the guard's chin.

He clenched his teeth against the jarring impact and the wet, gurgling noise that followed and pushed on toward Baldy, who looked a lot less bored now. Baldy backpedaled into the wall, clawing for his sidearm.

"You son of a—"

Baldy's words turned to a grunting whoosh of air as Jarek planted a hard boot sole in his chest. He added a kick to the side of the bastard's head to keep him down, then lunged for the first guard he'd kicked, who was recovering from the sea of spilled tools. He drove a knee into the side of the guard's head, crumpling him into a slack heap.

He panted heavily through his nose, cursing Baldy's gag, and looked around for something, anything, to quickly sever his bonds.

The hallway door burst open.

He spun around, preparing to throw himself over the chair in some manner of wild aerial kick. There was a flash of red eyes, and then Seth Mosen cleared the chair and hit him in a flying tackle.

The world became a blurred, confused series of brutally solid impacts with Mosen's bulk, the wall behind him, and, finally, the hard concrete floor.

Considerable pain clawed its way out from his disorientation. He rolled onto his back and gasped into his gag at the pain the movement sent lancing through his right shoulder.

The two guards from the hall were already inside the room, poking and prodding Baldy and the others back to awareness.

Mosen frowned down at the unconscious guard beside him and prodded him with his boot, then shot Jarek a grin that made his insides shrivel.

"If you want a job done right . . ."

"Tell me about it," Jarek tried unsuccessfully to say past his gag.

It wasn't like he had anything of substance to add anyway. He was too busy working to close his fingers around one of the tools he'd landed on—the one that felt mercifully similar to the handle of a box cutter.

Now he just had to figure out how to use the damn thing without being blatantly obvious.

He considered trying to scoot over to prop himself against the wall, but before he could move, Mosen bent down, gathered a handful of his shirt and one pants leg, and plucked him off the ground as if he weighed no more than a sack of potatoes. Ripping sounds from his shirt confirmed that he was in fact still a nearly two-hundred-pound man, but Mosen didn't seem to pay the fact much mind as he moved around the chair and tossed Jarek roughly down on it.

To his surprise, Mosen tore the tape from his mouth before moving to secure his legs. He caught the awkward kick Jarek aimed at his face and forced Jarek's leg down to the chair with the strength of a pneumatic press.

Jarek's tongue and throat were burning with effort by the time he managed to spit out the wadded bandanna and take a luxurious, full breath.

"You been hittin' the weights, Mosen?"

He continued struggling, mostly to buy time, as he set to work extending the blade of the box cutter and trying to shift it into a workable position without stabbing himself.

"Or has that Overlord of yours been letting you dip into his special stash?"

Mosen ignored him and gestured for one of the Reds to come help him with the straps.

"Look," Jarek said as one of the guys he'd kicked came around and grabbed aggressively at his left leg. "I like you guys and all, but I'm not sure I'm ready for this kind of adventure yet."

His voice might have stayed level, but as Mosen secured the strap on his right ankle and impatiently reached over to secure his left leg for his struggling assistant, Jarek felt the first wave of deep, genuine terror.

He'd been tortured once or twice before—okay, exactly twice, and despite what he might tell Pryce or anyone else, he hadn't emerged the same person from either encounter. The look in Mosen's cold eyes, coupled with the feeling of the second strap tightening down on his ankle, brought those memories too close to the surface.

He clenched his jaw and got to work with the box cutter, moving the tool back and forth in maddeningly tiny sweeps until the first tie gave way.

Baldy came around to join Mosen at Jarek's feet.

"What do you want with Carver?" Mosen asked.

He took a steadying breath. "He owes me a Coke. What do you think I want with him? You can't piece that one together for yourselves?"

He shifted the little blade and began working on the second tie with a sinking feeling that this escape plan was going nowhere. At least not before a few hours of agonizing pain. Still, he wasn't about to throw in the towel while he still had some angle to play.

Mosen gave Baldy a meaningful glance. Baldy began rooting around on the floor, collecting his tools on the metal tray with the air of a chef gathering the ingredients for a cake.

Mosen laid a hand on Jarek's right shin. For a second, the gesture was merely creepy. Then came sharp, piercing pain as Mosen pushed his thumb against his tibia hard enough that he thought the bone might actually break.

Strapped down like this, anticipating much worse to come, he couldn't help but buck against his restraints and let out a pained grunt.

"Come on," he half-shouted. The second tie gave way to his cutter. "You know what I'm doing here!"

Mosen squeezed harder. Jarek gnashed his teeth. His leg was going to break, and he was going to end up trapped in the Fortress like Michael. Al and Pryce had been right.

He forced himself to begin sawing at the third tie anyway.

Mosen opened his mouth just as an alarm buzzed through the room, echoed a second later by the same sound from the hallway. His grip on Jarek's leg loosened as he exchanged a confused look with the others. The alarm blared again.

The sound was like music to Jarek's ears, and he found himself chuckling at the spark of hope in his chest and the beginnings of a plan in his head.

Mosen stepped around the chair and brought his face close to Jarek's. "What the hell is this?"

Jarek beamed his best devil-may-care smile. "You don't really think I'd come here without a backup plan, do you?"

Of course, that was exactly what he'd done, but none of these guys knew that.

"Bullshit," Mosen said.

Jarek looked up, squinting in mock concentration. If he could get this freakishly strong bastard out of the room (preferably along with a few of his cronies), maybe he could make use of his soon-to-be-free hands. "You hear that, Mosen?"

Mosen frowned, listening. Jarek did the same in earnest and was surprised to detect the faint report of distant automatic gunfire.

What the hell was happening out there? Could it be the Resistance coming to collect Michael? Unlikely. A rival outfit seemed even less likely, mostly because the Red King didn't have rivals. Except for the Overlord, who was actually his boss.

He managed to keep his mischievous superiority act rolling as Mosen focused back on him and the alarm continued to blare.

"Here they come!" He waggled his eyebrows as if he knew what he was talking about.

A second later, two of the unmuted comms in the room crackled out the same message: "Intruder on base, last seen breaching the northeastern patrol outlet."

He couldn't have asked for more perfect timing. But had they said "intruder"? Singular?

Now wasn't the time to worry about that.

For a second, Mosen looked as if he might just tear into Jarek with his teeth. Then he turned to Baldy. "Keep him secure, and don't fuck it up this time." He pointed over Jarek's head and added, "You three, with me."

With that, Mosen turned on his heel and strode out of the room, his chosen men hurrying after him.

That left Jarek with Baldy and two Reds to deal with.

The third and final tie fell to the box cutter's blade.

"Strap his arms down," Baldy said. He returned to his inspection of his instruments, looking fully intent on continuing where Mosen had left off.

Jarek wasn't about to give him the chance.

The temptation to strike at the first guard who stepped within reach—to draw his sidearm and turn it on the others—was incredibly strong, but it was driven by fear. Mosen and the three he'd taken would still be plenty close enough to hear the gunshots, and they'd come running if that happened. He might be able to get free and armed well enough in time to take them, but why risk it when he could do better?

"Huh," Baldy said. It might have been paranoia, but Jarek got the impression he was looking for the missing box cutter.

It didn't matter now. The Red on the left drew a hunting knife from a sheath on the front of his vest and leaned in to reach for Jarek's bindings.

He exploded into motion, catching the guard's knife hand with one hand and sweeping out with the other to open the Red's throat with the box cutter, drawing a slow river of blood and a sequence of disgusting, wet slurping sounds. He stripped the knife from the Red's hand. No time to be appalled.

In one motion, he shoved the bloody Red back toward Baldy while aiming a reverse-grip stab at the second Red with the borrowed knife. The Red on his right managed to get an arm up to intercept his attack.

He dropped the box cutter freeing one hand to deal with the block. He caught the Red's wrist and gave a twist and a yank as he threw his other elbow into the guy's ribs twice. On the third strike, he flipped the knife around in his hand and stabbed upward, sinking the blade under the Red's chin.

Too much time, his instincts screamed. He'd taken too much time.

He didn't think about it—he hurled the hunting knife to his left. Only as the blade left his hand did he get a look at Baldy. The torturer had been about to shoot, and now his eyes were wide.

Jarek didn't wait to see how his throw would fare. He snatched up the box cutter and attacked the leather tethering his legs to the chair.

"Fuck!" cried Baldy to his left.

A clatter of heavy metal on concrete.

One strap down.

Shuffling to the left.

"—ing son of a bitch."

The light scrape of metal sliding over concrete.

Two straps down.

He vaulted off the chair, box cutter clutched in a reverse grip, and came down on Baldy just in time to knock his gun hand aside and stab him in the side of the throat.

He clenched his teeth at the spurt of dark blood that hit his right thigh, warm and wet through his pants. He held Baldy's eyes, watching as the torturer's struggles weakened from the furious thrashing of a sadistic bastard to the pathetic floundering of a lonely, frightened man.

Baldy stopped struggling.

Jarek swallowed and stood up, an odd combination of victor's pride and abhorred nausea swirling through him.

"Phase One complete, assholes." His voice sounded flat in his ears.

He bent to scoop up the hunting knife he'd thrown at Baldy, not really sure whether the blade had found a mark or if the projectile had simply stunned him. From the other Red, he took an old H&K MP5 submachine gun and an extra mag, which he tucked in a pants pocket.

He cracked the door open and listened. It was hard to tell past the buzzing alarm pulses still pouring from the speakers, but he couldn't make out any more gunfire.

Maybe they'd already taken care of whoever the hell had been crazy enough to storm the Fortr—

The pieces came together at once in his mind. The events at The Rath, Michael's reaction to them, the comm broadcast, and an intruder. Singular. One crazy-ass intruder . . .

The same person who'd been crazy enough to pick a fight with an entire pub's worth of hardened thugs?

"And so the plot thickens again," he mumbled.

If that *was* the arcanist out there, and if she was still alive, she'd be after Michael as well. Whatever their business was, he couldn't imagine it was going to make his life easier. He'd busted his ass and now killed three men to find out what Michael knew, and he'd be damned if he was going to let anyone jeopardize getting Fela back now.

Time to move.

He checked outside once more, stepped into the hallway, and set off for the brig, moving like a ghost in the fog.

CHAPTER SIX

G unfire roared down the hallway. As spent bullets clattered
to the floor and the temperature dropped another several
degrees around her, Rachel decided she might have to
rethink the design of the bullet catcher—or at least get used to
wearing something warmer than her worn leather jacket. Assuming
she made it out of the Red Fortress alive in the first place.

Things had been going so smoothly until a minute ago. She'd had
her quiet route planned. She'd nearly had the door unlocked. Skip
ahead two minutes, and now there was a trail of wreckage behind her
and a Fortress' worth of men bearing down on her.

She threw herself behind the cover of an inset doorframe, not
wanting to rely too heavily on the catcher and end up freezing to
death before she reached Michael.

The key, she decided, was to keep moving to warmer patches of
air, but that wasn't easy with this much hot lead flying in her direction, especially when she still wasn't sure the device wouldn't simply
miss a bullet or two at some point. Even so, she needed to keep
moving before the rest of the damn base arrived on top of her.

She gritted her teeth, pointed her staff blindly around the corner,
and fed a wallop of energy from her batteries through the glyph that

resembled a tiny sun. Even around the corner and through closed eyelids, the flash was bright. Down the hallway in the direction the staff was pointed, the effect would be monumentally stronger, like being at the epicenter of half a dozen lightning strikes.

Through the muffled ringing the gunfire had left in her ears, she thought she heard a few startled cries at the arcane flash. Time to move.

She whirled out from cover, staff at the ready. Four men lined the hall, weapons partially lowered as they shook off their disorientation. The closest of them fired a few blind shots that struck the wall unnervingly close to her.

She thrust out her open hand, pulling from her energy stores, and the two closest men slammed into each other headfirst.

One of the guys at the end of the hall must've recovered enough to see it happen, because he took careful aim and fired over his fallen allies. Two bullets pelted into the catcher's field and dropped to the floor, sending a chill through the air. She raised her staff and unleashed a strong telekinetic blast in response.

It caught the shooter full on, rocketing him back into the wall. His partner wasted no time in scrambling behind the corner for cover. She shifted her aim and sent a more focused blast.

Unseen force tore through the corner of the wall and drove the gunman across the hallway in a rain of concrete chunks and a cloud of gray dust.

She tromped down the hall as quickly as she could, panting and leaning heavily on her staff as the sheer volume of energy she'd just slung caught up to her. The staff alleviated some of the exertion that came with heavy-duty channeling, but she still had her limits. She'd have to pace herself if she wanted to have anything left on the way out.

The last gunman was recovering as she reached the end of the hall. She dealt him a solid blow with her staff and turned left down the next hallway.

A surge of panicked energy seared through her exhaustion at the sound of voices crying after her. Coming into the Fortress might be the last mistake she'd ever make. She clenched her teeth and told that tiny voice in her head to shut the hell up and get moving.

First, though, she needed to shake her incoming tails.

She turned right down the next hallway, which was mercifully empty, and ducked through the second door on the right as the voices drew closer behind her.

A broom closet. Wonderful.

She closed the door behind her, plunging the space into darkness. Footsteps pounded closer outside. The darkness pressed in around her, squeezing tighter and tighter with each approaching boot fall. Her fingernails dug painfully into her palm.

Then the footsteps were receding, continuing down the hallway. She forced herself to breathe.

Off to a great start.

She reviewed the directions she'd extracted from the patrolman, slipped out of the closet, and doubled back to continue her original direction. She did her best to extend her senses as she ran, scouting ahead for imminent threats. It wasn't the easiest thing to do while moving, and the result was far from perfect, but the effort at least enabled her to duck out of sight of a group of six men moments before they caught sight of her.

A minute later, she came across a man retying his boot as his partner bickered at him that now was a hell of a time and that he'd better hurry it up. She didn't feel particularly accomplished or proud when she managed to take them down, but at least she managed it before any shots were fired.

She passed a hallway and caught sight of the busy central hub she knew from her brief mental tour opened up at the heart of the facility. Apparently it acted as a marshaling ground too, judging by the din of voices and activity drifting out. At least she was getting close.

She crept carefully on until she'd passed the hub, then hung a right. The Red Fortress wasn't exactly teeming with direction signs pointing the way to the brig, but a couple of minutes later, she spotted the barred door she'd been looking for.

It was open.

She thanked her lucky stars and hurried into the antechamber of the quiet brig. By the time she returned her attention to her extended senses, it was already too late.

A guard had already emerged from a room she'd passed. He slammed the barred door shut and winked as its lock engaged with a heavy *click*.

She thrust her staff toward him with a growl, and his smirk flashed to shock as he rocketed upward and slammed into the hard ceiling. He fell limply back to the floor, a slow shower of dust following in his wake. She turned to face the door to the cell block.

Now that she took the time to properly explore with her senses, the situation was quite obvious: nine minds lying in wait among the cells. They might have been prisoners but for the armor and weapons she could feel on them.

She couldn't sense Michael, but that was to be expected. The Resistance had seen to it that his mind was shielded from telepaths like her. Her gut told her he was near, and that was enough.

A rush of hope welled up but was quickly tamped down by the realization that she'd just walked straight into a trap. Why else would so many armed men be lurking around the brig and waiting to close her in? They'd been waiting for her, which meant they'd figured out what she was after. She probably had that asshole Tom to thank for that.

It didn't matter now. She was here, and so were they. And if her gut was to be trusted, so was Michael. That was all that really mattered.

She tightened her grip on her staff and stepped into the brig proper. She swept out with her senses again. Three men on each side behind the first group of cells, and three more in the back right corner of the room. All waiting for her.

Did they already know who she was, what she could do?

She thought about making a big boom to show them, then decided advertising her presence to the rest of the base was unwise. Something subtler, then.

With a wicked grin, she raised her staff and focused her mind.

Then she drove the weapon toward the floor as hard as she could. At the last second, she directed the energy of the blow into one of the staff's glyphs, adding a pinch of energy from her battery stores for good measure. The staff jarred to an oddly silent halt, the only sound that of the rushing air that sprang into existence and swept through the brig.

The currents weren't strong enough to do much more than yank at clothing and ruffle hair, but judging from the way the men shifted around in her senses, the display succeeded at unsettling them.

"Hey, assholes," she called, doing her best to keep the waver out of her voice. "You took someone I care about. I'm here to take him back. That simple. Get out of my way, and I won't hurt you."

She wasn't really sure she meant the last part, but it seemed like the right thing to say.

A chuckle drifted from the back of the brig, alone at first but soon joined by another voice, then more until the whole brig was laughing it up.

So much for the easy way.

Another voice pitched in then, not with a chuckle but with a series of frantic, muffled cries. It was a voice she couldn't miss.

Michael.

That did it.

She rushed forward. The first few men caught sight of her and opened fire. She blasted the one on her right as bullets began to slam into the catcher's invisible barrier. He crashed into the bars of the next cell with a gross crunch. She spun the staff around and gave the same treatment to a shooter on the left, never stopping.

The remaining men opened fire from both sides as she cleared the first cluster of cells. By the time she reached the center of the intersection, a trail of spent lead lay on the floor in her wake. The air around her had grown frigid enough that her breath condensed in front of her, and a breeze stirred through the room as air pressures attempted to equilibrate.

The incoming fire momentarily faltered as she drew directly

between the pairs of shooters on either side. Then three more men emerged from behind the next group of cells and opened fire.

She cursed and darted right, putting the cover of the cells between her and the newcomers while also closing on the pair of men there. Her approach apparently overrode their concern over catching their allies in the crossfire, because both shooters opened fire again. Spent bullets fell to the ground in front of her, and she blasted one of the men into the wall. She closed on the second, shifted her grip to the end of the staff, and brought it around in a sweeping arc aimed at his raised rifle.

One last shot roared. Burning pain lanced across her left shoulder, then thudding impact as her staff slammed into the guy's rifle and arm. A cry escaped her as she whipped her staff back around. This time she found the bastard's head.

She reached for her shoulder and cursed when her hand came away streaked with blood. Shock gave way to terror as a pair of strong arms wrapped around her. Hot breath on the side of her face and arms constricting around her like a pair of pythons sent her into a panicked frenzy. Her staff clattered to the floor. She clawed at his hands and forearms. She'd just pulled her wits about her enough to stomp the holy hell out of the guy's foot when something struck the side of her head.

The world exploded into a disorienting blur of shapes and colors and pain.

Rising above the pain, though, she felt anger—hot, indignant fury at being struck, at feeling utterly powerless against the strong arms that held her like a vise. She embraced it, forging it into the iron of her will as she reached out, drawing energy indiscriminately until she felt she would explode with it.

She let it go with a wordless yell. Telekinetic force exploded outward from her like a bomb, tearing through the air with a clap and a boom. The two Reds blasted away from her like dolls caught in a hurricane.

A wave of exhaustion rolled over her. She bent to scoop up her staff and fell to one knee, her vision swimming with spots.

Move! she screamed at her suddenly uncooperative body. *MOVE!*

She planted her staff and pulled herself back to her feet.

Footsteps behind her. She spun and let loose a blast of force before she even had a chance to properly aim.

The attack clipped one of the three men advancing on her, sending him corkscrewing through the air. The effort sent her staggering back down to one knee. One of the others kicked her staff aside and descended on her, taking her throat in one hand and driving her smoothly to the floor.

Her head slammed to the concrete, and she sputtered for breath as her vision danced with stars. The hand tightened around her throat with an iron grip.

As she struggled weakly and looked up through her darkening vision, she could've sworn her attacker's eyes were glinting with a reddish hue as he grinned a wolfish grin and cooed, "My, my, what a bad girl you've been."

CHAPTER SEVEN

Something barked at the edge of Rachel's awareness—a crack of thunder, followed by two more in rapid succession. Gunshots. Whose?

She reeled in her extended senses and pulled herself back to her body. Her attacker lay slumped over her, two-hundred-plus pounds of warm, dead weight.

A soft thunk and a groan.

"Mmm." Michael's voice, thickly gagged. "Mmm!"

"I know, dude," someone said to her left in a loud whisper. "Phase Two!"

She couldn't see past her attacker's bulk. She pushed at him, her head swimming. Something warm dripped onto her neck. The guy on top of her had a neat bullet hole in the side of his head.

She jerked reflexively, her stomach turning over, and pushed again, frantically.

A dark-haired man appeared at the edge of her vision—the same guy she'd seen being hauled into the base, she realized. "It's all right, sweet—"

He cut off in mid-sentence, whirled around, and raised a weapon toward something she couldn't see. Three more shots cracked out.

She struggled harder. With a mighty heave, she rolled the slack body off of her just as the dark-haired man lowered his weapon and turned to face her.

She extended a palm toward him, preparing to reach out and wrap him in her will. The guy clearly wasn't on team Red, but he seemed to be one to shoot first and ask questions later. She wasn't keen to wait to find out what he thought of her.

She extended her senses. Nothing. Apparently, her surprise showed.

He raised a single finger for pause, holding a knife reverse-grip with the other digits, then he let his gun hang loose on its sling and reached up to tug his shirt collar down, revealing a lean chest and a tattoo of a simple kite shield set in a circle.

A glyph?

An easy grin slipped over his mouth. "Call me superstitious, but I do what I can to avoid surprises, sweetheart."

Her frown deepened. His grin followed suit. Did this guy know what she was? Either way, he was an ignorant fool if he thought that glyph would protect him.

He let go of his shirt and took his weapon back up.

In a moment of heart-wrenching panic, she let out the energy she'd gathered in a tidal rush of force that sent him flying. He hit the ground rolling, then thumped to a halt against the wall behind him.

"How's that for a surprise, asshole?"

She scrambled to her feet and over to Michael's cell as quickly as she could manage and placed her hand over the lock. Michael scurried to the side of the cell, crying something through his gag, but his concerns were unnecessary. As exhausted as she was from so much channeling, blowing the lock would've been a pricey way of saving a few seconds.

Instead, she let her mind trickle into the keyhole like hot wax, creeping through every nook and cranny until the tumblers aligned and the cylinder simply turned with the faintest application of tele-kinetic force.

She pulled the door open with a creaky groan, then spun as the stranger cleared his throat behind her. He held his knife and gun ready but not quite pointed at her.

They eyed one another uncertainly. Then Michael came scrambling out of the cell to plant himself between them, his eyes seething with frantic energy. The stranger lowered his gun further as Michael stepped into the line of fire.

Rachel kept a wary eye on the gun—a gun he'd just killed three men with, she reminded herself—and rested her staff in the crook of her arm long enough to rip the tape from Michael's lips and fish the balled-up rag out of his mouth.

The instant the gag left his mouth, Michael cried, "Holy crap, can you guys take it easy for a minute?"

"She started it," the guy said, his weapon completely at ease now.

"What are you, five?" she asked.

"What are you? Uh . . ." He snapped his fingers. "Dammit! Thought I had something. Who the hell is this chick, Mikey?"

"Who the hell am I?" She glanced at Michael and back at the other guy. "Who the hell are you?"

"Rachel," Michael said, "this is Jarek Slater, my, uh, acquaintance."

Jarek the 'acquaintance' held up a hand. "Easy there, Mikey. I need space to breathe."

Michael tilted his head in a gesture of defeat. "Jarek, this is Rachel, my sister."

His dark-eyed gaze flicked back and forth between her and Michael. "Not to be a dick, but is there a stork or a frisky milkman in that story somewhere?"

Well, there was a fresh one. Black and white siblings? How could it be?

"I was adopted, asshole."

Tall, Dark, and Dickish nodded, tapping at his chin. "That actually explains a lot."

She tensed, but Michael grabbed her arm. "Easy, Rache. He's a dick, but he's on our side for now."

"I'm right here, guys," said the dick.

Michael ignored him and nodded toward the trail of blood on Rachel's left shoulder. "Are you okay?"

"I'm fine." She didn't look away from the newcomer. He felt like trouble. Professional trouble. "And we don't need this asshole watching our backs until he can stick that knife in them. I can get us out."

He placed a hand to his chest, looking more amused than affronted. "Like, right here. Look, sweetheart, Mikey's not leaving my sight, and unless I missed some masterful plan that doesn't revolve around waving that there magic stick around until the big bad Reds go away, you do need this asshole's help."

Every muscle in her body clenched. "I don't know who the hell you—"

"Holy crap, you two," Michael said, his voice a low hiss. "There are people coming to kill us right now, remember? Can you reel in your egos for ten minutes?" He held up his bound hands. "And maybe untie me while you're at it?"

"There are always people coming to kill me, Mikey. But fair point."

So that was a no on the reeling-in of the egos for Mr. Tough Guy, then. She tensed as he stepped closer to Michael, holding out his knife, but then he twirled the blade in his hand and offered it to her handle first.

"I imagine you don't want me sticking this anywhere near his front or back," he said in response to her uncertain stare.

She looked at the knife for a second, then pointedly turned away from the blade to grab Michael's wrists. "So you have a plan then, tough guy?"

"Working on it, sweetheart," he said.

"If you call me sweetheart again . . ."

She poured heat from the surrounding air into a single point on each of the two ties on Michael's wrists. An acrid smell wafted through the air as it swirled from the sudden temperature differential. Michael's bindings fell to the floor. She turned back to Mr. Tough Guy.

"... I'm gonna break your nose."

He barked a laugh. "Joke's on you. I think it's already broken."

She gave him a deadly smile. "I can wait."

"Can we just get out of here?" Michael said, rubbing his wrists and shaking his arms loose. "The Reds will be here any second." He went to look for a weapon.

"Fine," she said. "It's Jarek, right?"

"If 'asshole' is becoming cumbersome, sure."

She pointed with her staff. "Well lead the way, Jar—"

Jarek snapped to sudden attention, closing his eyes and cocking his head as if listening. She focused and caught it as well: the faint sound of approaching voices and footsteps.

"Yeah," he said. "Yeah, I think I will."

He jogged toward the brig entrance, pausing on the way to pluck the comm from the wrist of the man who'd nearly strangled her and slip it on.

She spread her hands. "Was there a plan, then?"

Michael gave her a wide-eyed shrug and set off after Jarek. She shook her head and followed, mumbling under her breath.

Ahead of them, Jarek stuck his head into the hallway and yelled, "Help! I've got 'em cornered!"

Her blood went cold. The traitorous bastard!

Outside, the sounds of approaching Reds quickened at his call.

She pointed her staff at Jarek, prepared to blow the son of a bitch through the wall.

He flattened himself against the wall, placed a finger of his knife hand to his lips, and then whispered, "Phase Three!"

He gestured that they should take cover behind the first cluster of cells.

Boots pounded outside the brig. There was no time to ask what the hell he was talking about. Michael pushed against her, shuffling her behind the cover of the cells. She lost sight of Jarek the moment before the first of what sounded like at least four or five Reds entered the brig.

She held her breath, waiting for the shouts and gunfire that would accompany Jarek's inevitable discovery.

One of them spoke in a tense, gruff voice. "Where the hell are —hey!"

That was her cue.

She sprang around the corner to see Jarek yanking his knife from one Red's throat and lunging after another. Every gun in the room (at least five of them) tracked toward him, but no one managed to get a clean shot before he closed on his next target.

He moved with brutal efficiency, stabbing and kicking his way into the pack. He somehow managed to grapple and dodge at just the right times to prevent any of them from getting a clear shot at him.

That didn't stop them from trying.

Sporadic gunshots cracked out, none of them hitting their intended mark, especially not the one that sent another Red to the ground, clutching at his leg. Jarek's knife had just found its third target when one of the Reds slammed into him with a hip-level shoulder tackle that drove him into the wall. The last standing Red moved forward to catch Jarek's knife arm in both hands before Jarek could thrust the blade down at the first attacker.

She drew energy from her batteries and gathered her will.

Ahead, the Red with the shot leg was taking aim at Jarek's pinned, helpless form. Jarek kneed the guy wrapped around his waist right in the groin and threw two hard punches into the second guy's ribs. He dropped the knife from his pinned right hand, caught it with his left, and plunged the blade between the second Red's ribs.

The man fell to his knees with a thick grunt, and the leg-shot Red abandoned his hesitations and pulled the trigger.

A burst of gunfire roared out. Five slugs slammed to a halt a few inches in front of Jarek's chest and throat.

The Reds and Jarek all stared at the hovering slugs for a few stunned seconds.

"Well, that's new," Jarek said.

She closed her fist and yanked it back with a rough jerk—and with it, the barrier she'd constructed.

The last Red staggered back from Jarek and fell beside the shooter on the floor, who threw an arm back to prop himself against the invisible shove.

Jarek raised his slung submachine gun from his side.

Three cracks of thunder later, the room was quiet.

"Well," Jarek said, half panting, half groaning, "I think that went swimmingly." He pointed the knife at Rachel. "Neat trick, by the way."

She hefted her staff. "I'm just full of them."

"I'll bet you are . . ." he murmured, eyeing her a little too intently.

"Eyes up here, *sweetheart*." She waved to Michael that the coast was clear.

"All right, all right." Jarek ran a hand through his hair as he glanced through the brig entrance, then back to them. "Let's move, then."

Three men lay dead beside the guy she'd knocked out in the short hallway beyond the brig's antechamber. She could only assume they'd been Jarek's handiwork on his way into the brig, which put his body count at—Jesus, did it even matter? The guy was cold and clearly dangerous. He seemed to be on their side right now, but she wouldn't be taking her eyes off of him anytime soon.

At the junction outside the brig, she turned right, nudging Michael along beside her.

"Other way," Jarek said, grabbing her staff arm at the elbow.

She tugged her arm free. "I came this way. I don't know where that leads."

"Brilliant," he said. "Follow the same route in and out. They'll never see that coming!"

Angry heat rushed to her head, but before she could deliver the retort brimming on the edge of her lips, Jarek said in a level tone, "I know what I'm doing." He grimaced and touched at a tear in his shirt over his left shoulder. "Just trust me."

She nodded toward his shoulder. "Did you get shot back there?"

"Twinsies," Jarek said, pulling his hand from the shoulder to reveal a bloody finger.

"Is it bad?" Michael said.

"Not nearly as bad as the next one could be," Jarek said, holding her gaze as he tilted his head to the left hallway. His eyes beseeched her. "Plan. Trust me."

She glanced at Michael, who gave a small nod.

"Not for a second," she said as she moved to follow him.

That only made the cocky bastard grin.

They left the junction at a run. For all his talk about having a plan, she wasn't entirely convinced Jarek knew where he was going, but he sure as hell acted as if he did. He led them up to the second floor and left out of the stairwell.

A minute later, they turned a corner into a stretch of hallway that opened to a suspended catwalk crossing through the Fortress' central hub.

The hub was around fifty feet high and wide open aside from the catwalks spanning its far edges. Among other things, the area held two medium-sized airships. Four large, interlocked panels set in the hub's high ceiling looked as though they could part to allow the ships to pass.

Most importantly, though, the room below was positively crawling with armed men either standing guard over the potential getaway vehicles or rallying to go track down the Fortress's escapees.

They halted at the edge of the railed metal walkway. It was woefully exposed—and their only way of proceeding forward.

"What the hell'd you bring us this way for?" she whispered by Jarek's ear. "You're not seriously thinking about stealing one of those ships."

"Hell no," he whispered, turning back to look at her.

The motion put his face within inches of hers. She leaned back and swallowed, trying to pretend she hadn't felt a light trill in her chest.

"That's crazy talk, sweethea—uh, yeah, even if those doors were open, it'd—"

A lurching groan sounded from the panels in the ceiling, which began to slowly open to the Newark sky with a loud, steady hum of motors.

Jarek's eyebrows drifted upward. "Huh. Guess now's the time to go for it."

She was opening her mouth to express just how wholeheartedly she disagreed with that line of thinking when he started across the walkway.

Shit.

She traded a shocked look with Michael, and they both set off after him across the metal walkway. She stepped lightly, hoping the noise from the opening panels would cover their tracks.

Dozens of armed Reds filled the area below them. All it would take was one wrong glance and they'd be screwed, but all eyes were trained toward the splitting ceiling.

Halfway across, a flicker of movement drew her attention to the opening panels. A figure was plummeting through the gap toward the ground fifty feet below. Despite the fatal height, he didn't flail or cry out; he simply waited to land, arms and legs at ready positions as the air attempted to rip his long coat from his body. His long, rust-red coat.

Could that be—

The man's eyes flared with a violent scarlet glow, clearly visible even across the enormous room. She watched with morbid fascination as he slammed into the concrete floor with a thud and the sound of crumbling stone. A small cloud of dust and pulverized concrete shot up around him.

Like everyone else, she'd heard plenty of ghost stories about the raknoth over the years, but as she watched that figure stride out of the dispersing debris cloud, fiery-red eyes alight and apparently unperturbed by the bone-shattering force of his landing, she couldn't deny what she was seeing.

She was looking at a raknoth, and she could only assume it was the Red King.

The King's attention settled on a group of Reds waiting nearby in silence. Even from across the room, she could feel the tension as the raknoth approached them. Above, a large, vaguely avian airship began descending into the hub, presumably the ship the King had jumped from.

One of the Reds stepped forward from the cowering huddle. For a second, it looked like the King might speak, but then he grabbed his subject by the hair, yanked the man's head to the side, and plunged his teeth into the side of his neck.

The sounds of the descending airship and the men below covered Rachel's gasp.

The Red King's eyes pulsed brighter. Crimson blood rolled down the man's neck, yet he didn't fight as the King lapped it up.

Shock and revulsion filled her.

Then the Red King's head snapped up like a predator catching a scent, and revulsion shifted to alarm.

The King pushed his meal back toward the other men, who caught the bloody man and steadied him. The King paid no mind, sniffing at the air.

Shit. Had he sensed them? Had he sensed her?

Jarek signaled they should move.

She took two steps after him, and then something slammed against her mind like a falling iceberg. The presence was vast and powerful and alien, and she barely managed to hold her defenses together under its devastating attack. It could only be one thing. She sank into her mental space, scraping and clawing to find some purchase, but the raknoth's mind was relentless in its drive.

This wasn't a fight she was going to win. Her cloak. She needed to activate her cloak.

Keeping all but the barest scrap of her mind fixed on holding the Red King's telepathic invasion at bay, she struggled to find her comm with slow, awkward fingers. With painstaking concentration, she swiped a command over the comm's surface.

The mental pressure vanished as the cloaking glyph on her neck-lace activated. She gasped, feeling the weight lift from her.

It was only then she noticed that she'd fallen to the walkway. Michael was clutching at her arm with wide, panicked eyes.

"Have to go," she said, her voice a weak croak.

Below, the Red King was pointing up at them, and dozens of Reds were turning toward them as the raknoth bellowed, "Bring them to me!"

CHAPTER EIGHT

As much as Jarek didn't understand what the hell had just happened, he was pretty sure about a few things.

Thing one: they were totally exposed in the middle of the walkway with several dozen armed men all staring at them, probably moments away from getting their shit together and opening fire (although Red-Eyes down there had said "bring them," not "kill them").

Thing two: they needed to run, and one-third of their party already looked as if she'd just run a hundred miles with lead bricks for shoes.

Things one and two added up to thing three: they were at least a little bit screwed.

"Come on!" He helped Michael haul Rachel back to her feet. "Move, move!"

A roar filled the room, every bit as ferocious as a lion's. Below, the Red King darted forward with alarming speed. After a few steps, the raknoth gathered himself and Jumped—with a capital J, Jarek's mind noted—toward their little walkway huddle.

He numbly registered that the leap would carry the raknoth across the sixty or seventy feet between them to land on the walkway. Then he raised his MP5 and fired.

"Mikey!"

Michael fumbled with his weapon, but he wasn't going to be fast enough. The Red King was on the downward arc of his trajectory now. Jarek fired another burst, and another. He could tell at least some of the shots were landing by the raknoth's small, mid-flight jerks. The bullets didn't seem particularly bothersome, but Jarek could have sworn they sent ripples of green across the raknoth's skin like some kind of reactive armor.

He let loose on full auto, hoping to at least cut the King's flight short. Even a raknoth had to fall prey to simple physics, right? Maybe so, but it wasn't enough.

Then Michael's gun roared out beside him.

The raknoth gave a savage cry as he came up short of the walkway, dropping down, reaching, reaching . . . and caught the edge of the walkway with a single inhuman hand. It was a sickly shade of green with the texture of reptilian scales, each finger sporting a vicious-looking claw.

The walkway groaned under the sudden load, the metal under that monstrous hand deforming from the impact.

How strong was this thing?

Jarek leaned over the railing and emptied his last few rounds into the King's face. He caught a glimpse of sandy blond hair and mostly human features, aside from the disturbing glow of the eyes and the darkening patches of green, before the raknoth tucked his face away from the gunfire.

This time, he was positive the bullets had hit, and just as positive they had barely affected the raknoth, aside from making him sprout new splotches of green scales across his neck and face.

Thing four: the raknoth were every bit as terrifying as the stories he'd heard.

The Red King yanked himself up and made a grab for Michael's leg with one hand. Michael jumped back. The raknoth clamped onto the walkway and began pulling himself up properly.

Rachel thrust the tip of that oddly winding staff into the Red

King's face an instant before the end detonated with a booming flash of light.

There was a screech of metal and an angry roar.

Jarek tried too late to shield his eyes, his vision already bleached with light. Something pressed against his side, and he heard Rachel's voice through the ringing in his ears.

"Move."

He didn't argue. As his vision began to resolve, he saw Rachel ahead, pushing Michael along ahead of her. The Red King was blessedly nowhere in sight.

Of course, the King's absence cleared the line of fire for all the Reds below.

He kept his head down and ran as at least a dozen weapons opened fire together. Rachel dropped back, yanking Michael with her, and put herself between the guns and their little band.

It was almost comical to see the small blonde tugging around the big black guy, but when the spent lead slugs began clanking down to the walkway in their wake, Jarek decided that Michael had good reason to comply.

The air unmistakably chilled around them as they ran unharmed through the swarm of lead.

They reached the end of the walkway and fled into the cover of the next hallway.

Jarek bent over and braced his hands on his knees. Thing five: apparently arcanists were pretty damn real and also a little scary themselves. He'd heard plenty of rumors and hearsay, but he'd never really believed. His views were changing pretty quickly. As usual, Pryce had been right. Now Jarek just had to stay alive long enough to tell him so.

They ran down the hallway side by side.

Michael hissed, "Was that—"

"Telepathic attack," Rachel said. "Yeah. Pretty freaking strong one too."

She still looked more than a little pale. Pryce had insisted on multiple occasions that arcanists couldn't simply bend nature to their wills for free, that there had to be some equivalent, thermodynamically feasible exchange. Apparently he had been right about that too.

"That was the Red King?" Michael said, panting now.

Jarek swapped his spent mag for a fresh one as he led the way around a corner. "That or there happens to be another one that's decided to run around in a ridiculous coat and call himself a—*shit!*"

A stairwell door burst open ahead of them and two men swept into the hall, weapons raised. Jarek raised his MP5, but Rachel stepped in front of him and Michael. She pointed her staff, and the two Reds went tumbling back through the doorway to crash into more allies, judging by the disgruntled cries.

Rachel slammed the stairwell door shut, wedged it closed with her foot, and applied the tip of her staff to the latch. The air in the hallway grew cooler even as the metal around the door handle glowed red-hot. A muffled yelp came through the door—probably someone burning their hand on the opposite handle, he thought with a grin. As suddenly as it had appeared, the red glow drained out of the door and the temperature in the hallway returned to normal.

Moving on instinct, he pushed Michael forward and lunged to yank Rachel aside.

She glared at him. "What the f—"

Muffled gunfire barked out, denting the door beside them. A few bullets tore their way through.

She looked from the door to him. "Right."

The gunfire ceased, and something—maybe a boot—slammed against the door. The door held. Rachel had melted the components of the door's latching mechanism into one solid piece, effectively locking the door for good unless someone hit it hard enough to shear through the fused metal. Someone like an angry raknoth, for instance.

"Not half bad," he said. "Let's move."

The monotony of the hallways didn't help with the directions, but he was at least eighty, maybe seventy percent sure he was leading them southwest. They'd be fine.

A loud crash echoed down the hall, not unlike the sound an angry raknoth might make kicking down a locked door. Jarek led them down the next stairway and picked up the pace, waving Michael and Rachel onto the ground floor.

Down the hallway. Another left. Another right. They had to be getting close.

"I sure hope you guys can both swim," he said.

Michael glanced over. "Why does that—oh."

Jarek smiled. "Oh, yes."

Ahead, the top left half of the next hallway was lined with translucent polymer windows. The windows afforded a view into a small indoor dock. There were only a few boats sitting in the dark water, all small and in varying states of disrepair, but it wasn't the boats he cared about.

He pulled open the first door they came to and hurried the others in, uncomfortably aware of the proximity of voices behind them now.

The water would feed into the Passaic River. More to the point, it would feed out of the Red Fortress. The only problem was the bay door that would in all likelihood be locked. Luckily, he'd had the foresight to swipe Seth Mosen's comm, and he was reasonably sure its ID would grant them access, assuming the bay door didn't require an additional code.

It did.

"No, no . . ." He swiped the comm past the receiver again, which refreshed the same message: "Please enter your personal access code."

"Stupid"—he kicked the wall—"shit!"

"'I know what I'm doing,' he says," Rachel said. She was leaning on her staff, looking like she desperately needed a nap or some form of sugar. "'Trust me,' he says. What's the plan now, asshole?"

He bit back an angry retort and held up a finger, thinking.

The controls were digital, but the locks themselves were mechanical, and he'd seen what Rachel could do to locks.

He nodded at Rachel's staff. "You pop the locks, we lift?"

She spread her hands in a gesture that said *What the hell else am I gonna do?*

"That's the spirit, Goldilocks."

He met her glare with his best grin. He was tossing away Mosen's comm and the knife he had no easy way of carrying into the water when he caught motion through the translucent panes of the dock's inner wall. The sounds of approaching Reds echoed oddly off the water's surface.

"Shit," he whispered. Then, louder, "They're coming. Everyone in. Now."

He dropped down into the dark water, trusting that they'd follow. The coolness of the water embraced his tired body. It was deeper than expected; he found the bottom only at the lowest point of his plunge. The waves of Michael and Rachel entering the water rocked him on the way up. He surfaced and moved to find a handhold on the side of the pool.

Michael surfaced and managed to get his own handhold just before the door opened, letting in the sounds of numerous Reds in the hallway outside. Rachel was flailing a few feet away, encumbered by her staff and her leather jacket.

Michael tried and failed to reach her.

Jarek caught her fingertips and pulled her to him, trying to convey the strongest shush he could with his eyes. Her expression was hard to read in the darkness as he drew her in and wrapped his arm around her waist to keep her afloat.

Her body pressed against his, warm and soft in contrast to the stagnant water. Above them, footsteps plodded toward the water and paused.

He stopped breathing.

"Clear," a voice said after what felt like minutes but must've been only a second or two.

Grumbles. Shuffling footsteps. Sounds of the Reds moving on. Then, finally, silence.

She let out a careful breath against him, and his focus precariously teetered away from listening to the retreating Reds. His senses filled with the sweet scent of her closeness and the racing of her heart against his sternum.

"We clear?" she asked, the air of her whisper teasing lightly at his wet cheek.

They were, as far as he could tell, but instead of saying that, his lower anatomy decided to go with, "Are you seeing anyone?"

She pushed away, electing to go back to her sorry version of treading water.

"Seriously, dude?" Michael hissed from the darkness.

Jarek allowed himself a small grin. "I know! Jesus, guys, can we act like professionals here and just focus on getting this damn door open?"

"You have problems," Rachel whispered from the darkness.

"Tell me about it." He began swimming toward the bay door. "Like this door, for instance. If you can pop the locks, I can hold it while you and Mikey scoot under. We should probably go down together."

"You'd like that, wouldn't you?"

"Is that a no in the 'seeing someone' column, then?"

There were a few swishes from Michael's direction. Then, again, "Seriously, dude?"

"Not my fault!"

"Can we just get this over with?" Rachel asked.

"You'd like that, w—" Before he could finish, she took a deep breath and vanished beneath the dark surface of the water. "Shoot. Let's go, Mikey."

He dove down, guiding himself along the surface of the bay door with his hands in the dark. On his way down, he felt more than heard a pair of sharp clicks reverberate through the door, followed a second later by another pair. The arcanist must've done her job, then.

He grimaced in the dark as his hands tracked down along a steadily grimier door. Finally, he found the bottom and arranged himself into an effective pulling position.

It was only then that he realized the hiccup in his plan. Down there in the nearly complete darkness, they weren't going to be able to see one another and make sure they'd all made it through. But that was assuming the door even opened in the first place. First things first.

There was no hope of effectively coordinating with Michael. He dug his fingers under the slimy edge of the bay door as best he could and heaved. Even partially submerged in water as it was, the door wasn't light. He pulled harder, and it began to budge upward, inch by inch. He adjusted his grip, shifted his footing, and pulled again. Halfway through his pull, the door began moving faster, and he assumed Michael had found his side and pitched in.

By the time the door was high enough for him to maneuver underneath it and prop it on his left shoulder, a good thirty seconds had passed. His lungs were burning with exertion.

The water outside of the bay door was slightly lighter, but not enough to afford any real visibility. So he remained crouched at the bottom, pinned under the heavy door, heart racing and lungs burning, hand outstretched as he waited for some sign of the others' passing.

Something brushed against his hand. An arm. A leather-sleeved arm. Rachel. A small hand found his, tugged once in the direction of the river, then let go.

Did that mean Michael was already on the other side? He must be. Maybe.

He considered inching his way over to check, but the door was heavy, and he was running out of air. He'd made the decision to try anyway when the weight on his shoulder shifted and pressed down harder. That had to have been Michael leaving his post on the other side of the door. That was the only explanation, right?

He waited another lung-burning fifteen seconds to be sure, then shimmied out and toward the river. When he broke the surface, Michael and Rachel were already near the end of the short, walled-off inlet, looking back uncertainly.

The sweetness of his first breaths was soured by Rachel's impatient wave.

Why the hell had he even been so keen on waiting for the two of them?

"This is why we work alone," he mumbled as he swam quietly over to them, ignoring the fact that Al wasn't there to hear him.

"You get lost down there?" she whispered as he drew up to them.

"Just making sure I didn't lose my new business partner," he said, looking pointedly at Michael. "Also, I forgot: Phase Four."

With that, he pushed past them to join the flow of the river.

They floated downstream like deadwood under the moonlight. With the extra weight of her soaked leather jacket and staff, Rachel had it the worst attempting to keep afloat. Between their soaked clothes, wet boots, and general, bone-deep weariness, they swam with all the grace of drunken hippopotamuses.

Behind them, the Red Fortress was alive with activity as men scoured the base and cars hit the road to look for them. He waited until they'd floated nearly half of a mile and rounded an appreciable bend before he decided their chances of being spotted were low enough.

He signaled an end to their tactical float, and they extracted themselves at the edge of what had once been a park but was now a small field of mostly bramble and wild grass. No one was quick to do anything but lie in the thick foliage and catch a few merciful gulps of warm summer air.

"Mikey," he finally said, extending a closed fist toward the younger man lying beside him.

Michael's shadow shifted, his head turning from Jarek's face to his fist and back.

Jarek plopped his head back down to the tangle of weeds and wild grass with a wide smile. "Operation complete."

CHAPTER NINE

W hat Rachel wanted more than anything was a hot shower, a good meal, and a couple of years' worth of sleep.

What she got instead was a long night of slinking from shadow to shadow under Jarek's paranoid, arguably insane direction. And her sopping-wet jacket didn't help either.

"It's been like a goddamn hour," she whispered softly to Jarek as they peered around the corner of an abandoned home, checking the next stretch of road. "If we haven't seen them yet, you really think they're out here?"

Instead of answering, he held up a single finger. She was on the verge of reaching out to snap said finger when someone gave a low whistle from a truck she hadn't noticed.

Four men, all well armed, came shuffling out of the nearby houses to pile into the truck.

He waggled his eyebrows at her. "Oh, they're out here, Goldilocks."

After that, she didn't argue so much.

After her years living in Unity, Newark at nighttime was a spooky sight, a dark, empty husk of a city that told mostly of lives dead and gone. They scarcely spoke as they trekked through dusty lots and past a gamut of old homes and other buildings that ranged from run-down to scorched wreckages. Under Jarek's lead, they stuck mostly to the shadows, being especially careful to avoid the streetlights that intermittently lined the crumbling pavement of the old streets.

In another hour of walking (or, more accurately, sneaking), she saw a grand total of eight people outside their homes. Jarek guided them into the shadows or behind the cover of fences or old cars while each of those eight people passed. The caution seemed a tad ridiculous, but Jarek just said something about how people talk, and neither of them saw fit to press the issue. Better safe than sorry.

As sparse as the pedestrians were, there weren't many signs of occupied homes, either. The few small gardens they stumbled upon were inevitably hidden from street view, and none of those houses had lights on inside. Her father had once mentioned something about how people in the cities tended to rise and fall with the sun these days because lit homes ran the risk of drawing the attention of passing marauders.

She gazed at the dim shapes of ruined buildings as they went and tried to imagine how the place had looked before the Catastrophe, when there had been flowers in the gardens and children playing in their augmented realities. Back before the raknoth had culled the world population from nine billion to one with the push of a few buttons.

The story had spread across what remained of the world with as many variations as there were tellers. She'd heard stories about how the creatures ate people whole and others about how they only drank the blood of humans. That one might actually be true, considering the way the Red King had ripped into his own man earlier.

Some claimed the raknoth had come from space and had been hiding away on Earth for thousands of years, while others insisted they'd been sent by God himself as a reckoning for humanity. No one actually knew how or why the raknoth had nuked the world into oblivion, only that they had done it.

She hadn't even fully believed the raknoth were real until tonight. She shuddered, part from the chill of her wet jacket and part from the memory of the fury in those blazing red eyes and the raw power of the alien mind that had sought to invade hers. The thing had been an absolute monster—one of the very monsters her brother had signed up to wage war against.

She could see why Michael wanted to stop the raknoth. He'd only been five when the bombs had fallen, but he'd grown up utterly surrounded by constant reminders of the hurt the creatures had inflicted on the world. She'd suffered plenty of hurt herself, but most of that had come before the Catastrophe. Once John Carver had taken her in, she'd been too preoccupied making sure she didn't lose another home and another family to think about running off to join some foolhardy crusade.

As fun as tonight had been, somehow she wasn't too upset at the thought of getting Michael the hell out of Newark and taking the next five or so years to calm her amped-out nerves. She might have to find them another car, as getting close enough to the Red Fortress to recover the one she'd been using didn't seem like the wisest idea right now. She'd probably be able to find an abandoned solar car some-where. God knew the Catastrophe and the long winter that had followed had left plenty of them lying around, and a lot of them still functioned, especially once the debris had begun to clear from the atmosphere.

For now, though, lying low, licking their wounds, and getting an hour or two of sleep all sounded like good enough places to start. While she didn't trust Mr. Tall-Dark-and-Handsome ahead, he seemed to be their best bet for avoiding the Reds while they did that.

When they reached the dusty span of an old park, Jarek announced they were almost there. They skirted around the mostly barren clearing of the park, cut north for one last, spooky block, and arrived in front of a plain gray metal door.

Jarek walked in as if he owned the place. She traded a hesitant look with Michael and followed him in, keeping her staff ready.

The space inside was small and unremarkable, a palette of beige tones from floor to ceiling that somehow managed to be both soothing and depressing. The only thing that stood out was the large bulletin board on the wall, overflowing with pinned papers ranging from handwritten notes to honest-to-god wanted posters that looked as if they'd come straight from the rootin'-tootin' Wild West.

She tensed as a door sprang open at the back of the room.

"Honey, I'm home!" Jarek called.

The man who stepped into the room was a dead ringer for Albert Einstein's evil twin gone mad scientist (and starting to bald).

"And I see you've brought guests." The man's eyes scanned her and Michael briefly before fixating on her staff.

"Long story." Jarek cocked his head. "Okay, maybe not so long. Mostly, lots of asses pulled out of lots of fires—some nicer than others."

"The asses or the fires?" the older man asked, still studying her staff.

Jarek gave a bark of laughter. "Pryce, you old rascal, you!"

She cleared her throat.

"Ah, right," Jarek said. "Guys, this is Jay Pryce, tinkerer extraordinaire. Pryce, this is Michael and Rachel."

"Utterly intrigued, I am sure," Pryce said, stepping forward to offer his hand.

"Uh, thanks?" She slowly reached out to take his hand.

Pryce didn't really shake her hand so much as hold it up for closer inspection. His curious eyes flicked back and forth between her hand and her staff. This guy's wheels were definitely turning. Did he know about arcanists too?

Jarek rolled his eyes. "You'll have to excuse Pryce. He thinks he's a scientist or something."

"Sorry." Pryce released her hand with a guilty grin. "It's nice to meet you." He offered his hand to Michael. "Both of you. I've heard your name mentioned more than a few times, Mr. Carver."

Michael took his hand, and they exchanged a more conventional handshake.

Pryce looked back to Jarek. "So, the Red nation is combing the city for you."

"You already heard about it?" Jarek said.

"No . . ." Pryce stroked his chin. His eyes flicked over her and Michael once more. "But I don't see how they couldn't be, considering that you were clearly there and now you're here. So. You come to grab your things, or is there some other wonderful reason you decided to pay me a visit with an angry army on your back?"

Jarek grinned and offered Pryce his submachine gun. "Don't pretend like you don't love it. Where else could you find this kind of excitement?"

Pryce snatched the weapon from Jarek and studied it dubiously. "Oh, the glory."

She couldn't quite place a finger on what the relationship was between these two. It was almost like father-son but without the responsibility or obligation. Whatever Pryce might be to Jarek, she just hoped he had food and maybe a soft place to lie down for a few hours.

Jarek seemed to be stalling. "Well, I guess if you'll bring my comm, I can just call the ship in and we can, you know, be on our way, or . . ."

"Oh, don't be ridiculous." Pryce pulled a comm and an earpiece from one of the many pockets of his tool-laden shop apron and handed them to Jarek. "Any luck finding our girl, by the way?"

"That's the question, isn't it?" Jarek slipped on the comm and popped in the earpiece, then clapped Michael on one shoulder. "I held up my end of the deal."

Rachel's stomach fell. "What deal?" She looked at Michael. "What did you promise him?"

Michael shifted. "I think I know how to find—"

"Think?" Jarek said.

Michael pursed his lips. "I know how to find something that belongs to him."

She stared and waited for more. None came. "Aaand what the hell is this 'something' that you're willing to sign up with this . . . person over?"

Jarek touched a hand to his chest as if mortally offended. She wasn't amused. If Michael was indebted to this asshole, that could make their return to Unity more difficult.

"Jarek lost his exosuit," Michael said. "Hux and I found it when we, uh, knocked over a shipment from the Reds to the Overlord." A shadow crossed his face. "Hux stashed what we found in his safe place before . . . before they found him."

Her apprehension bled away at the grief on his face. She'd never met Michael's mentor, but she knew he'd looked up to Huxley with fierce respect, and they'd been friends as well.

"Sorry, man," Jarek said. "You two were pretty close, I take it."

She was almost surprised to see what looked like genuine sympathy on Jarek's face. Maybe he wasn't utterly heartless.

Michael nodded, then gave a little shrug. "Nothing to do now but make sure it wasn't for nothing."

Jarek clapped a hand on Michael's other shoulder. "Hallelujah, man. Let's get cracking on finding this safe place, then."

"I suppose you could all stand to sit down and breathe for a minute or two," Pryce said. "I can't help but notice you could all benefit from medical treatment."

That brought the pulsing ache of her bullet-grazed shoulder back to the forefront. It wasn't bad, but it could certainly use cleaning and dressing.

"A drink might not hurt either," Jarek said.

"A medical professional might feel otherwise," Pryce said.

"Guess it's good you're just a crazy old geezer, then."

She looked away to stifle a smile as the two shared a fit of amused chuffing. Grown-ass man-children though they might be, even after the night they'd had, there was something mildly charismatic about Jarek and Pryce.

"Well, c'mon back then." Pryce turned to stroll to the back of the room.

Jarek hesitated. "You're sure? We do have some serious heat on us."

"Sure, sure. Where else am I gonna find this kind of excitement?"

Jarek gestured for her and Michael to go first, mumbling something about crazy old bastards.

Michael followed Pryce, and she and Jarek fell in behind. When they reached the door, each paused to see who would go first. Then they both did, shouldering into one another with almost perfect synchrony.

She scowled at him. He stepped back and offered the right of way with a dramatic bow.

"Sexist," she grumbled.

He winked at her.

She rolled her eyes and stepped through the door into a workspace that was much larger than the front room and chock-full of all kinds of stuff. That was the best word for it: stuff.

An astounding variety of tools decorated the wall over a large, L-shaped work bench. Across the room, several metal shelves hosted an eclectic assortment of items including electronics, garden fertilizers, blocks and bars of different metals, and various other raw materials. Behind the shelves, another long bench housed a grab bag of lab equipment: scales, glassware, a microscope, and a few other machines she wasn't sure about.

Pryce strolled past two large tables in the center of the room that were heavily laden with more stuff to a dark, tightly winding spiral staircase in the far corner. "Upstairs?"

"Perfect," Jarek said behind her. "As long as there's—wait, what?"

She turned. He was touching his earpiece, his brow deeply furrowed.

"Patch it through," he said.

His eyes darted back and forth, focused somewhere far away as if he were reading text that wasn't there. After a moment, he seemed to remember the rest of them.

"Local broadcast," he explained.

He reached down to touch his comm. A crackling voice filled the shop.

"—as gone on long enough."

Despite the crackle in the line, she recognized the voice. She'd only heard him speak four words that night, but they'd stuck with her, right in the place where all of her darkest nightmare material hung around.

The Red King.

"You have twenty-four hours to return the nest," he continued, "at which point we will grant you amnesty and allow you to leave the city. Refuse this offer, and you will be opening the world to horrors like it has never known before. You have no idea the power you meddle with. Twenty-four hours. Do not make us find you."

With that, the line went silent. The silence lingered as they traded looks and tried to puzzle out what exactly they'd just heard.

"Say, Mikey," Jarek finally said. "I'm thinking now might be a swell time for you to tell us what the hell it is you stole from the Reds."

CHAPTER TEN

"Here's the thing," Michael began.

Jarek braced himself. Here it was. Good news never started with "here's the thing." What if Michael couldn't really get him to Fela? What if he'd busted his ass and brought the entire Red army down on his own head for nothing?

He let out a breath, leaned back into the soft armchair, and found a practiced semblance of relaxation as Michael continued.

"We're not really sure what we found."

"The nest, apparently," Al said in his ear.

"The nest, apparently," Pryce unknowingly echoed from the small kitchen space that adjoined his cozy but perfectly adequate living quarters, where they'd decided to hold council once he'd seen to their wounds.

Jarek stifled a smile. It was good to have Al back, even if he and Pryce were redundant at times. Being without Al for any amount of time always felt wrong after all these years, as if he'd left a physical part of himself behind.

He took a long sip of whiskey. The liquid fire passed down his throat, leaving behind tingles that spoke of spices and cherries. He watched Michael over on the couch next to Rachel, waiting for him to get to the point.

"Honestly," Michael said, "it was kind of dumb luck that we stumbled onto the thing at all."

Jarek sipped the delicious whiskey again and rolled a hand in a *let's hurry it up* motion.

"So what exactly did you find?" Pryce said. "Other than Fela, that is."

"There were some munitions and other supplies," Michael said, "but the main thing—the thing I assume the King was calling the nest —was a, well, some kind of device. It looked kind of like a giant metal egg standing on its base, almost as tall as me. At first I thought it was just a weird statue or something. It didn't have controls or anything like that."

"But?" Pryce said.

"But when I touched it, I felt something. There was this low buzz, like the thing was on or using power or something. But there was something else too. It was like"—he frowned, scratching at his dark bush of hair—"like the thing was trying to communicate. Like it was partially conscious or something. I don't know. I just know that it felt powerful and that the Overlord wanted the thing in his possession. Badly."

Rachel frowned at Michael. "Do you think it was trying to reach you telepathically? The way I used to try?"

Michael considered. "I guess it kind of reminded me of that. But my glyphs would've stopped that kind of thing cold, right?"

Jarek ran a hand through the back of his hair and tapped his foot on the ground, resisting the urge to tell him to hurry the hell up and tell him what any of this had to do with Fela.

"I don't like the sound of this, Michael," Rachel said.

"And how, I wonder, would such a device 'open the world to horrors it's never known before?'" Al said quietly in his earpiece.

That was a good question, but not quite as good as where Fela was and how he was supposed to get her back.

He polished off his whiskey and reached for the bottle. On the couch across from him, Rachel took a sip of her own whiskey, wrinkled up her face, and failed to suppress a small cough. He grinned. Michael shot a frown her way.

"Right, then." He leaned back with a fresh glass and propped his feet up on the worn wooden coffee table between them. "Giant, mind-bending metal egg thing. Fascinating stuff."

"Eloquently said, sir," Al said.

He ignored Al. "Now why the hell is the Red King threatening us with doomsday over this thing, and, more importantly, what does any of this have to do with my suit?"

Michael fixed him with a serious look. "I have no idea what he meant by that, but this could be big, Jarek. Bigger than you or Fela. We're talking about potentially stopping the raknoth here. About getting this world back on track. Can't you see that?"

"You know," Jarek said, "I've probably heard people make claims like that a dozen different times now. It's always something big, always the turning point you've all been waiting for. It's bullshit, Mikey. You're sitting on a giant egg. That's it. You have no idea why they want it. And even if you were right and this was the time for us to all hold dicks together and fight the raknoth, you know I'd be a hundred times more useful to everyone if I had Fela. So before we get high on dreams of saving the world, first things first: where's my suit?"

Michael shifted in his seat. "Like I said, I don't know, exactly."

"Right. But I take it you know who does."

"I do." Michael took a deep breath and let it out before finally meeting Jarek's gaze. "But it's Alaric Weston."

"What?"

That wasn't good. That was the opposite of good. The man who knew how to find Fela just so happened to be a legend who'd disappeared like a ghost years ago. "You've gotta be kidding me."

Michael shook his head.

"Fuck. Fuck!"

"Not good," Al agreed in his ear.

Pryce placed a food-laden tray on the table and sat in his own armchair beside Jarek. "Did you say Alaric Weston?"

"That can't be your only lead," Jarek said.

Michael looked down at the thick white carpet between them, his expression that of a dog who'd just crapped on said carpet.

"Who's Alaric Weston?" Rachel asked.

"He's kind of the father of the Resistance," Michael said, not looking up.

"The absentee father," Jarek said. "Who hasn't been seen or heard from for at least, what?"

"Five years," Pryce said. He took a sip of his own whiskey and calmly began to assemble a sandwich from the tomatoes and cheese and homemade bread on the platter in front of them.

"Five years!" Jarek set his whiskey to the side and leaned in to follow Pryce's lead. He'd been content enough to enjoy the sweet fire of Pryce's homemade whiskey as he waited, but now that the scent of fresh-baked bread was hitting him full blast, he was ready to eat. Busting out of fortresses was hungry work, it seemed, because the others quickly followed suit.

"I have to say, Mikey," Jarek said around a bite, "I really hope the next seven words out of your mouth are, 'I know where Alaric Weston is.'"

"That's six words, sir," Al said in his ear.

He paused and began counting off on his fingers. "Jarek. I know where Alaric Weston is, Jarek. Make my day, Mikey."

"I know where Alaric Weston is," Pryce said. He took a bite of his sandwich and shrugged. "Or where he went, at least."

That came as a surprise. Jarek knew Pryce had been acquainted with Weston on some level, but he was pretty sure they weren't pen pals these days. And of course, Pryce just had to milk his delicious intel for all it was worth.

"Thanks for speaking up sooner, ya old goat," he said. "So where'd the big bad rebel go?"

Michael leaned forward. "Resistance intel—"

Jarek snorted.

"—puts him in Deadwood."

"South Dakota," Pryce said at Jarek's questioning look. "That would be my strong guess too, but I don't think finding him's the real problem. It's getting him to come back here that's going to be the hard part."

He didn't know much about Weston's disappearance save that the guy had bailed after his role in the Resistance had gotten his family killed. Jarek could fly to South Dakota himself, no problem. But opening this particular can of worms?

There had to be another way.

"Are you sure we really need Weston to find this place?"

"That's what Hux told me before he . . ." Michael's eyebrows knitted together. "He said Alaric was the only other person who knew. He was going to show me the place someday, but that's . . ." He sighed. "Yeah. Weston's our best bet."

"And we're sure Al can't get a fix on Fela?" Pryce said. "Even knowing she's probably somewhere in the city?"

"No dice," Jarek said. "Believe me, we've tried, and—oh, come on, Al." He rolled his eyes at the confused looks Michael and Rachel were shooting him over their sandwiches. "Might as well say hi."

Al's voice came out of the comm's external speaker now. "Um, right. Hello! I'm Al."

"Hi," Rachel said, her eyes shifting back and forth uncertainly.

Michael stared at the comm. "Is that . . ."

"My robot sidekick, yep," Jarek said. "Moving on: Al's done his best, but Hux must've shielded this safe place of his, because we've got nothing. Al's also . . ."

He actually felt bad saying it. Despite what the few who knew about him might've thought, Al had feelings too—real feelings.

" . . . not at my best, sir," Al said. "Not running on this confounded ship's computer."

"He almost crashed the ship a few weeks ago," Jarek said.

"The computer?" Pryce said. "Or the actual ship?"

"Well, you know, when one goes . . ."

Al sniffed. "It's a rubbish computer, sir! I've no space to stretch my legs in here."

"I agree," Jarek said. "Which leads us back to needing Fela."

"Well that's a fine pickle, then." Pryce tucked the last bite of his sandwich away.

Michael and Rachel were still staring at Jarek's comm.

Rachel cleared her throat. "You're telling me this Al guy is, like—"

"An artificial intelligence construct, if you please," Al said, "though 'Al' will do fine. Alfred, actually, is the name."

"I'd heard rumors you had some kind of lost-gen AI riding around in that exo," Michael said, "but I didn't know—wow, man."

It was clear from the looks on their faces that this revelation was going to take a minute to process. Normally, he'd say that was fair enough, but right now, Jarek wanted answers.

"Look, I get it. I'm pretty awesome and everything—"

"I believe I'm the one inspiring awe, sir," Al said.

"—but can we please get back to figuring out how to find our stuff so we can all be a step closer to going on our merry ways?"

Michael held up empty hands. "I think we have to find Alaric Weston."

"I think *you* have to find Weston," Rachel said, nodding at Jarek. "Michael told you what he knows." She looked at Michael. "You can tell your precious Resistance too, but there's no reason you need to stick your neck out again."

Michael stared uneasily back and forth between them.

Jarek polished off his whiskey, glad for its warmth beginning to ease through his limbs.

This was bullshit. Worse, this was bullshit he didn't see any clear way out of. A lead was a lead. Especially when it was the only lead.

He poured himself a fresh glass. The drink was the only thing in the room that could make him feel better about any of this. Pryce gladly took a pour as well.

"You know what?" Jarek said. "I think she's right, Mikey. No reason to risk our bacon. You should head for the hills—right after your people find Weston and give me my suit back." He nodded to Rachel and offered her the bottle. "Everyone wins, right?"

"Should you really be drinking with the Reds looking for us?" Michael said.

"If I stopped drinking whenever someone was looking for me, I'd be sober till the day I died. You know what they say about all work and no play . . ."

"It's the leading cause of healthy livers everywhere?" Al said.

Pryce snorted.

He wiggled the bottle at Rachel. "A friendly drink. No one wants Mikey sticking his neck out for no reason."

When she hesitantly extended her glass, her left sleeve rode up her arm. She fixed it in an instant—a practiced, reflexive motion—but not before he caught a glimpse of the raised, pale lines of old scars on the inside of her forearm.

He wordlessly poured her drink, storing the information away, then held the whiskey out to Michael with a grin. When the younger man declined, as Jarek knew he would, he poured himself more instead.

"So what do you say, Mikey? What can the Resistance do for us?"

Michael fidgeted with his hands. "In the next twenty-four hours? Probably not much. Both of our ships were down for repairs, last I knew."

He stared at Michael for a second, then tilted his head back and cackled. "Both of them? You broke-ass jokers are down to two ships?"

Michael scowled. "We've shifted to more of a ground fleet. Airships are too easily spotted these days anyways."

"Not to mention they get you places way too conveniently. Where's the fun?"

Michael rubbed at his temples. "Let me call in to update them and see what they can do, but I know they're going to ask if you're willing to help find Weston. In return for the suit, of course."

"Oh, of course," Jarek said. "Naturally. Because my braving the Red Fortress to pull your sorry ass out clearly isn't payment enough for the return of my own property."

"Our back is kinda to the wall here," Michael said. "We're trying to help this world."

"Forgive me if I don't get all dewy-eyed. I've heard a few too many despicable people say those words."

"Boohoo for you, then," Rachel said. "You could walk away from all of this as easily as Michael can. Sounds to me like you just want a reason to bitch."

Jarek straightened in his chair and glared at her, his pulse throbbing in his temples. "Actually, I can't just walk away from this." He turned to Michael. "You know what? I'll find Weston for your band of bumbling idiots, but you're gonna see to it that I'm paid for the effort."

Michael nodded emphatically. "I can do that. I can definitely do that."

"So you're a mercenary," Rachel said to Jarek, folding her arms. "That makes sense."

He jabbed a finger in the rough direction of the Red Fortress. "You didn't seem to have a problem with my methods when I was saving your ass back there."

She leaned forward, jaw tense, ready to rise.

Pryce calmly stood and made a point of gathering up their plates and the tray. The action dispelled some of the tension in the air. "If Jarek's a mercenary, he's not very good at his job."

Jarek sipped his whiskey and leaned back in his chair, reclaiming his practiced calm.

"What I'm still wondering," Pryce continued, "is why the raknoth care so much about this nest object."

Truth be told, it was a mildly interesting question. He wasn't entirely sure he cared about the answer, but it was mildly interesting nonetheless.

"What are they even gonna do after twenty-four hours? Put the Resistance in time out? Declare war against the people they're clearly already at war against?"

"I'm more concerned with what this nest will do after those twenty-four hours," Pryce said. "It sounded like the threat was planetary, not specifically against the Resistance."

"I agree, sir," Al said. "Though it almost sounded to me as if he was warning us that this nest was the threat, not the raknoth themselves."

Jarek barked a laugh, then shrugged as they all looked at him. "What? No one thinks a giant psychic doomsday egg is worth a laugh?"

Apparently not.

"Maybe the freaking thing hatches," he said.

Pryce stroked at his chin. "Maybe so. There's only so much damage one thermonuclear device can do. I mean, they already played that hand and we're all still here, right?"

"Unless this device transcends our technology," Al said. "The raknoth *are* aliens."

"We don't know that," Pryce said.

"Most likely," Al amended.

Pryce didn't argue.

"They're probably just trying to scare us into handing it over," Michael said. "I think they don't want us to have it because it's dangerous to them. Maybe it's full of information we could use to finally get the upper hand."

"Here's a novel idea," Rachel said. "What if we just walk away and let the creepy alien egg rust in the secret safe place? Maybe the raknoth throw a tantrum. Maybe nothing happens. Either way, the raknoth lose their toy, and we don't get ourselves killed. Problem solved."

"Unless it's a time bomb," Al said quietly.

"Yeah," Jarek said. "You can't go through life just walking away from ticking time bombs, Goldilocks."

She glared at him. "Says the guy who only cares because his stupid exosuit is in there."

"That"—he held up a finger—"plus the children. We can't let a big bomb go off around here."

"This place is dead!"

"There are close to fifteen thousand people left in the Newark area," Pryce said. "Plenty more across the bay. Most of New York fled this way when the bombs started falling."

Rachel's mouth worked soundlessly for a few seconds, and she sat back with a huff. "That still doesn't mean you need Michael for any of this."

She clearly wasn't going to drop the idea, though Michael didn't appear to have any interest in fleeing. Jarek might have to sleep with one eye open tonight in case Rachel got it in her head to attempt a rescue via kidnapping.

Pryce set the dishes down in the sink with a clatter. "Michael may be exactly the one who's needed. Whoever goes is going to have a hell of a time getting Alaric Weston to come back by choice after what happened here. Jarek isn't Resistance—or much of a diplomat."

"I resent that, old man," Jarek said. "But you may have a point. Still, you'd think someone who cared enough to start the Resistance might be able to set personal grievances aside when the doomsday threats start flying, right? Especially if it means sticking it to the raknoth one more time."

"I never really got why Weston left in the first place," Michael said. "I mean"—he glanced at Rachel—"if I lost my family to those bastards, I'd—"

"That's not why he left," Pryce said. "Not the entirety of it, at least. Alaric did lose his wife and son to the raknoth. The part most people don't know is that his son isn't dead. He's the one who killed his mother."

Jarek turned around to look at Pryce full on. "Dude killed his own mother?"

"From what little I gathered, it wasn't really his son anymore. The raknoth got to him. Changed him."

"They got into his head?" Rachel said.

There was a terrifying thought.

"More than that, maybe," Pryce said. "I've heard stories about them . . . altering people. Making their servants more like them."

And there was a more terrifying thought. He thought about Seth Mosen's uncanny strength and the creepy red glint in his eyes. Was that what had happened to him?

"As far as I know," Pryce continued, "the raknoth still have the boy under their thumb somewhere. I think that's why Alaric left. Because he was terrified he might have to face down what was left of his son someday."

"That makes more sense," Michael said slowly. "My God."

He couldn't say he disagreed with Michael on that one, but even so . . .

"Everyone has to face down their demons eventually."

It came out sounding more bitter than he'd intended.

Rachel arched an eyebrow at him.

He pushed down the unpleasant memories fighting to emerge and shrugged. "What? I'm just a heartless mercenary. I don't know any better."

He swiped the whiskey bottle from the table and stood, no longer in the mood to talk about any of this. The simple act of standing dropped the curtain on the work the whiskey had been doing behind the scenes. He felt good.

He started for the stairs. He'd sleep in the shop, let Rachel and Michael sort out their business.

"We have enough fuel for a round trip to South Dakota, Al?"

"Affirmative, sir."

"Good. Tomorrow, then." He paused at the top step and glanced at Pryce's back where he stood at the kitchen sink. "Assuming you don't mind us grabbing a few hours of sleep here, old man."

Pryce raised a soapy hand and gave him a thumbs-up over his shoulder.

"Right. Thanks." He looked at Michael. "Better get some sleep, Mikey. We should leave before sunrise."

"*You* should leave before sunrise," Rachel said.

It wasn't going to end, was it?

"Mikey's not leaving my sight until I have my suit."

Michael nodded, looking perfectly happy with the news.

Rachel rose to her feet, hands curling to fists. "The hell he isn't."

She looked as if she were contemplating throwing him through the roof, and Jarek wasn't sure there'd be a damn thing he could do about it if she did. Pryce had turned around to watch the scene, wariness and curiosity warring for control of his features.

"Rache," Michael said softly, taking her left wrist in his hand. "This is my choice. If you drag me back to Unity, it's going to have to be kicking and screaming."

She finally dropped her glare and looked down at Michael, her face tight and slightly flushed with drink.

That was Jarek's cue.

"Think I better let you crazy kids talk this one out," he said, starting down the stairs. "Just don't skip the sleep, Mikey. The adventure starts tomorrow."

CHAPTER ELEVEN

"What the hell, Michael?" Rachel said once Pryce had abandoned the remaining dishes and retreated to another room.

"I have to do this, Rache," he said. "I have to see it through. I'd say it even if it was just for Hux, but I have a feeling this is a lot bigger than that."

"Oh, good!" she hissed, her face hot with frustration and whiskey-fueled fire. "You have a feeling. I was afraid you were risking your life for nothing!"

"Rache—"

"Look, last night was fun and everything, but I'd rather not have to storm another fortress for you. You need to get out while you still can."

A silence passed between them, and she found herself wishing she hadn't had those two heavy drinks.

"This isn't one of your comics, Spongehead," she said. "Those people weren't fucking around back there. And where the hell was your precious Resistance? They hid under their rock while the Reds tortured you."

"It's not like that, Rache. They didn't—"

"Didn't what? Didn't know where you were? It took me less than two days to crack that one, Michael, and I barely even know where the fuck I am right now. A fucking mercenary came to pull you out of there of his own free will before your Resistance friends so much as raised a finger. I don't like him, but at least he didn't leave you to die. You can't go back to 'friends' like that."

How could he not see that?

"Rache . . ." He reached out to touch her arm.

She shrugged it off, too irritated for contact.

"The rest of us can't do the things you can, Rache. Busting me out of the Red Fortress would have taken everything the Resistance has and then some. We're severely outgunned here. It's why I need to make sure what Hux and I found doesn't go to waste. I promise they were trying to find a way."

She snorted. "Jarek didn't have an army. Where were his excuses?"

That put a deep frown on Michael's face. It probably caused him physical pain, hearing his sister praise the morality of a man like Jarek Slater over that of his precious Resistance. But so what? Jarek might be a dick—scratch that, he *was* a dick—but she couldn't deny that things might've gone much differently at the Fortress if he hadn't been there.

Then again, maybe this was all just the whiskey talking.

"That's different," Michael finally said. "Jarek might not be like you, but he's—Jesus, he only did it because he thought I could help him find his suit."

"What is it with this suit?" she said. "What's the big deal?"

"Do you remember those Iron Man holos I used to read?"

She nodded. He'd had his head buried in every holo comic he could get his hands on for the better part of their childhood.

"It's kind of like that. He's damn near unstoppable in the thing, and as far as we can tell, he's the only one who can use it—not that that's stopped anyone from trying to get hold of it. Plus there's the whole thing with Al."

She frowned. That entire thing had been unbelievable. She still wasn't entirely convinced it hadn't been another person on the line screwing with them for kicks. But if this suit of Jarek's was real, why not Alfred the AI too?

"Where the hell did he even get his hands on that kind of tech?" she said.

He shook his head. "No idea, but he sure wants it back."

That was obvious enough. Which also meant he wouldn't be likely to just forget about Michael and leave him be, not until he got his precious suit. Still, she could handle Jarek. And once they got back to Unity, it wouldn't matter anyway.

"Do you know how to contact Jarek?"

"We have some mutual contacts, I think."

"Good. Then we should leave Newark. Now. You can get word to Jarek or the Resistance from Unity if you're really so desperate to help them."

Jarek was camped out downstairs, but she had other ways of getting them out of the building. With a little luck, they could be back to Unity by noon tomorrow.

Michael reached over to take her hand. "Rache, it's not that simple."

She turned a hard look his way.

He held her gaze. "This is my decision. I believe in this. You can't keep trying to protect me forever."

"Not if you're so damn set on getting yourself killed." She pulled her hand free of his grip and set her jaw. "I'm not leaving you to go on a freaking road trip alone with that trigger-happy idiot."

Understanding and alarm flooded his eyes. "Rache, I don't want you to—"

"Oh, no. You don't get to have it both ways, Spongehead. If you're so set on seeing this thing through, you don't get to tell me to sit out." She grabbed her staff and moved to the top of the stairs. "If you go, I go. That's the deal."

She started down the stairs.

"Where are you going now?" he called.

"To make your stubborn ass a shield in case I'm not there the next time it gets shot at. Try to get some sleep."

"Rache?"

She paused.

"Can I borrow your comm? I need to check in with my people."

Of course he did. She stripped off her comm and threw it to him, maybe harder than necessary, then continued down the stairs. "We're not done with this conversation, Spongehead."

SHE FOUND JAREK SPRAWLED OUT on an armchair he'd pulled over to one of the worktables close enough that he could prop his feet up on the table's bench. The half-empty bottle of whiskey sat on the table in front of him. His eyes were closed and his breathing light, but she couldn't tell if he was asleep or not.

She decided she didn't care and went over to inspect the supplies on Pryce's extensively stocked shelves. The invitation Pryce had given to "make themselves at home" before he'd disappeared upstairs might not have included the use of the shop area, but she didn't need much, and he didn't seem like the type to begrudge someone a few scraps when it might be a matter of life and death. She gathered what she needed, found a rotary engraver from the giant wall of tools, and returned to the worktables.

She paused next to the larger table, frowning down at the still lines of Jarek's face and the shallow motion of his breath. He didn't look particularly peaceful for a sleeping man, but how would he? He'd killed at least nine men back at the Fortress, and given the ease with which he'd done it, she could only imagine how many more corpses he'd left in his wake over the years.

It was a disturbing thought, and yet she didn't feel this was a hardened murderer she was looking at.

Whatever. If she was going to be watching Michael's back around Jarek, it wouldn't do to start worrying about his soul.

She was about to turn to her work when he said, "Take a picture." His eyes came open in a way that told her he'd been awake all along. "It'll last longer."

She managed to stifle her surprised jolt, but she still sucked in an audible breath. The sound ignited a wolfish grin that spread to his eyes.

Asshole.

"I'm coming with you," she said.

"Much as I'd love to have you along, sunshine, there's no need for that. I'll keep Mikey safe. You can go home and not worry a single golden hair. Or maybe *you* just want a reason to bitch too."

She dropped her cargo on the table and pointed her staff down at Jarek's sprawled form. Maybe it was the remnants of the whiskey talking, or maybe she was just pissed at the Spongehead's bad judgment, but she couldn't take this shit right now.

He frowned at the tip of the weapon as it settled in front of his face. Then he burst into motion, tugging the staff aside and springing to his feet so fast she didn't have time to so much as blink. He pinned her to the table with her arms tucked uselessly at her sides.

She bucked against him a few times, reaching for her power. His grip loosened. She looked up to find him watching her with an expression that was hard to get a read on. Slowly, almost gently, he released her. He held his hands up but didn't step back more than an inch or two, which left him firmly planted in her personal space.

She held his dark eyes. Her pulse quickened, a thrill she'd almost forgotten stirring in her chest. Need burned in his eyes. Any moment, he was going to kiss her—she could feel it. Would she kiss him back if he did? Or would she put his well-formed ass through the wall twenty feet behind him?

"I, uh . . ." His eyes searched her face in a way that seemed utterly unlike everything she'd observed of him since they'd met. "I think we may have gotten off on the wrong foot."

Goddamn right they had. She wasn't sure why that made her angry, but it sure as hell did. She clenched her fist, enclosing him in a cocoon of her will, and shoved him back into the table five feet behind him. She squeezed harder, intensifying the pressure of his cocoon.

"So you're . . ." he managed to squeeze out between breaths, "saying you would like to come then?"

"Goddammit." She relinquished her hold on the energy.

He slumped back against the table with a little puff as she scooped up her staff.

"You're a child," she said into the silence. "You know that, right?"

He didn't answer. Instead, he inspected the pile of scraps she'd laid out on the table.

She waited for the inevitable: the paltry attempt he'd make to salvage his pride or mark his territory and establish his dominance. That was what guys like him did, right? She'd learned from experience it was best to smack down the bullshit before it took root. But the attempt didn't come.

"How are you hitting me past my glyph?" he finally asked. "Is my shield faulty?"

She frowned. "That's the first thing you wanna know?"

"Considering I might be stuck for the time being around an arcanist who wants to kick my ass, yeah. That's the first thing I wanna know. Why? Were you expecting me to ask what it's like to have *powers*?" He wiggled his fingers for dramatic effect.

Dammit all to hell, she was fighting to keep herself from mirroring his grin. Something about the stupid thing was infectious. Worse, he was right—that was exactly what everyone asked when they found out about the things she could do.

"Your glyph is fine," she said. "There's just more than one way to toss around an asshat."

He chuckled, and she felt that stupid grin tug at her mouth.

"My mind is safe, though?"

She arched an eyebrow at him. "I don't know if I'd agree with that assessment, but you're guarded from telepathic influence, at least."

He nodded. "Great. So what are the ways?"

"What?"

"What are the ways one tosses an asshat?"

She considered. There wasn't any great reason not to tell him. If she did end up needing to wipe the ceiling with him, nothing she told him would help him much anyway.

"Well," she began.

He held up a finger and looked back toward the spiral stairs. "Is that you up there, Pryce?"

There was the sound of a clearing throat, and then padding footsteps and light creaks as Pryce began descending the staircase. "What are you two up to down there? I hope you're not making a mess of my supplies."

"It's like you read a book called *Things Grumpy Old Men Say 101*," Jarek called back. "And don't pretend you weren't eavesdropping, you old weirdo."

Pryce shot them a guilty smile as he drew into view and made his way over to the table. "Couldn't sleep. Too curious."

"What's it like being you?" Jarek said, looking at him as if he were an alien.

Pryce ignored him and turned to her. "Care to sate an old man's curiosity?"

"What, are you an enthusiast or something?" she asked.

Jarek laughed. "You have no idea."

Pryce shrugged. "I am a man of many fascinations. An intellectual polygamist, if you will."

She looked between the two of them, then shrugged and gestured to the bench. She grabbed a small metal plate for her pile of scrap and sat down on the bench opposite them.

Jarek watched with interest, but Pryce looked like a kid whose parents had told him Santa was coming.

"The most efficient way to exert telekinetic influence over something is to form a direct connection with it," she began, reaching out with her mind to find the little plate and trickling a tiny bit of her own body heat into it, shaping it to do her will.

The plate rose smoothly from her fingers to float between her and her audience.

"This kind of connection wastes less energy." She concentrated, picturing the piece in motion, and it began to weave a figure eight through the air. "And it also makes precise control a lot easier."

Pryce was staring, eyes wide and mouth agape.

"Freakin' Jedi," Jarek said.

The bulb paused in midair. "Freakin' what?"

He looked at her as if she'd sprouted a third arm from her forehead. "Have you not seen . . . ?"

The smile she'd been holding back finally spilled over her face. "Of course I've seen *Star Wars*. Jesus."

"Oh, thank the maker," Jarek said, placing a hand to his chest. "I mean, otherwise, what's the point?"

Pryce nodded his silent agreement, his eyes still fixed on the floating plate.

"Do you wanna hear the rest or not?"

"Apologies, master," Jarek said. "Do continue."

"So. When someone—let's say an insufferable mercenary—decides to get cute and shield something from an arcanist's mind using a glyph or whatever, I can't form that direct connection, which means I have to get creative."

Jarek listened attentively now, genuine interest in his eyes.

"Different arcanists handle these things in their own ways. I've heard of people resorting to calling wind, for instance, but that's kind of a shitty workaround. I basically conjure up a solid wall in my mind and push that against the shielded space. Or maybe into it. It's kind of abstract, but . . ."

She willed the plate to resume its figure eight, this time fixing it in a hard case of her will, not unlike she'd done to Jarek a minute ago. The plate wove through the turns, its flight noticeably more jerky than before. At each turn, there were tiny sounds as if the plate were striking a physical surface in the thin air.

"It's clunky and less efficient than a direct connection, but it works."

"I'll say. Felt like I'd been hit by a car back in the brig."

Pryce arched an eyebrow, glancing between them.

She let the plate drop back to her open hand. "Yeah, I was a little revved up at that point. And you didn't seem to be taking prisoners."

"Not a problem," Jarek said. "I would've done the same thing if I had Jedi powers."

She set the plate back on the table. "I didn't say I was sorry about it."

He smiled. "I know."

They regarded each other in silence.

"I'm not so sure about this Jedi talk, either," she said. "Arcanism might be on the mystical side, but at the end of the day, it's bound by energy conservation just like the rest of the universe."

"*Star Wars* was based in this universe."

She threw her hands up in exasperation. "Whatever, man. You know what I'm trying to say. I'm not tapping into some magical energy here. It's all give and take."

"I knew it!" Pryce said, thrusting his hands into the air.

She couldn't help but smile at his fervor.

"Yeah, yeah," Jarek said. "Keep it in your pants, old man."

"You first," Pryce mumbled.

She cleared her throat.

Jarek turned back to her. "So do you have to kill us now that you've told us all your secrets?"

"I wouldn't say *have* to," she said. "Sometimes I do things just for the fun of it. And that was hardly all of my secrets."

"Intriguing." He waggled his eyebrows at her, then glanced down at his comm. "Think it's better if I hear the rest of them later, though. I'm useless without my beauty sleep." He stood, his expression leaning toward serious. "We're gonna leave in a few hours. You should sleep too if you're coming with us."

She nodded but made no move to stand. As much as her body craved sleep, she needed to at least get the glyph etchings laid down on the new catcher tonight. The actual enchanting she could always do on the road—or in the air.

Pryce remained seated as well. "Caught between the Resistance and the whole Red nation, the fate of Fela and who knows what else hanging in the balance. What have you gotten yourself into this time, son?"

"Agh, who knows," Jarek said. "As long as I get Fela back, everything else can burn, for all I care."

"Spoken like a true mercenary," she said.

Jarek gave her a lazy two-fingered salute and turned for the stairs.

"He doesn't mean it," Pryce said quietly.

"The hell I don't, old man." Jarek's voice rang down as he disappeared above.

Pryce smiled a weary smile, then turned his attention to the scraps she'd laid out from the pile. "And what are we doing with these here?"

Maybe she should feel bad for dipping into his things, but Pryce didn't seem put off in the least.

"Enchanting." She picked up the engraver with a flourish, unclipped her own catcher, and handed it over to Pryce. "Making a copy of this thing."

He turned the catcher over in his hands. "And what does this doodad do?"

"It pulls thermal energy from the air to stop incoming bullets."

It was hard to say it in a way that didn't sound ridiculous out loud.

Pryce paused his inspection to look up at her. "Well, I'll be damned. It just boggles the mind."

"I guess it's easy to start taking this kind of stuff for granted." She conjured a small sphere of nebulous green light into existence over her palm and watched Pryce, so clearly fascinated by all of this. She smiled, relishing the electric tingles the minor channeling sent racing through her body.

He set the catcher back in front of her so he could clap his hands. "Amazing."

"If you say so." She released her hold on the light.

"And it's all equivalent exchange? Energy in equals energy out?"

"If you're really good, yeah, but less skilled arcanists tend to waste a lot of energy."

"Makes sense, but there must be some limit to . . ." He shook his head and leaned back. "I'm sorry. Someday, I'd like to ask you eight thousand questions about how all of this works, but Jarek's right. You should sleep while you can."

She watched him extract his legs from the bench. "You don't do this very often, do you? Take people in like this, I mean."

A sad smile crossed his face. "I won't say Jarek's family. We don't have family anymore, he and I. But he's a good kid, no matter how hard he tries to hide it. Better than he himself knows, I sometimes think."

She pushed down the urge to ask if they were talking about the same Jarek. The way Pryce talked about him, the almost gentle way Jarek had reacted to her threats . . . Maybe there was an ounce or two more to the guy than his dangerous jackass routine let on.

She picked the etcher back up. "I need to get these etchings done tonight, but I can talk while I work. The concentration part doesn't really come till later."

He inclined his head and sat back down, settling his elbows on the tabletop and propping his chin up on intertwined fingers.

"He lost his parents in the Catastrophe?" she asked, starting on the first glyph.

Pryce studied her and nodded. "Been on his own ever since, for the most part. He was on a short stint with a merc outfit when I first met him. That didn't end too well."

"For him?"

"For them."

When she glanced up, he looked ten years older. "Sounds like there's a story there."

"Oh, yes. That's where he got his nickname, actually."

"His nickname?"

"In a lot of circles, they call him the Soldier of Charity. When he has Fela, at least."

This time, she couldn't hold it back. "We're talking about the same Jarek, right?"

He chuckled. "There's a reason his nickname isn't the Czar of Teamwork and Sensitivity."

She smiled back. As a general rule, she didn't really trust anyone until they had damn well earned it at least thrice over, but occasionally she decided she liked certain people. Jay Pryce was quickly making his way onto that short list.

"I'll keep that in mind."

"He's been through a lot," Pryce said. "Seen too much. He might not play well with others, but his heart's in the right place. Assuming I have any right to say what that place is."

She put the finishing touches on her third glyph. "Why are you telling me all this?"

Pryce showed her a tired smile. "Because you seem like you might care."

Well, that was sobering. She swallowed, and whatever dam had been staving off the exhaustion picked that moment to break inside her.

"Sleep." Pryce waved at the table. "You can take all this tomorrow— the engraver too. Get some rest."

Apparently he'd seen the dam break too.

She sighed and gave a hesitant nod.

He left as she began to gather up her supplies and returned a few moments later carrying a small leather satchel. He held it out to her.

"You're sure?"

He shrugged. "Feels nice to help someone while I can."

She thanked him and scooped the table's contents into the satchel's main compartment.

"Why don't you use my bed tonight?" he added.

She stiffened, her defensive reflexes kicking in. "I'm not stealing an old man's bed. I can sleep on a couch or in a chair just like those people up there with the man bits."

"Oh, I've no doubt of that, but I probably won't sleep tonight now anyway, and if I give the bed to Jarek, he'll probably just bleed all over my nice white sheets."

He met her uncertain look with a friendly smile. "Let an old man pamper a lady for a night. I won't tell if you won't."

She smiled and finally gave a shrug. "Have it your way."

She climbed the stairs, not the least bit excited about flying off tomorrow to stick her head into business that wasn't hers. Then again, if even a tenth of the people around Newark were half as good as Pryce, maybe there were worse ways to risk one's neck than trying to make sure the place wasn't about to become the new raknoth ground zero.

She laid down on Pryce's soft bed, her entire body weeping in relief, and decided that these were questions for her tomorrow self to figure out. Within the minute, sleep took her.

CHAPTER TWELVE

No one talked on the short walk to the ship the next morning, partially out of fear the Reds would still be out looking for them and partially by merit of the ridiculous predawn hour that Rachel wasn't entirely convinced could even rightfully be called morning. To top it all off, she'd had just enough whiskey the previous night to leave a dull ache in her head.

Yes, it was just as well that no one talked. She couldn't imagine anything Michael or Jarek would have to say right then would do anything but piss her off more.

A sleek-looking ship was waiting for them when they arrived in the still mostly dark space of the overgrown park.

"Baby," Jarek said, patting its hull, "you'll never believe the week I'm having."

In response, the rear hatch let out a few pops and began to descend into a boarding ramp.

The ship looked as if it might have been a military design—not that she was an expert. Its body was about the size of a small trailer home, but the sleek angularity of its matte black hull panels and compact wings whispered promises of stealth and speed nonetheless.

She absentmindedly reached out to touch the hull, more to appease a vague curiosity than to learn anything of value.

"All aboard," Al's voice said quietly from inside the empty ship as the boarding ramp touched down.

Yep. The whole artificial intelligence thing was definitely going to take some getting used to.

Jarek strode up the boarding ramp with the air of a child who wanted to show off his favorite toy but was scared to admit he cared what anyone thought.

How the hell had that guy ended up in possession of a fancy ship, a fancy battle suit, and a freaking artificial intelligence?

Inside, the ship was just large enough to constitute a cozy living space, which was exactly what the first compartment looked like—minus the "cozy" part.

A small, stiff-looking cot lay against the right wall. At the foot of the cot, a faded brown recliner faced a film-screen TV that hung over the drawers on the opposite wall of the cabin. Beyond the drawers was a tall locker with an obscenely large sword hanging along its side.

"What the hell is that thing?"

He followed her gaze and gave the giant sword an affectionate pat. "It's my Big Whacker."

Of course it was. Talk about overcompensation. The thing looked far too heavy to be effectively wielded, but maybe that was where this suit of his came in.

Rachel eyed the rest of the ship. The bare-bones kitchen space and the separate compartment that must've been a small bathroom were the last stops before the bulkhead that separated the cabin from the cockpit.

"So you live here?" she asked.

"Sometimes, yeah." Jarek ran a hand through the back of his hair. "Most of the time, I guess."

She stared at him. "Who are you?"

He shrugged. "I'm awesome. Don't worry about it."

"Not what I was implying."

Michael cleared his throat. "It's a heck of a ship, Jarek."

"Yeah," she said, her tone flat. "Really cool. Seriously."

"Oh, bite me, you wiener hats," Jarek said. "And I'll remind you that you don't need to be here, Goldilocks. I'm not even rightly sure I remember anyone inviting you. Feel free to step off at any time."

"Happy to, just as soon as Michael steps off with me."

He threw his hands up and turned for the cockpit. "It's like my life is stuck on some shitty broken record." From the cockpit, he called, "Come strap in for takeoff. Or don't. See if I care."

"'Weiner hats,'" Michael murmured beside her. "What does that even mean?"

"I don't know. But you totally are one."

"Glad to see we're all going to be mature adults on this trip."

She stalked up to the cockpit.

The cockpit only had proper seats for two, the pilot and the copilot, but there were benches against the bulkhead to either side of the doorway, complete with harnesses in case the ride got bumpy. She eyed Jarek lounging in the captain's chair, then turned to plop down on the left bench.

"Prepare for takeoff, Al," Jarek said. "Whoa!" he added as Michael came into the cockpit and moved to the copilot's chair.

"What?" Michael said.

"That's Al's chair, muchacho. Show some respect."

Michael shot her a confused look. "Oh, uh, sorry."

"Oh, really, sir," Al said through the cockpit speakers.

Jarek regarded Michael with a stern expression. Then his face cracked into a smile. "Just screwin' with you, Mikey. Whaddaya think, I'm some kind of crazy person? Strap in."

Michael did so, moving far more cautiously than the task merited.

"You secure back there, Goldilocks?" Jarek asked. "God forbid we lose you."

She pulled on her harness, shot him her sweetest smile, and gave him a middle-fingered thumbs-up.

Jarek beamed at her, then stomped one of the pedals in front of him.

Rachel's stomach lurched as the ship shot smoothly into the air.

Jarek peered over his shoulder, winked, and turned back to the controls. The whooshing sensation in her abdomen shifted directions as the ship accelerated forward and banked to the left.

Maybe his heart was in the right place (she still wasn't sold on Pryce's word there), but that didn't make Jarek any less of an asshole.

They leveled out of the turn and continued accelerating.

"All yours, Al," Jarek said. "To Deadwood, we go."

"Got it, sir. We can be there in as little as three hours."

Jarek unfastened his harness. "No hurry. Just wanted to clear Newark before anyone with eyes could see us. No reason to show up knocking on Weston's door at five in the morning over there." He looked back at Michael and Rachel. "You guys might as well get some sleep if you can."

As lovely as that sounded, she had a bullet catcher that needed finishing.

"Maybe we should figure out what the plan is before we get there," Michael said.

Jarek rolled his eyes. "Don't be such a boy scout, boy scout. We'll tell the guy what's up. And if that's not good enough, we'll knock his ass out and drag him back with us. Shit, I don't know. It'll be fine."

"And what if it's not?" Michael said. "What if he's armed and not agreeable? What if he's not even there? What if he's surrounded by civilians and decides to put up a fight?"

"Or," Jarek said, "what if he's surrounded by innocent, armed civilians riding giant teddy bears with gumdrops for eyes? Then we're really screwed."

Michael's brows knitted together. "What? The point is, we have no idea what we're walking into here, so we need to be ready for anything."

"Well, yeah," Jarek said. "Hence the giant gumdrop-eyed teddy bear mount contingency."

Michael's peaceful exterior was beginning to crack.

"Boys . . ." she said.

Michael stood. "You're a real handful, you know that?" He left the cockpit before anything more could spill out.

Jarek watched him go, trying and failing to contain a grin.

She scowled at him and leaned over to glance into the back cabin. Michael had plopped down into the recliner, arms crossed moodily across his chest. Irritated as he was, she knew he'd be asleep within minutes. The Spongehead had always slept like a rock.

She, on the other hand, would not be asleep within minutes, which meant she'd be stuck with Jarek Slater. Wonderful.

"I'm using your shower," she announced.

"Need help?" Jarek said. "It can get awfully confusing in there with all those dials and knobbies."

"Somehow, I think I'll find a way."

Cramped and lukewarm as it was, the shower was a godsend. It had been what, two days? Three? Too long, for sure. There'd been too much. Everything was blending together into one long, unpleasant trip. However many days it had been, it felt pretty damn good to be at least half clean for a few minutes. Returning to her dirty clothes tarnished the experience, but it was still something.

Michael was lightly snoring when she stepped out of the tiny bathroom, and Jarek was standing in the dim cabin, stripping off his dark, torn Henley. She caught a glimpse of a morbidly mesmerizing collection of scars on his lean, well-muscled torso.

Then he shot a wink at her, and she headed for the cockpit with a sigh.

There didn't seem to be any obvious work surfaces on the ship, so she settled down on the floor facing one of the benches and began unpacking the scraps she'd scrounged from Pryce's odd emporium.

Jarek stalked into the small bathroom and thumped around in the shower for a few minutes, whistling a tune she didn't recognize. A few minutes later, he plopped down in the pilot's chair sporting a fresh maroon Henley and smelling of soap and deodorant. He proceeded to occupy himself with some stupid game on his comm holo.

"You can do that over here," he said some time later, tapping at the flat space of the console in front of the copilot's chair. "Whatever that is."

She didn't look away from the glyph she was etching. "It's called enchanting in most circles. And I'm fine down here."

"Oh, right. Enchanting. Should've known. So what're you—"

"Getting ready to make another one of these." She held up her own bullet catcher. "It basically detects incoming bullets and stops them if they're gonna hit the person who's wearing it."

He swiveled his chair around, interested now. "So that's how you were doing that. You know, I've deflected a few bullets with a sword before . . ."

"Not without help," Al said quietly. "And it's hardly proved practical, sir."

Jarek frowned at the disembodied voice. "Whose side are you on again, Mr. Robot?"

"I'm trying to keep my brother alive," she said, "not win a competition."

"It's still a competition, Goldilocks. I'm just not your opponent."

She met his eyes. Was that true? It was and it wasn't, depending on how she looked at it. She turned back to her work.

"So how does it work?" he said after a while.

She put the final touches on a glyph in the shape of an eye before looking up. "In a nutshell, it's kind of like writing code. Except instead of text commands, I use glyphs. Then I power them up. It's complicated."

He scooted over to the adjacent bench and picked up her own catcher for inspection. "And you can track an incoming bullet with a few of these glyphs? I'm not a physicist or anything, but that sounds like some complicated shit to parse out."

"Well said, sir," Al said. "I was wondering the same thing, though."

Rachel allowed herself a small smile. "A lot of it comes down to how accurately I can focus my intention when I empower each glyph."

"Sounds quite subjective," Al said.

"There's a reason I was still scared to get shot at."

"Wimp," Jarek said.

She rolled her eyes.

"So all of this comes down to energy in and energy out?" Jarek asked.

"If you're really good, yeah, but most arcanists tend to waste a lot of energy, even on the basic stuff."

"And how many arcanists would that be, roughly?" Al said.

"You're awfully curious about all this for a robot and a hardened mercenary," Rachel said.

"Well, you're our first," Jarek said, wiggling his eyebrows. "Plus Pryce would kill us if we didn't come back with answers to some of his questions. The guy has so many of them."

She set down the piece she was working on and rotated to face Jarek. "I've only ever met three other arcanists, the one who helped train me when I was young and two who passed through Unity a grand total of three times over fifteen years. So I don't think there are that many of us around these days, if there ever were."

"Is it an inherited trait?" Al asked.

"Christ, I don't know." She waved impatiently. "I'm not a professor of arcanism. But my mother was gifted too, so maybe."

She started etching the last glyph in the silence that followed.

"So even if it's energy in versus energy out," Jarek said, "there's gotta be some kind of limit, right? That's one of Pryce's favorite thought experiments. I listened to him ramble for half an hour one time about how you guys must essentially be like power lines."

"He's a clever man."

"And he knows it. So what does it feel like, being a power line?"

She finished the glyph and set her tool down. "Channeling. That's what we call it. It's kind of like a shock that pours through your entire body, like this wave of . . . not heat, I guess, but—"

"Energy?"

"Sure," she said. "Let's go with that."

"Kinda sounds like an orgasm gone horribly wrong."

She snorted. "Jesus, you're a child. I dunno, the light stuff can actually be kind of soothing once you get used to it, but it gets pretty intense when I cut loose."

He gave her a wolfish grin. "You're not really disproving the comparison."

There was no avoiding it: anything she said at that point could and would be used against her in a court of bad innuendoes.

Al cleared his throat, despite presumably not having one. "Is it dangerous? Channeling more energy than you're equipped to handle?"

"So I hear," she said. "I passed out once when my eyes were bigger than my battery, so to speak, but apparently people have died from that kind of thing before. Hearts giving out and such."

"It just gets better and better." Jarek said.

She narrowed her eyes at him.

"So your mom," he said. "Was that before the Catastrophe?"

She stiffened and mentally cursed as she realized she'd started rubbing at her left forearm with her thumb. She occupied her hands with packing up the pieces of the new catcher. With the engraving done, the next steps would require careful focus, and she clearly wasn't going to find that here.

He held his hands up. "Whoa! It's okay. Forget I asked."

"Sorry, I just—"

"I get it." He shifted to bring his legs up on the bench and rest his back against the wall. "We should try to get some sleep. Why don't you take my bed for a couple hours?"

She arched an eyebrow at him.

He held up his hands. "No funny business. You know, unless you're asking for it."

She held his gaze, searching for her retort. Seconds passed. Why didn't he look away? Why didn't she? What did it say about her that his eyes drew her like magnets even after she'd seen him cut half a dozen throats last night?

It didn't matter. Whatever awful ideas her libido might have, she would stomp them out like the destructive pests they were. Besides, she had work to do, work that she might actually get done if he'd shut up and go sleep on his cot.

"I'm not stealing your sorry excuse for a bed," she said. "I can rough it just as well as you."

"I dunno, I like it pretty rough."

"It never ends with you, does it?"

He nestled his head against the back corner of the cockpit and closed his eyes. "It always ends with me."

It didn't sound like a cute joke.

She studied the lines of his face. What was he talking about? Banter? Relationships? Or something else entirely? Something told her it was the latter. The demons he must be carrying on his back—

He opened one eye. "Go. Sleep."

She shook her head and turned back to the beginnings of the catcher on the bench in front of her. "Take the cot, you chauvinist pig. I have work to do."

He smiled but made no sign of moving.

"Much as I hate to interrupt," Al said. "I thought you two might like to know that we'll be encountering some turbulence ahead."

She suppressed a dark urge to laugh.

If only Al could tell her something she didn't know.

CHAPTER THIRTEEN

Deadwood, South Dakota, was the alleged birthplace and long-time home of Alaric Weston and, according to Pryce, the one place the man would've run to after the metaphorical shit had hit. Studying the town in front of him, Jarek could see why. By all appearances, Deadwood was a charming, thriving little town. That wasn't something people got to say much these days.

At the time of the last pre-Catastrophe census, Deadwood's population had been about fifteen hundred. Who knew how those numbers had held up over the past fifteen years, but enough homes and stores and cars looked in good repair down there for him to believe Deadwood had simply gone on living in its cozy little mountain valley.

Michael and Rachel plodded down the boarding ramp behind him.

They both looked tired, even though Michael had slept straight through the entire flight.

Jarek had woken long enough to (unnecessarily) direct Al to set the ship down on the southern crest nestled between the two forks of the Y-shaped valley in which Deadwood had been built. After that, he'd grabbed a few more hours of sleep before coming out to scout.

Rachel had still been blearily, stubbornly awake when he'd risen the first time. He'd felt some small satisfaction to find her curled up in his cot when he'd woken the second time, but judging from the pallor in her face, she must've risen to get back to her enchanting since Jarek had left the ship. Or maybe she was just that tired.

"How's it look?" Michael said, rubbing the sleep from his eyes.

"Oddly intact," he said, "except for the fact that I haven't seen a single damn person for the past half hour."

There'd been a bustle of activity in the streets below when he'd first risen to look, but it hadn't lasted long. Everyone had seemed to be headed to—

"Church," Michael said. "It's Sunday."

Son of a bitch. Of course he hadn't thought of that. Attending church had become a dangerous practice in most places once the marauders caught on that Sunday services made easy targets. But up here in the mountains, far removed from what population hot spots remained, it made sense.

"Where were you on that one?" he murmured softly.

Al made a sniffing sound in his earpiece. "Perhaps if I had proper eyes out there and wasn't relying on your hodgepodge scouting report, sir."

Reason 5,093 they needed to get Fela back.

Now that he was closer, Michael's dark features looked reserved but not overtly unfriendly. Nothing like a beauty sleep to cure a bad case of the mopes.

"Church, sure. Good call, choirboy."

Michael reached for Jarek's binoculars. "There's no winning with you, is there?"

"Nope!" He handed Michael the binoculars and turned to Rachel. "You look like you need a cookie."

She gave a noncommittal grunt by way of reply.

"Touché."

He pushed past her to walk back to the ship and went to the locker in his cabin. He patted the giant blade of the Big Whacker affectionately, and then he withdrew his black synthetic gun belt from his box of goodies and strapped it on, drawing the holster straps snug on his thighs. His trusty old Glocks and a couple of extra mags were still loaded in the belt from last night, but he grabbed a third pistol and an additional mag for Michael.

Before shutting the locker, he paused, gazing thoughtfully first at the firearms on his person and then at the smaller sword resting in the vertical space inside the locker. They were just going to talk . . .

Ah, hell, how often did that work out? Plus, his ammo stockpile wasn't going to last forever.

He slung the sword over his shoulder, closed the locker, and went to join the others.

Outside, Rachel eyed his armaments dubiously, her eyes lingering on the hilt of the sword. It was a good blade, one of his favorites—formed from a single piece of steel with a straight, medium-length blade and a no-frills hilt wrapped tightly with thin green paracord for grip and thickness. It had been a gift of sorts from Pryce shortly after they'd met.

Michael's eyes widened in surprise or maybe horror when he turned and got a good look. "Dude, we're not looking to pick a fight here! And a sword? Seriously? Why?"

Jarek offered Michael the extra pistol and mag. "You're the one who was harping on being prepared. I have a sword because people tend to think twice before poking guys who walk around with swords strapped to their backs. Plus"—he raised his hands in a shrug—"they don't run out of bullets. And I might need to cut someone."

"Ten minutes in Deadwood, and he thinks he's a rootin'-tootin' cowboy ninja," Rachel said from behind them.

"Sweetheart, you have no idea. Whoops, that's a slip on the S word there—force of habit."

"I'll bet."

He drew one of his pistols halfway from its holster. "Did you, uh, want one of these fellas? I have one more in there."

She frowned at the pistol and hefted her staff. "I think I'm better off with this here whackin' stick, cowboy. Doesn't run out of bullets either."

He gave the hilt of his sword an affectionate pat. "Can't beat that. And you two are all magically bulletproofed now, I assume?"

A dark look crossed her face. "About that."

She pulled the small, glyph-etched metal disk of her bullet catcher off the back of her belt, checked the dial on its surface, and offered the device to Michael. "I want you to keep this on you until I finish yours."

Michael stuck the pistol and extra mag into his pockets and took the disk. After a few seconds inspecting it and a glance at Rachel, comprehension spread across his dark features. "That wasn't you stopping those bullets back at the Fortress? It was this thing?"

She nodded. "I've been playing with that prototype for a while now. Turns out it actually works."

"Wow, Rache." He looked at the device in his hands. "This is amazing! But I can't take it"—he offered the catcher back—"not when you might need it."

She pushed the little disk back toward Michael and waved her staff. "I have other ways, if it comes to that."

Michael stared at the device, unconvinced.

"Shit," Jarek said, "I'll take it if you won't, Mikey. I think it's your turn to get shot, anyways."

Rachel glared at him while Michael shrugged, slid the catcher onto his belt, and pulled his shirt down over it. It made Jarek's own backside feel woefully vulnerable.

Reason 5,094 they needed to get Fela back.

"Man," Jarek said, kicking at a tuft of wild grass. "When do I get one?"

Rachel shot him a wolfish grin. "Convince me I don't want you getting shot."

He ran his hands along the front of his body as if presenting a particularly breathtaking piece of art. "You're telling me this isn't reason enough?"

She snorted and was about to say something when Michael aggressively cleared his throat. "Time to go, then?" His eyes flicked back and forth between the two of them with irritation, or reprimand. Or could it have been jealousy?

"Let's hit it," he said, shooting Michael his most jovial grin. "The door please, Al."

There was a faint hum and a series of sharp clicks as the ship's boarding ramp closed and locked.

"Thanks, sweetie."

"Save it for Alaric Weston, sir."

The three set off along the long, widening crest headed for the narrow point where it descended to the town. Several stubby trees sprouted up amid the hilltop's wild grass. As the slope gradually angled downward, their numbers seemed to multiply, covering the hillside with pleasant shade and greenery.

"I'm not sure what's creepier," Jarek said quietly as they picked their way through the trees, "how freaking quiet it is down there, or the idea that it's that quiet because everyone's at church."

"You scoff," Michael said, "but the teachings of the church are something this world needs now more than ever."

"Half of the people that went all stabby-looty-rapey on the world when things went to shit were God-fearin' Christians, you know," he said, picking his way over the trunk of a fallen tree and turning to watch the others scramble over. "But that's not the point. I'm just saying I have a bad f—"

A pair of gunshots rang out in quick succession somewhere off to their left. *Crack. Crack.* Maybe half a mile away.

"—a bad feeling about this, guys. A real bad feeling."

They all waited for several seconds to see if more shots would follow. For now, all was quiet.

"So." He drew one of his pistols. "Probably that way, then?"

Michael yanked his own pistol out of his pocket, slightly wide-eyed. "Marauders?"

"Only one way to find out."

They set off in the direction of the shots. Jarek set their pace at a careful trot. They were on the clock—the gunshots had established that—but they'd have a better chance of handling whatever they might find if they avoided running full speed into it off the bat. Plus, running downhill through thick foliage wasn't exactly conducive to rapid travel, at least not if one preferred not to break one's neck.

The slant of the hill grew steeper, and a highway came into view at the bottom. He picked his way over and around shrubs, downed trees, and other obstacles. The shallow wound in his shoulder awoke with a steady ache as his pulse picked up from the exertion.

They'd just reached the crumbling highway when another shot rang out. And there—the faint trace of a scream from the same direction. It sounded terrified, not pained, and it hit him straight in his anger button.

On the other side of the empty highway, they cut toward the heart of town, skirting the line of dilapidated wooden fences separating the road from the back yards of several houses. After a few properties, the fences ended and the space to their left opened into a paved parking lot. It was backed by a small brick building that was, like most of Deadwood, in surprisingly good shape.

He led them across the lot to the corner of the building and pressed up against the warm brick wall, listening. The murmur of voices was unmistakable now. Slowly, cautiously, he peered around the corner.

Michael had been right. It looked like most of the town had been at church when marauders had rolled into town and caught them with their collective pants down.

Eight men were herding the townsfolk out of the church. The marauders were all armed, mostly with shotguns, pistols, and a couple of old lever action rifles. Given that the frightened townspeople were still filing out the doors at either side of the building's front, there were probably at least another five or six marauders inside, maybe more.

"Shit."

"What is it?" Michael whispered.

"You were right about church," he whispered back. "But we also have at least a dozen marauders over there, and it doesn't look like they're here to praise the Jesus."

"Shit," Rachel agreed.

"We have to help them," Michael said.

He pinched his temples between thumb and forefinger. Of course they had to help them. What the hell else were they supposed to do?

Much as he'd rather have nothing to do with it, he'd never managed to find the shut-off switch to that incessant voice in his head that demanded he stand up for the weak and the helpless when assholes came knocking.

He glanced at the cowering townsfolk again.

No walking away from that; they were just too damn pathetic.

He could see a few potential approaches, none of which seemed fantastic. He gnashed his teeth as one of the marauders smacked a graying man to the ground.

Getting clear lines of fire probably wasn't going to happen, and fighting around defenseless innocents was never a good plan. Scratch that; it was a totally shit plan, especially when the baddies were perfectly willing to use innocents as human shields. He was far from above half-cocked plans, but if they wanted to take these guys down without getting everyone killed, they needed a better plan than rushing in, guns and staff blazing, and hoping for the best.

They needed a distraction.

He met Rachel's steady gaze. Maybe she could whip up some arcane chaos. He was about to ask when a voice rang out ahead, cutting through the frightened murmurs of the townspeople and the confident jeers of the marauders alike with surly authority.

"You boys'd be saving yourselves time if you kicked off to the next town now," the new guy said. He was older, by the sound of it, with a bit of a drawl. "Ain't much here worth your time, I'm afraid."

The guy had balls, Jarek had to give him that. He glanced around the corner again. Judging from the direction the marauders had turned their weapons, the guy was approaching from the next road over, the one running right in front of the church. The adjacent building hid the guy from sight, but on the much brighter side, it looked like the universe had decided to give them that distraction.

"Let's go," he murmured to the others before creeping across the gap between their building and the next in a low crouch.

"Well, look at this, boys," one of the marauders called.

Jarek took cover behind the first of several cars parked beside the building. Rachel and Michael piled in beside him.

"We have a real, live fucking cowboy here on our hands! I think you're selling your town here short, old man. I see plenty here that looks worth enjoying."

Jarek pointed Michael's attention to the service ladder bolted to the building next to them on the side opposite the church. He slipped Michael an extra mag from his belt. Michael nodded and dipped behind the building. Once he made it to the front edge of the rooftop, Michael would have a great line of fire. With any luck, one or two of his shots might even be clear. Fingers crossed.

Jarek gestured for Rachel to follow him and began slinking toward the church, moving between the wall and the line of parked cars.

He'd missed the mystery cowboy's reply.

". . . got a lotta balls, old man, I'll give ya that, but you need to shut your fucking mouth and get over here with the rest of these good people before I get bored and start shooting."

Jarek stopped at the second to last of the cars next to the building. Cars typically made for pretty shitty cover, but two would be better than one if bullets started flying. Rachel hunkered down next to him as he leaned forward to get a look between the hood and the corner of the building.

"Son of a bitch," he whispered.

The mystery cowboy of many-balled repute was a dead ringer for the man in the two pictures they had to go by. Rachel's hand pressed lightly on his left shoulder as she leaned around to look too.

"Son of a bitch," she agreed softly.

Standing in the dead center of the road, twenty or so yards away from the marauders, was Alaric Weston.

CHAPTER FOURTEEN

Alaric Weston stood with his arms crossed, the battered, grayish-brown long coat he wore billowing lightly in the faint breeze. He wasn't particularly tall or built—hell, underneath his gray beard and his stringy gray hair, he looked at least sixty, if not older—but even at a distance, Rachel could see the hard resolve in the man's face.

"And you called me a cowboy," Jarek murmured, his cheek nearly touching hers.

She met his eyes for a moment, then they both snapped back to the scene as Weston called, "These boys hurt anyone, Bobby?"

"M-M-Mark's dead," came a reply, high with fright.

"Stupid, Bobby," the head marauder said.

She wasn't an expert, but the sound of a gun hammer being cocked was recognizable enough. A cloud of tension coalesced in the following silence, a heavy, tangible pressure that would only be alleviated in one of a few ways.

"Get ready," Jarek mumbled next to her.

Ready for what, exactly? She swallowed and gripped her staff more tightly.

Jarek hopped to his feet and began waving his free arm around like he'd spotted an old friend in a crowd. Aghast, she half stood to pull him back before anyone noticed, but it was too late.

"Alaric, you old coot!" he cried. "I've been looking for you everywhere!"

Dozens of heads, marauder and hostage alike, whipped around as if connected on a single track.

She was too focused on the several guns rotating to face them to notice said old coot had moved until the gunshot roared and the two rightmost marauders fell to the ground.

Two?

Things clicked into place a second later as she saw Weston had a revolver in each hand. Two shots so perfectly synchronized they had sounded like one.

As soon as her mind caught up with that, all hell broke loose.

Weston fired again, but his next shots must've missed or hit armor, because none of the marauders fell. Instead, they began to return fire.

Jarek's pistol cracked out beside her.

"Take cover, Deadwood!" Weston cried as he fired another pair of shots and ducked out of sight behind the building next to them.

The few hostages who hadn't already hit the dirt promptly did so.

She was gathering energy in preparation to defend their position when Jarek yanked her down behind the car with him.

She slapped his hand away. "Asshole!"

He opened his mouth to say something, but the air filled with man-made thunder. Shattered glass rained down on them as a tidal wave of marauder lead sought them out. A few bullets tore through the car door beside her. Her head buzzed as she pulled a barrier into existence between them and the car.

"Great plan!" she shouted, glaring at Jarek. "Really fantastic stuff!"

He calmly pointed a finger upward. A second later, three steady, well-paced shots rang out from the top of the building next to them—Michael, she realized.

On the crack of the third shot, Jarek poked his head up long enough to fire two shots. She rose beside him, holding her barrier in front of her and partially in front of Jarek. Weston's and Michael's weapons rang out again to their right.

"Inside!" the marauder leader snapped, yanking one of his men along as he scurried for the stairs. "Get inside!"

A third man turned to join them and promptly fell to a shot from Michael or Weston. More shots followed, kicking up chips of concrete and brick around the leader and his sole getaway partner as they cleared the crowd and scrambled up the front steps.

Next to her, Jarek let out a long, deliberate breath. His gun cracked once, and the marauder leader stumbled and fell on his way through the doorway. The second marauder scurried into the church, pulling the door shut behind them.

Rachel reminded herself to breathe as her heart began climbing down from record speed.

Then a girl in the crowd screamed.

An icy knife twisted in her stomach as a marauder who'd taken cover in the crowd stood, yanking the dark-haired girl who'd screamed up roughly by the throat. He hunkered behind her, firing a few blind shots from his revolver as he staggered back toward the church.

The ice in her stomach melted into a bubbling rage that rose up and propelled her from the cover of the car.

"Rachel!" Michael called from above.

The marauder's surprise gave way to a sneer as he took her in and turned his gun on her. What harm could this little blond chick be, right?

She would show him.

She extended an open palm toward the cowardly bastard without breaking stride. He pulled the trigger. Thunder clapped, and a lead slug crumpled against thin air five feet in front of her. The harmless lead clanked to the pavement at her feet. The stunned marauder tried again, to similar results, and dead silence descended on the yard.

"What the—" he said quietly. "What . . ."

He yanked his human shield tighter to him and jammed the

muzzle of his gun against her head. "I'll kill her! Stay the fuck away from me!"

The girl's eyes were wet with tears, but she didn't make a sound. Rachel met the girl's eyes and willed her to be brave. The marauder jerked her tighter, digging his pistol into her temple, and the girl let out a soft whimper.

She wrapped her mind around his hand like an iron glove and yanked it away from the girl with vicious force. Something in his shoulder made a loud *pop*, and he staggered back, crying out as his pistol clattered to the ground.

She pulled more energy and turned her hand palm up to focus her will. Waves of electricity crackled through her as she lifted the bastard eight feet into the air. He flailed and cried out in undignified protest. Beneath him, the girl scrambled clear.

She turned her palm over and slammed the thug to the ground. He groaned, feebly shifting to pick himself up. She took care of that for him, then slammed him down again, a wordless cry boiling out of her throat. She panted, preparing to lift him up a third time, intending to bring him down harder yet.

"*Rachel!*" Jarek bellowed.

Then something crashed into her from behind.

It should have hurt more, hitting the ground. Something helped break the fall. An arm. Jarek's arm. He was lying next to her. What the h—

Gunfire erupted from the front of the church, tremendously loud and fully automatic. The voice of a second weapon joined it. Jarek, lying prone on his stomach beside her, was already squeezing off several rounds in return.

The enemy fire abated for a moment, replaced by shouts and the sounds of shattering glass. Jarek was somehow already on his feet, pulling at her arm.

"Move." There was a level intensity to his voice that set her feet scrambling.

They took off for the front of the church, keeping low. More gunfire cracked out from behind as Michael and Weston covered their advance. The gunmen didn't manage much more than a few potshots from the church windows before she'd bounded up the steps and out of their line of fire.

Jarek was right on her heels. He methodically tucked an empty mag into his belt and slid a fresh mag into his pistol, then he holstered it and reached back to draw his sword with a smooth, practiced motion. The edge of the blade glinted in the sunlight.

"Plan?" she asked.

"Stick 'em with the pointy end." He drew his left pistol. "Or something like that. Cover me?"

No matter what his words said about him, the guy clearly had some idea what he was doing. She nodded.

Jarek moved to the right of the double doors, indicating she should mirror him. Satisfied, he reached over and yanked the right door open, and she immediately learned why he'd taken the time to scoot them clear of the doors.

Gunfire roared from within. Bullets slammed into the heavy wooden door. Some stopped there, but several tore through the thick wood, showering them with splinters and dust.

Through the chaos, Jarek caught her eye and wiggled his eyebrows.

Christ, was he enjoying this?

He held his gun hand up to point his index finger at his own eye, then he wiggled it toward the church, raising his eyebrows. It wasn't the most inspired sign language on the planet, but she took his meaning nonetheless. Before the door across from her had completed its slow swing closed, she jammed her staff through the crack and began pulling energy.

He gave her a wink and said, "Give 'em hell, Goldilocks."

She was surprised to feel her mouth pulling into a tight grin as the energy built inside her. She met his eyes and let loose with her finest arcane flashbang.

Blinding light flashed out of the narrow door crack, along with a resounding crash of thunder. Jarek was already moving, tearing the door open and darting through. She rocked back to her heels as the fatigue hit.

Inside, crisp, controlled shots were quickly joined by shouts and more sporadic gunfire.

She cleared her head as best she could, wrapped herself in a tele-kinetic shield, and slipped into the church after Jarek.

Two dead marauders waited for her inside. She jerked her gaze up the hallway at the sound of another gunshot just in time to see a third man crumple to the thick red carpet. Jarek stood over him, smoke dissipating from the barrel of his extended gun.

Another marauder leaped into sight and swept a tiny, vicious-looking sawed-off shotgun toward Jarek. The shotgun roared, but Jarek had already ducked past the marauder.

The dark wall spit sawdust as the shot tore into it. Jarek swept his sword up. A shudder rippled through Rachel as the blade passed through the marauder's arm and everything from the elbow down unceremoniously flopped to the carpet, gun and all.

The man stared in shock at the place where his right arm used to be. Jarek placed a solid kick into his side, and he toppled to the ground, twisting to clutch at his fresh stump. An agonized scream escaped his throat. Jarek kicked him in the side of the head, leaving him unconscious or at least stunned out of his misery.

"Come on," Jarek said.

She felt hypnotized. His blade was oddly free of blood after having passed through all that flesh and cartilage. It seemed such an odd thing, that—

Jarek clucked his tongue twice, tugging her back to the present. "They made their choices. No time to hold back. Come on."

He vanished around the corner at the end of the hall. She squeezed her eyes shut for a long second and then followed at a hard run.

She pulled up at the corner to the deafening chaos of two gunmen firing at Michael and Weston from the windows of the next hallway. One of them had an assault rifle of some kind and the other, an old bolt action.

Jarek leaned out of an empty doorway ahead, pistol raised. The closer of the two gunmen, the one with the bolt action, turned. Jarek fired twice, the crack of his pistol paltry in contrast to the roar of the assault rifle down the hall.

His first shot went wide, kicking up a puff of drywall dust next to the first gunman's head. The second shot found the man's throat. The gunman fell against the wall, a horrified expression frozen onto his features as he clutched at the bleeding mess of his neck.

By then, the thunder had quieted as the second gunman turned to see what was happening. Jarek took a hurried shot and missed, and then the thunder promptly resumed. Jarek threw himself through the doorway he'd been using for cover as the wooden doorframe exploded into showers of sawdust and splinters.

With his first choice of targets behind cover, the gunman turned to her. She made like Jarek and threw herself back around the corner. A stream of hot lead tore into the corner behind her, and she scooted away. No reason to tire herself butting heads with an assault rifle when there were perfectly good walls, right?

The hallway fell silent. Was the gunman reloading? Or just waiting?

Jarek must have been wondering the same thing. Maybe if she distracted the gunman . . .

She pulled her barrier back in place, took a deep breath, and stepped into the hallway—just as the gunman slammed a fresh magazine home. His rifle tracked toward her. Before he could fire, Jarek appeared and sent three shots at him. The first went wide. The second and third must've struck his armored vest, because he jerked back but swept his rifle back toward Jarek.

She dropped her defenses and let loose a telekinetic blast that caught the gunman like a small wrecking ball and threw him through what remained of the window.

Hopefully Michael and Weston would handle the guy from there, if he was still conscious and functioning.

Tingling fatigue licked at her limbs. She leaned heavily on her staff.

"Defenestration by magical whackin' stick." Jarek nodded approval from the splintered doorway. "Classic."

She kept her eyes on the end of the hallway as she gathered herself and moved forward. He fell in beside her.

"You just wanted me to know that you know what 'defenestration' means, didn't you?"

"Gotta use them there big words when I can. People need know me talk real good."

She fought down a smile. Why did that even make her want to smile?

"God, it's unbearable."

"The charm?"

She spared a glance at his impish grin. "Sure. We can go with that instead."

Was that what it was? Was she charmed by this man?

She'd have to deal with that irritating thought later.

They drew up to the sanctuary doors. There was a muffled thump on the other side and a few shouts.

She held the back of her hand out to Jarek's chest to signal him to pause. If he had questions, he held them surprisingly well as she closed her eyes and reached out with her extended senses.

Her mind brushed against pinpricks near the head of the room. "Two at the front of the pews. Both armed. One seems to be in a lot of pain."

"I would think so," he said. "I shot him in the ass."

Through the door, there was another loud thump and then a muffled voice: "No, you idiot! He shot me in the ass!"

She traded an unbelieving look with Jarek, fighting down the surreal fit of giggles that threatened to burst free. Every scrap of humor evaporated as she cast her senses up to the altar and felt a dozen young, frightened minds.

"Kids." She felt as breathless as if she'd been kicked in the gut. "Sick bastards fell back to hole up using the kids as cover."

Jarek sobered in an instant. "Son of a bitch."

"What do we do?"

His gaze shifted from her staff to her eyes. "Can you shield us without that thing?"

She nodded.

"Then we give them what they want. They don't know what you can do yet. Follow my lead, and please don't let them shoot me."

She nodded again.

He searched her face. "This isn't the part where you just let them take me out, right?"

Was that real concern in his eyes? For a second, he actually looked vulnerable, and she actually wanted to reach out and tell him not to worry.

The second passed. She broke their eye contact and reached for the energy to conjure their barrier. "Just keep close to me. And no sudden movements unless you're ready to abandon the shield."

"Fair enough."

The doors parted easily. The butt-shot leader lay on one of the pews at the front, groaning in pain but managing to keep his pistol trained at the altar, where a dozen boys and girls ranging from five or six through the early teens cowered. A second marauder stood watch behind them, but he looked like he was seriously thinking about making a run for it instead.

At the sound of their entrance, marauder number two whirled to face them, jumpy as could be.

She showed her hands. Beside her, Jarek did the same, letting his pistol hang loosely on his finger by the trigger guard as he held his hands up.

"Easy, guys," he said.

The marauder leader swiveled to face them from his pew, keeping his gun trained on the altar. "Who the fuck are you people?"

"It doesn't matter." Jarek took a few slow steps forward, waiting for her to match each step. "It's just us now." Slowly, carefully, he bent and dropped his sword and pistol onto the thin gray carpet.

She followed his example, carefully maintaining their barrier as she tossed down her staff.

He nodded to her, and they slowly walked forward side by side, hands raised.

"Your posse is dead," Jarek said. "You have nothing to gain by doing this."

"That's far enough," the leader said, his voice thick with pain.

Jarek took one more step forward and stopped. Slowly, he removed his second pistol with thumb and forefinger and tossed it into the pews. "There. Our weapons are down. You two are free to slip out the back and be gone. Leave the kids and go."

The marauder behind the altar took a small step toward the back exit, clearly thinking about it.

The leader shot an uncertain glance that way, then looked back to them, his face pulling into a sneer as he turned his gun their way. "You think you're better than us? Walking in here and shooting up our crew when we're just trying to survive too? You can go fuck yourself."

"Dude. Not only did you decide to raid what might be the only half-decent town left on the planet . . ."

Jarek was slowly moving left into the pews as he spoke, keeping them moving without actually approaching the marauders. She followed closely, not yet sure what his angle was.

" . . . you did it on a Sunday while the good folk were at church, for Christ's sake. Or, you know, not for Christ. Whatever." He spread his hands. "I think that goes a bit beyond just surviving, don't you?"

The marauder leader only glared at him with murderous eyes.

"I get it, man," Jarek went on. "At some point, you had to eat. You had to do what you had to do. But then you just kept on doing it— taking and taking and killing and killing. You couldn't stop, could you? I bet it even got easy, didn't it? Pulling the trigger? No problem. At least until you had to lie down to sleep at night."

"Shut up," the man said, fanatic energy creeping into his eyes. "Shut up and hold fucking still!"

Jarek paused and raised his hands higher in emphasized surrender. "You know what? I tried to reason with you, but fuck it."

She caught it then: the faintest flicker of motion at the doorway leading out of the front right corner of the sanctuary. She did her best not to react.

Beside her, Jarek sat down in the pew. "Everyone wants to blame this shit on the raknoth. I say it's people like you that have kept us in the dark ages for the past fifteen years."

That's when Alaric Weston strode in from the corner opposite them with his dark revolvers raised, one for each marauder.

By the time they caught a hint of his presence, it was already too late.

A few of the children screamed, but their peers saw to them, quieting, soothing. After it became apparent they were more or less okay, her attention shifted back to Weston.

He stalked toward them, guns still drawn if no longer pointed at anyone. She shifted her barrier to cover them as he approached, although her head buzzed and her limbs were beginning to feel heavy with the prolonged effort.

"Hello again," Jarek said. "Thought I saw you lurking back there. You're, uh, not gonna try to kill us now, are you?"

Weston stared at them, his dark eyes stoic. "Son," he said finally, holstering his revolvers in a smooth movement, "I don't know who the hell you are, but I reckon I owe you a thanks rather than a bullet. Now, can you two help me get these kids outside?"

She released her barrier as Weston went to the altar to begin restoring order.

"Whew!" Jarek patted the spot over his heart. "Guess that's a no on the killing us thing, then. Go, team!"

He bounded over to help with the children. She watched him go and couldn't help but wonder: would that no stay a no once Alaric Weston found out why they were here?

CHAPTER FIFTEEN

J arek fancied himself a hard man, more or less. He'd certainly been known to rough it often enough. But as he shifted his numbing butt on the thick stump that was his seat at Alaric Weston's round wooden table, he decided that proper chairs wouldn't have been too much to ask for after having saved the day.

Michael was pointing at him. "You're telling me that you, Jarek Slater, talked your way through a hostage situation?"

He shrugged. "I was gifted with a silver tongue, Mikey. I'm not sure why you're so surprised."

Michael glanced at Rachel, who sat at the table with them as they waited for Alaric's return.

She gave her own shrug. "Yeah, as long as you consider having two marauders gunned down in front of a roomful of children a victory, Jarek totally nailed this one."

He held his palms upward. "Hey, no one died. You know, except the guys who—ah, I'll take it anyway."

Michael leaned his elbows on the sturdy bulk of the table and frowned. "I'm not seeing it."

"Ye of little faith," Jarek said, sitting on his stump as sagely as he could manage.

Michael rolled his eyes and looked around the room for about the trillionth time in the past hour. "Well, I hope that silver tongue's ready to make the hard sell to Alaric when he gets back."

It wasn't hard to tell that Michael was restless. He understood. Fighting was stressful enough, and they had what might very well turn out to be the hard part still ahead. Repetition, like obsessively looking around a room over and over again, could be soothing. It could help convince someone they were doing everything they could despite not really doing anything at all. But try as he might, it wasn't as if Michael were going to suddenly spot Alaric hiding behind the bread box or under the table.

They'd barely had the chance to exchange more than a sentence with Alaric, but saving an altar-full of kids had a way of breaking the ice. He'd asked that twitchy Bobby kid who'd nearly been executed before the fighting started to show them to his cabin and insisted they take a breather while he helped the townsfolk cart the surviving marauders to their small jail, which turned out to be next to Alaric's house anyway.

According to Bobby's ceaseless chatter, the location wasn't coincidental.

When Alaric had fled the east coast five years prior, he'd apparently arrived just in time to liberate the town from a violent batch of would-be rulers. When they'd realized he was a local returned home, they'd named him sheriff. He'd refused the badge but accepted the call of duty. As thanks, they'd pitched in as a community to build him the rustic cabin they were sitting in, made with wood cut from the trees of the very hillside next to them, if you could believe it. (Thank you, Bobby.)

Maybe the kid's verbal flatulence wasn't unreasonable given he'd almost been killed thirty minutes earlier, but Jarek had a sneaking suspicion that Bobby never really stopped bouncing off the walls, near-death experience or no.

At least the kid had shown them to the food before scurrying off. A large bowl of beans and a few glasses of water later, Jarek was sated and well prepped for flatulence of the nonverbal variety.

After another twenty or so minutes of idle chatting, heavy boot steps sounded on the porch. The screen door screeched open, and Alaric Weston strode into the room.

He went straight to the wooden rack by the door and unburdened himself of his battered long coat in a way that was clearly ritual for him, revealing a simple shirt of some light beige, rough-spun fabric. Next, he made as if to remove his gun belt, then thought better of it and came to settle on the last of the four stumps at the dining room table. He brushed his stringy gray hair off his forehead and behind his ears.

The four of them sat still for a long moment, silent but for the sound of Alaric's steady chewing. God knew what he was chewing. Maybe tobacco leaves.

"Right, then," Alaric finally said. "You're Resistance?"

Michael nodded. "I am."

More chewing. "Figured as much. We don't get many new folk 'round here." He looked at Jarek, then at Rachel. "Especially not ones that can stop bullets in thin air. Much as I appreciate the help back there, I made it clear to Hux that I was done with the fight. Not much left to say there."

Michael looked down at the table, his face tight. "Hux stepped down from Command a while back. Sloan wormed his way into replacing him before I got there."

Alaric's expression darkened. "Nelken and Daniels still there?"

Michael nodded.

"Well, they knew the score too, so either they've succeeded at shoving their heads so far up their asses that they forgot, or something's seriously wrong."

"We've got a pretty big problem," Michael said. "And you might be the only one who can help us."

"Although I think you're pretty spot on about the heads-in-the-asses thing too," Jarek said. He smiled and shrugged at the stern look Michael shot him. "Just one outsider's opinion."

"You two are freelancers?" Alaric asked, looking from him to Rachel.

"Just friends," Rachel said.

"Rachel is my sister," Michael said, earning him a frown from Rachel.

The honesty didn't surprise Jarek. Michael was a believer, and Alaric had basically founded the Resistance. Michael would probably have licked Alaric's boots if he'd asked. Plus, pedigree aside, Michael was about to ask something of the guy—something that wouldn't be easy or pleasant for him. A little honesty probably didn't hurt their chances.

"And Jarek," Michael continued, "is—"

"His indentured love slave," Jarek said. "Wait, no, I'm getting my roles all mixed up again."

"Jarek is a mercenary who is astoundingly unclear on how being a mercenary works," Rachel said.

"That," Jarek said, holding a finger up for pause, then dropping it back down and nodding his agreement, "is actually pretty true. Thanks, sweetheart."

A flicker of surprise (among other things) shot through his core as she gave him a sultry wink. The very next moment, order was restored to the universe as she waved her hand in a shooing motion. An invisible hand shoved him backward. His stump tipped over, but he managed to land in a deep squat right behind it.

She rolled her eyes as he grinned, righted his stump, and plopped back down.

"She doesn't like the S word," he explained to Alaric.

Michael was clearly not amused. "Getting back to the matter at hand . . ."

Alaric, who clearly was amused, turned the fading spark in his tired, dark eyes back to Michael. "What is it you think I can do for you?"

"Well . . ."

"I got it," Jarek said, holding a hand up. He turned to Alaric. "Mikey and your mutual pal Huxley stole one of the Red King's toys and stuck it in a safe because they thought they could use it against the raknoth, but now"—he hesitated, realizing he'd just talked himself into the corner of breaking the news of Huxley's death—"they can't get to the goods, and we got a call from the Reds saying that it's gonna be Doomsday 2.0 up in here if they don't get it back in"—he glanced at his comm—"twelve-ish hours, and uh . . . what?"

Alaric had stopped chewing. He turned to Michael, his mouth in a tight line and his brows fighting to meet. "Hux is dead, isn't he? That's why you're here."

It took Michael several seconds to meet Alaric's eyes. "I'm sorry."

Alaric sat back, his eyes somewhere far away. After a while, he chewed once. Then again. His jaw slowly built pace like an old steam engine until he finally grimaced and said, "Well, shit."

"Yeah," Michael said.

Alaric came back from whatever distant place he'd ventured off to and focused on Michael, his expression stoic but not unkind. "What did he lock up in there? What could possibly be so important?"

Michael proceeded to spit it out: how he and Huxley had found the strange egg-shaped device, how the thing had felt when he'd touched it, how desperately the Red King and the Overlord wanted it back, the doomsday warning—all of it. Rachel and Jarek pitched in on the more recent parts.

Alaric listened patiently, chewing all the while.

"I don't know what it is you've found," he said when they'd finished, "but it seems to me the lady has the right idea here. This nest thing is already buried. All you have to do is walk away."

"What?" Michael said.

Alaric studied Michael, sympathy creeping into his expression. "The Resistance isn't going to take those monsters down, son. Probably never was. I learned that the hard way. You wanna help? Find some people that need helpin' and give it to them. Find someplace you can forget the vamps, and forget them."

Michael looked as if he'd just stumbled onto a dead pet. Jarek didn't blame him. It wasn't easy, finding out that one of your heroes has given up the good fight. He'd found that one out the hard (and violent) way back around the same time he'd met Pryce.

Of course, if this old cowboy didn't play ball, Jarek could also kiss

Fela goodbye for the foreseeable future—maybe forever. Despite whatever Al might say, that wasn't an option.

He leaned forward. "While I generally agree with the philosophy, old-timer, it kind of falls to shit if this whole doomsday threat pans out."

Alaric shrugged. "Vamps'll do a lot worse than lie to get what they want. You really think they'd be the ones trying to prevent something terrible from happening to the planet after what they did?"

"They do live here." He shrugged. "Maybe they're feeling some bomber's remorse."

"I don't buy that for a damn second."

"Either way, this might be one of those if-there's-even-a-slight-chance kind of scenarios."

Alaric looked out the window toward the small jail. "I can't leave this place. Especially right now."

"We're talking about a day trip here, man. It's not like we're asking you to throw in and reroot your life."

Alaric narrowed his eyes. "And what exactly do you get out of this? What's your angle?"

Jarek might've given any number of lies at this point, but the one that probably wouldn't fly was that he was here out of some noble urge to save the world.

If the world were actually in danger, who knew? But he was less than convinced.

"I'm trying to help a friend get his home back," he finally said. "Long story."

Alaric pursed his lips, his gaze flicking between all three of them. "I could tell you where Hux would've hidden your nest, but it wouldn't do you much good without me."

Michael nodded. "Hux told me he booby-trapped the place."

"That might be an understatement. And if he didn't give you access, I'm assuming it'll be my credentials you'll need. My finger-prints, my voice, and my retinas, which all means you'll be needing me." He shook his head. "But I can't leave. These people need me."

Dammit.

He could see the wheels furiously turning in Michael's head as the kid tried to figure out what to say—what magical combination of words he could string together to make Alaric see reason. It wasn't just going to click into place, though; that much was clear.

Maybe it was time to strike a match under Alaric's ass.

"Are you sure about that?" he asked quietly.

Alaric's eyes narrowed slightly. "Sure about what?"

"That these people need you. You sure it's not the other way around?"

Michael started to say something, but Alaric raised a hand and he fell silent, looking about as tense as a cat in a dog pound.

"Son," Alaric said, his expression stony, "I appreciate what you did to help my people today, but you best be careful with your next words."

"Careful," Jarek said. "Like you today, when you strutted up to face a company of armed thugs on your own? What were you planning to do next? It was blind luck we showed up when we did."

Alaric's jaws slowed briefly, then sped up as if to make up for lost chews. "I'd have figured out something. I always do."

Jarek barked a short, harsh laugh. "You thought today might be the day, didn't you? And then us meddling kids had to come along and spoil everything."

"You don't know what you're talking about."

"Oh, please. I recognize a death wish when I see one."

Michael leaned forward. "Jarek, this—"

"Shut it, Mikey."

Michael rocked back. Rachel bristled.

Maybe he should just knock the geezer out and cart his ass back to Newark, but that would leave them still needing Alaric to show them where to go. Somehow, that didn't seem like much of an option. Besides, he wanted—maybe even needed—to see this washed-up old fighter cut the shit and admit the truth. He'd wring it out of him if he had to.

"Your people can survive twenty-four hours without you. What are you scared of, old-timer?"

"Son, you need to—"

"Funny you'd use that word so much, considering."

It was as if a switch had been thrown.

Alaric wasn't chewing anymore. His breath came in long, heavy draws. He locked stares with Jarek, murder in his eyes.

Jarek felt his own pulse quickening, his nerves crying that he should bolt for the door, or draw his gun, or do *something*.

"Get out," Alaric said, his voice trembling with barely controlled rage. "All of you."

"Jarek . . ." Michael said.

"You can't run forever," Jarek said, ignoring Michael.

"Out," Alaric said. "*Now!*"

"You can't escape him out here."

In the space of a second, Alaric was on his feet with a revolver drawn, cocked, and pointed straight at him. Rachel came to her feet too, staff in hand, but Alaric's eyes remained resolutely locked with his.

"My son is gone," Alaric said.

He leaned forward. "Say his name, then."

"Why are you doing this?"

"Say his name if he's gone," he repeated, his voice growing in intensity.

"Just go. Get out of here." Alaric's voice wavered, but his gun hand remained steady. Steady enough.

"Say it." He stood to lean over the table toward Alaric's revolver. "*Say it!*"

Adrenaline roared through his body as Alaric jerked the revolver and pulled the trigger.

In the small cabin and directly in front of the weapon, the shot was nearly deafening, but not so much that he missed Alaric's next words.

"SETH IS DEAD!" he roared, kicking over his stump as he turned for the door. He threw the screen door open hard enough that it crashed into the wall and bounced back, but he was already clear, stomping down the porch steps to storm off who knew where.

The bullet hanging in the air a few inches in front and to the right of Jarek's head fell to the wooden floor with a small *thunk*.

None of them moved for several seconds. Jarek ran a mental sweep of his body and came to the same conclusion his eyes had told him: he had not been shot. Given where the bullet had ended up after Rachel stopped it, Alaric had pulled the shot on purpose. It was something, but it didn't exactly quell the feeling that he'd just fucked up big time.

"Thanks, Goldilocks," he murmured, picking up his sword and slinging it over his shoulder.

"What were you thinking?" she said.

"Is he coming back?" Michael said.

Jarek looked at them with unseeing eyes. What *had* he been thinking? Digging into someone like that—someone he barely even knew . . . It didn't matter now. He was tired, and he was pretty sure that waiting around for Alaric to return wasn't in anyone's best interest.

"Hell if I know."

He started for the door as his hopes of ever recovering Fela began cracking at the foundations.

CHAPTER SIXTEEN

By the time they made it back to the ship, the sun was a couple of hours past the day's pinnacle. Jarek had barely spoken a word since Alaric's cabin, much to the irritation of Michael, who was clearly in full-on what-are-we-going-to-do mode. Rachel, on the other hand, simply radiated disapproval at the way he'd handled the situation.

Whatever. They could both shove it. He wasn't in this for the Cause, and he sure as hell wasn't in it for the Resistance. Now, more than ever, he just wanted to get back Fela and get the hell away from this bullshit.

Alaric had that part right, at least. It was a pretty damn big world, and screwing with the raknoth was purely optional. Hell, maybe those scaly bastards just wanted to be left alone themselves. Maybe they blew the whole world up trying to find some peace and quiet. Who knew?

"So what," Michael called as Jarek ascended the boarding ramp, "we're just going to hang out here and wait?"

"Unless you have a better idea." He grabbed the cleaning kit from his locker and pushed past Michael down the ramp. "Then yeah, I guess that's the plan for now."

He went around to the side of the ship and sat down, leaning back against a landing strut.

"Just leave it, Michael," he heard Rachel say in a low voice.

Apparently the advice didn't jibe with Michael's current mood, because the kid came stomping down the ramp and around the ship to square off in front of him, arms crossed and dark jaw set.

Jarek calmly laid out a cloth and began disassembling his pistols.

"So what were you thinking?" Michael said after several seconds of idle huffing and puffing.

"Well, I don't want 'em getting all rusty and whatnot," Jarek said, not looking up. "Glocks are pretty good, but—"

"Dammit, Jarek. This isn't a game, man. You know what could happen."

He looked up at Michael. "I really don't. Aside from me not getting back what's mine. You don't either, Mikey, so why don't you hop off that high horse and relax in the grass with the rest of us for a few minutes?"

"Boys," Rachel called, her tone that of an admonishing elementary school teacher.

"No, Rache, I'm sick of this jerk screwing with everyone and refusing to take any of this seriously just because he's mortified at the thought of actually giving a crap about anything other than himself and his damn suit." By the end, Michael was basically shouting.

Jarek let the bitter amusement seething in his chest creep onto his face. Apparently, Michael had been hoping he'd kowtow like a reverent, scolded puppy.

"This is why you're alone, man!" Michael cried. "I know it bothers you. It has to bother you." He regained some composure before he continued. "I'm fighting for something I believe in. You can mock that all you want, but until you find the courage to stand up for something yourself, even if it's not perfect, you're never gonna be happy, man. You're just gonna be this bitter wiseass who's too afraid to even open up long enough to—what? What's so freaking funny?"

Jarek tried to stifle the laughter that had threatened to bubble out during Michael's tirade, but he only half succeeded.

Michael's hands curled into fists.

"I'm sorry." Jarek dropped the pistol frame to the cloth with the rest of the parts and raised his hands in a pacifying gesture. "You're totally right. You've clearly had a lot more experience than me with how the world works. Maybe you could show me a thing or two. Like where are these unicorns I keep hearing about? And those fields where there's always sunshine and rainbows?"

Michael's mouth drew so tight Jarek thought his head might simply suck into his mouth like a vacuum and invert.

"Just give a shit about something, will you?" Michael said.

He stormed off to go do something on the ship—probably sleep, if the flight over had been any indication.

Jarek looked over to find Rachel frowning at him from the corner of the ship.

"Kids, right?"

"You're an asshole," she said, turning to join Michael on the ship.

He nodded to himself and resumed cleaning his weapons.

An asshole he may be, but at least he wasn't a naive little shit. The more he thought about what Michael had said, the more irritated he felt. Michael was a smart kid and he had a good heart, but he had no fucking idea what he was talking about. He didn't know where Jarek had been, what he'd been through. How could he? More than that, he was too damn young to appreciate just how much he didn't know.

He'd been like Michael once. Ten years ago, back when he'd thought he was going to return peace and prosperity to the world, starting with Boston.

Boston, believe it or not, had yet to enter its new golden age, and his naivety had earned him little more than hard lessons about the depravity of men, some serious scars, and that stupid freaking nickname. From the carnage, the Soldier of Charity had risen, wise enough to know that even the most well-intentioned of rulers had to shit somewhere.

He finished reassembling one clean pistol and slid it into his right holster.

Now, without Fela, he was just another schmuck—a particularly crafty, resilient one, maybe, but a schmuck all the same. Reason five-thousand and . . . whatever.

He didn't hear much from the other two for the next few hours. After cleaning his guns and oiling his sword, he stood for a stretch and found that Michael had indeed fallen asleep (in his cot, no less, the not-so-little bastard), and Rachel had returned to working on her second catcher.

He went back outside to occupy himself with a holo game until he grew too antsy.

Would Alaric be back by now? Who knew? The better question was how they were going to salvage things enough to get the ex-freedom-fighter back on board.

"Why didn't you tell me to pump the brakes back there?"

"Because I thought you were right about him, believe it or not," Al said in his earpiece.

"Man, that ship computer must really be bogging you down if you're finding yourself agreeing with me."

"I'm still not sure we were wrong, sir. You did resort to high-pressure tactics. He may simply require some time to reorient."

"That or he's busy carving my name in the bullet right now."

"Don't tell me you're afraid, sir."

"Not of Alaric."

Just of the crushing thought of never finding Fela. But he didn't have to say that part. Al knew.

"We should send Michael," Jarek said after a while. "Assuming his watchdog will let him off to play on his own for an hour or two."

"I'm not so sure about that, sir. I think you might still get through to Alaric if you two can make peace."

Over his dead body, most likely.

"Yeeeah. Or we send Michael first."

Al sighed. "Or that."

Playing make-up was all well and good, but he was pretty sure he'd surpassed even the leader of those marauders on Alaric's People I'd Like to Murder list. Much as the kid's high-and-mighty attitude was starting to irk him, Michael probably had the best chance at reaching Alaric.

He was standing to go pitch the idea to the others when his comm buzzed against his wrist.

It was Pryce.

News? Another broadcast from the Reds, maybe?

He accepted the call and waited as the feed struggled to establish through Deadwood's abysmal net coverage. Really, it was actually kind of impressive there was a signal at all this far away from major civilization. As it was, the holo sputtered with a few slow frames of aliased garbage before his comm automatically dropped the call to audio only.

"—arek!" Pryce's voice crackled through.

"Pryce. What—"

"Shut up and listen! No time. They're here."

He froze. "Who?"

"The Reds. They're coming for me. Must have tracked you here. You need to get Alaric and get out of there. No telling if they—"

There was a heavy thud, coupled with a sound of groaning metal. Was that Pryce's door? Or maybe the steel security hatch at top of the staircase? Shit, why couldn't his stupid comm find the signal to establish a video link?

A second thud, this one accompanied by a sharp *crack* and followed by voices and the squealing protest of metal hinges. Rustling sounds. The roar of a shotgun blast.

His insides shriveled, his mind whirling. There was nothing he could do. Not a damn thing. Only listen.

Another shotgun blast, and then someone said in a raspy baritone, "There is no need for that, Jay Pryce. You are not the one I am looking for."

"Move your ass, son," Pryce murmured. Then he cut the call.

An icy fist held Jarek's gut and refused to let go as the second voice registered in his mind. It was the same voice from the broadcast last night.

The fucking Red King had just kicked in Pryce's door. And it was his fault.

His jaw trembled.

It had to be his fault. What other possible explanation was there? Pryce had said it himself: the son of a bitch must've tracked him and the others to the shop. He'd been careful to avoid being spotted, but it wasn't impossible they'd been followed. Or maybe the raknoth had simply sniffed out their trail; he'd heard stories about their predatory prowess.

It didn't matter now. Pryce was in trouble.

"Al." His voice croaked out of his parched mouth.

"I'm here, sir," Al said.

The earth felt unsteady beneath his feet. First Fela, now Pryce. How could this be happening?

He had to do something.

But what?

"What do we do?"

"We need to find and access that safe house, sir." Al's voice was steady. It grounded him enough to think.

If the Red King wanted Pryce dead, there was nothing he could do about it at the moment. It would take him at least three hours to get back to Newark. The only chance he had of helping Pryce was if the King wanted the old man alive for something.

That seemed like a real possibility.

It wasn't any mystery what the King was after. He wanted that damn egg of his back, and probably their three heads on a platter at this point. Killing Pryce wouldn't get him what he wanted. No. Chances were good the raknoth intended either to torture information out of Pryce or to use him as a bartering chip to get Jarek and the others to play ball and give him what he wanted.

If Pryce made it through the next five minutes, getting him back would likely mean a fight with the Red King or turning over the device, which would also probably mean a fight. If it came to that, he was pretty certain Fela was his only real chance against a raknoth. Either way, they needed to get into that damn safe house.

Which meant they needed that damn cowboy.

He looked at the ship, machinations of trickery and kidnap flashing through his mind. Rachel had appeared at the corner of the ship. She watched him with a worried expression. Michael stepped off the ramp to join her.

"Was that . . ." she asked.

He nodded, heat rising in his chest and throat.

"What?" Michael said, looking back and forth between them. "What just happened?"

"They took Pryce," Rachel said, her eyes still locked with his. "The Reds?"

He nodded again, the heat bubbling over into deep anger.

"How did they . . ." Michael said quietly. "Oh, no."

Jarek slung his sword over his shoulder, scooped up the cleaning kit, and pushed past them onto the ship.

"They want the nest," Michael said from the ramp behind as he stowed the kit and reloaded his mags. "They'll try to use Pryce to get to us. Dammit."

He didn't bother answering. He turned to leave. Rachel stood in his way, hazel eyes staring up at him with intensity.

"What are you gonna do?"

"Find Weston," he said. "What's it look like?"

She searched his face, objections clearly hanging on her tongue.

"They were friends once, him and Pryce," he said. "Or something like it. He'll wanna help."

"And if he doesn't?"

He shrugged. "I'll bring him back after we're done in Newark."

She traded a look with Michael, whose dark forehead was crinkled with apprehension.

"Jarek," she said. "I don't—"

"Do whatever you want." He pushed past them and down the ramp. "Just don't get in my way."

One way or another, Alaric Weston was returning to Newark with them tonight.

CHAPTER SEVENTEEN

Somewhere along the line, something had gone fatally wrong.

Just a week ago, Rachel had been safe in Unity, keeping her head down with the best of them. She'd been worried about the wayward brother who hadn't returned her calls for several days, sure, but things had been good—stable, predictable, uncomplicated. Boring. Boring was good.

But then the world had walked up and shot Boring in the head.

Michael had continued to not return her calls. Worry had won out. For good reason, too; Michael had been in big-league Trouble with a capital T. From there, every step she'd taken had led her further away from the cooling body of her old friend Boring.

Part of her wanted nothing more than to be back in Unity, safe and bored. Maybe Michael didn't even need her here. Even if she hadn't been around to help, she had a feeling Jarek would have found a way to pull Michael out of the Red Fortress. The guy didn't seem to do well taking no for an answer.

As long as Michael had something that he wanted, Jarek would fight to keep him safe, even if only as an insurance policy.

Much as that last thought should have made her skin crawl, it didn't. Maybe largely because she wasn't sure she believed it anymore.

Despite having watched Jarek efficiently cut and gun down god knew how many men in less than twenty-four hours, she wasn't so sure Jarek was the cold, hardened mercenary he pretended to be.

He was perfectly capable of killing; there wasn't a hair of doubt about that. And he was beyond rough around the edges. But there was something else there at his center.

After everything she'd seen, she was starting to think Jarek Slater might actually be one of the good guys, as far as good guys went these days. And right now, he was alone and, she was almost certain, terrified for Pryce.

Poor Pryce.

"I'm going after him."

She was almost surprised to hear herself finally say it after thinking about it for the better part of an hour.

Michael looked up from the cot where he'd been sitting with his face buried in his hands. "What?"

"It's been like three hours," she said. "Pryce is running out of time if he isn't already . . . you know."

Michael frowned at her. "Since when do you care about Pryce?"

She reached for the ceiling with an eyebrow. "Seriously?"

"You've been trying to get away from this thing from the start." He looked out of the open ship hatch. "What's changed now?"

"What's changed now is that another good man's been pulled into this bullshit. I don't want Pryce getting hurt because of us."

"Are you sure it's Pryce you're worried about? You sure it's not Jarek?"

Instinctively, she reached for his mind with her extended senses, just as she'd always done when they'd bickered over the years. She'd never pushed too far, but brushing against the exterior—testing the emotional waters, so to speak—had always been by far the fastest and most effective way she knew to understand how her brother was feeling and to empathize with him.

But that had been then.

Now, the tendrils of her mind met a rigid wall of nothingness, a product of the gift the Resistance had stamped him with upon his initiation.

Frustration swelled through her.

"Jesus." She grabbed her staff and turned to face him from the top of the ramp. "You know what?"

Did she even know what? She wanted to say that he shouldn't have dragged her into this if he didn't want her taking sides and deciding to care, but he hadn't really dragged her in, had he? Sure, his being in danger had heavily weighted her choices, but they had been her choices every step of the way.

And now she was making another.

"I'm going."

Michael stood. "Hold up, I'll—"

"You stay. Let me deal with one moody child at a time, please."

She stalked off into the cool country air and the dwindling daylight, trying to ignore the little voice pointing out that there were in fact three moody children in their party right just now.

Dusk was thickening the sky like an ethereal curtain as she reached the tree line and began the descent to Alaric's cabin. Among the trees, it was dark enough to need to flick on her comm light to get down the hillside and back out under the slim crescent moon and the few stars that were making their appearance above.

A few townsfolk headed here or there by car or foot in the street, but for the most part, Deadwood was quiet. Alaric's cabin was dark inside, and Jarek was sitting on the front porch.

He didn't move as she approached. Maybe she'd made a mistake in coming here, but . . . No. No, she was a grown-ass woman, and she could sit on whatever porch she pleased. So she did, lowering herself down to the smooth wood next to a still-silent Jarek.

"No Alaric?" she said.

He gave a small shake of his head.

She sat still, enjoying the chirping of crickets and the whisper of a cool breeze as it rustled the greenery around them in the slowly fading light. It was actually kind of relaxing, life-or-death troubles aside.

After a few minutes of silence, Jarek finally turned to look at her. She could almost feel the heaviness resting on him. For a second, he looked as if he'd say something, but then he turned his aimless gaze back out to the country evening.

She reached out in the gathering darkness to find his hand. It was an impulsive move, and certainly not a romantic gesture. Just human touch—a quiet, warm reminder that he wasn't alone, even if the war raging inside of him was solely his own.

His eyes flicked toward her, though his head remained fixed forward. She sensed more than saw his mouth beginning to open.

"Shut up," she said quietly. "Just . . ."

Wordlessly, he turned his hand over so that his palm met hers. She swallowed as his fingers intertwined with hers, welcoming the growing cover of darkness as he squeezed her hand and heat flowed into her cheeks.

It wasn't a romantic gesture, she reminded herself. Never mind what her pulse said.

They sat quietly for a long while, hand in hand.

"Michael was right," he finally said. "I mean, he's naive and sophomoric, but I don't know what I'm doing here anymore."

She suppressed the urge to say something. He'd say what he wanted to when he was ready. She kept his hand in hers and waited.

"There's no winning. I cut down fifteen men, and you bet your ass fifty more are gonna step up to bat. And somehow, some way, the good people always end up getting dragged into the shitstorm."

He shook his head. "It's not a good feeling, you know, ending lives. Surprise, right?" He pulled his hand free from hers. "I lost count a long time ago of how many people I've killed trying to protect other people."

He swallowed audibly. When he spoke again, his voice was thick. "It's too much. The things I've seen people do . . . This world is so breathtakingly fucked, I don't even know where to start. And I feel tainted, like I'll never be free of it. I don't think I ever can be free of it."

"Jarek," she whispered.

"And now Pryce is dead, for all I know, just because I wanted to get

149

my goddamn suit back. And for what? So I can get back to doing this shit at full steam again?"

"Jarek."

He met her gaze.

"You saved lives today." She thought back to the kids in the sanctuary and the girl she'd freed from the marauder in front of the church. "We saved lives. Good ones. And maybe it's not forever. Maybe another raiding party rides in tomorrow and levels the town. We can't stop bad things from happening. But at least we gave them more time than they would've had without us." She shrugged. "It's not perfect, but it's something."

He contemplated her in the fading light. "Christ, when did you decide to join the scouts of America?"

She smiled. "Right about the time I saw your sad ass still sitting here."

"Right. Fair enough." After a pause, he added, softly, "Thanks, Rachel."

"Holy shit."

"What?"

"I think that's the first time you've ever called me by my name."

"Not true. I distinctly recall yelling your name in front of the church today. Just before I heroically saved your life, I might add."

"Oh, yeah. You mean just before you tackled me to the ground like a rampaging gorilla, right?"

"You're welcome. Don't pretend like you didn't like it, sweetheart."

She scowled and threw a light punch at his shoulder. He deftly brushed the attack aside in the dark, moving so that her hand somehow ended up in his once again. After a moment's hesitation, she relaxed, allowing his fingers to once again intertwine with hers.

They sat that way for several minutes before he said, "What about you?"

"What about me?"

"How are you holding up? You looked a little green at the gills back at the church."

"Yeah, well, believe it or not, I'd never seen someone dismembered in real life before."

"Hey, we don't have to talk about it. I just thought, you know, I'm airing my shit out, only fair to listen if you wanna do the same."

She slid her hand free and considered what it might be like to tell him what had been going through her head when she'd saved that poor girl today. How some tiny part of her had felt like maybe, just maybe, she could undo what had happened to her family (and to her) if only she could save someone else. How she'd felt shockingly little remorse when she'd helped Jarek cut through the rest of the bastards.

She'd never really talked to anyone but Michael and their dad, John, about the home invasion that had claimed two-thirds of her family and left her next to dead. Others had garnered rough ideas, but it wasn't something she willingly relived. Even with Michael and John, she'd never been able to say it all. How could she explain the animosity, the raw, unfettered hatred that had been unleashed on her, to people who were decent and good?

Somehow, with all the shit he seemed to have been though, Jarek might understand better than her brother and dad had ever been able to. But baring herself like that . . . Why did the thought alone sound so terrifying?

"I saw," Jarek said.

Confused, she followed his gaze and realized her thumb was tracing along her left forearm. She folded her arms tightly in front of her chest. Any crazy ideas of opening up to a complete stranger evaporated as more practiced responses took over.

She stood and walked down the steps.

"It's okay, Rachel," he said behind her.

It really wasn't. How could it be? That kind of trauma didn't just go into the vault for later recall, like the time you tripped and scraped your knee on the pavement. The reminder of how completely defenseless she'd been, of how completely her worth as a living, breathing person had been disregarded, was a constant weight on her mind. At times, it was suffocating. Even now, thinking about those memories indirectly, she felt the hot wetness of tears forming in her eyes.

"Suffice it to say that there's a reason I don't necessarily disagree with your killing career assholes," she said, managing to keep most of the waver out of her voice.

"Fair enough," he said, nodding. "I'm sorry for whatever happened. I'm not great at this whole talking thing, but for whatever it's worth, I'm glad you pulled through."

Justified as she might be, she wasn't accustomed to losing her shit, especially not in front of other people. She did her best to cover a wet sniffle with a forced chuckle.

"This from the guy who uses words like 'sophomoric' and 'defenestration.'" She turned her head to dab away the brimming tears. "Totally helpless. Clearly."

"I mean, I may have read a book one time, but . . ."

Silence stretched as the darkness grew thick enough to partially obscure his features from view.

"Have you ever thought about joining the Resistance?" she asked after a while.

"Not really," he said.

"Not even with a nickname like the Soldier of Charity?" She took a few steps closer so he'd see her small smile.

He seemed to snap back from somewhere far away. "Thought I heard Pryce talking about that last night. Well, if he told you anything about the guy who first called me that, you'll understand why I'm hesitant to jump onto any ship that sails on promises of a better tomorrow."

"What happened?"

Dark was falling in earnest now. She stepped closer.

"Long story short, a guy by the name of Connor found me when I was—"

His head jerked up like a dog who'd just heard someone at the door, and his hand slid smoothly to the pistol holstered at his right thigh. There was a low, mechanical cough from somewhere behind her and to the right. Then something stabbed into the back of her right shoulder.

"What the fuck?"

She reached for her shoulder. Her voice sounded strange in her ears, deep and weirdly distorted.

Her hand found a small cylindrical object protruding from her shoulder. She pulled, and the world lurched—no, she had. She saw a well-formed butt in front of her and realized Jarek had hoisted her over his shoulder. But why?

Two gunshots cracked out right beside them, then two more. Jarek's gun?

"Hold on, sweetheart," Jarek said from somewhere far away. He sounded like he was standing at the bottom of a pool.

The world spun around her as she managed to bring the little cylinder she'd pulled from her shoulder up close enough to see. A tiny dart. That wasn't good. Because? God, why was it so hard to think?

Because . . .

"Oh, shit," she murmured as darkness closed around her.

CHAPTER EIGHTEEN

Whoever said chivalry was dead was probably right.

Sure, Jarek was doing his best to protect a quickly fading Rachel, but if that meant she had to take another tranq or two to cover him as he hauled her up the steps and into Alaric's cabin, so be it. He couldn't very well help either of them if he went down too, could he?

Long live the pragmatists.

Once they were inside with the storm door shut behind them, he yanked a dart from Rachel's lower back and another from her lovely little rump. He searched around the dark room for options to their current predicament. There weren't many. Luckily, having an AI on board your getaway ship was a decent ace in the hole.

He set Rachel down on the table. "Hostiles, Al. Rachel's been hit with a tranq."

"Oh dear," Al said. "Shall I come for you, sir?"

Jarek bit down the urge to immediately reply hell yes, he should come for him. Instead, he took a glance out the closest window, keeping low. To the left, across the street, shadows moved—six, no, maybe eight of them. More appeared as their predecessors spilled across the street and fanned out into the yard and the small lot that separated Alaric's cabin from the town jail.

Who the hell were these guys? More marauders, coming to spring their men free? No, they were too organized, and the tranquilizers didn't fit that picture.

It didn't matter who they were right now. What mattered was getting out. A pickup would be messy at best with that many men out there, but it wasn't like tromping through the woods in the dark with Rachel slung over his shoulder would be a much better idea. These guys were equipped with tranq guns; what if they were packing infrared specs too?

He'd take his chances here. If it all went ass over teakettle, at least he'd go down in a blaze of glory instead of tripping on a shrub and breaking his neck in the woods.

"Okay. Save us, Mr. Robot."

Al's reply was lost beneath the voice calling, "Come on out, Slater. It doesn't have to get messy. Yet."

Was that . . .? It couldn't be.

He peered through the window again and caught sight of the silhouette. He groped for the leftmost switch beside the door, picking at random. Light poured out from the porch.

There was a glint of red, and his stomach fell to the floor as Seth Mosen materialized in the light of the front yard.

"Don't leave us waiting, Slater. I see you in there."

He ducked away from the window and dropped down beside the table, lightly slapping at Rachel's cheek for some response. No luck. He choked down a dry swallow and glanced back at the window, briefly wondering if any of the townsfolk would dare to step in.

Not good. This was not good.

He took a steadying breath and called out, "Seth Mosen, as I live and breathe . . . Didn't I put a bullet in that big old head of yours?"

"Mosen?" Al said in his ear. "Oh dear. Hold on, sir."

"Busy week," Mosen called. "Couldn't spare the time to go dying."

Jesus, did he sound that cheesy when he was making his own wise-cracks? He crossed the room and grabbed Alaric's coat from the rack.

No, he decided as he threw on the battered long coat, he was definitely craftier at practiced nonchalance. Way craftier.

None of that remotely explained how the hell Mosen was still breathing. But that was a problem for later, when they weren't pinned down by the Reds, as was the question of just how the hell they'd even found them here, though he had a sinking feeling that Pryce's abduction had played a role in the latter.

He moved back to the window and pinched the coat's sleeve experimentally. It probably wouldn't stop a tranq dart, but it was certainly better than his Henley.

"You know," he called, "in my experience, it's better if only one of us tries the wise-guy routine. Things get confusing way too fast otherwise."

A movement from the tree line behind the jail drew his attention to the right.

"Son of a bitch," he murmured as the slinking shadow drew close enough to resolve into the figure of Alaric Weston.

"Sir?"

"Alaric's back," he said. "This might be a hairy one, Al."

"When has it ever not been, sir?"

Fair point.

Mosen was just finishing some line or another about how he'd just have to beat the wise-guy out of him. What to do, what to—

"Seth."

Jarek froze at the sound of Alaric's voice in the quiet night. It wasn't the commanding, surly tone he'd heard him use before. Somehow, in that one word, he thought he heard fragility.

Mosen turned toward the voice, a more substantial red glow flickering in his eyes, and Jarek's breath caught as a string of thoughts fell into congruent order. *Seth is dead*, Alaric had shouted at him. Seth. Pryce's story about what the raknoth had done to Alaric's family, what they'd done to his son . . .

For the second time in as many minutes, Jarek found himself staring down an impossible conclusion.

"Father," Mosen called, his voice strong but his tone flat.

"Hold up a second, Al," Jarek said.

Alaric was walking into the open yard, hands not quite held up but clearly removed from the revolvers at his hips.

"Alaric's—shit, never mind for now. Just tell Michael to be ready and get your ass down here when I give the signal. Code word: party. Or rave."

"Acknowledged, sir."

Outside, Alaric stopped a few feet away from Mosen. His usual stony expression looked as if it might melt and ooze off his face at any moment. Mosen's back was turned toward Jarek, so Jarek couldn't see his reaction as Alaric slowly reached out a hand.

Judging from Alaric's expression, it wasn't good.

He cracked the window to listen.

"—have they done to you?"

"Given me gifts beyond anything you could ever hope to, Father. I've become far more than I could have been as your son."

"Those aren't your words," Alaric said. "They're his. That's the Overlord talking."

Mosen tilted his head back and let out a high, bitter laugh.

The situation clearly wasn't improving. He'd better make his move.

He holstered his gun and gave Rachel one last hopeful shake. Aside from the tiny groan that rumbled out of her, there was no response.

"And this is why I work alone," he said as he gathered up the sleeping arcanist and hauled her back onto his left shoulder. He turned for the door, brushing the long coat open to draw his gun back out.

Opening the door with Rachel slung over one shoulder and a pistol in his free hand wasn't particularly graceful, but he managed. "Howdy, boys! Long time no see."

He didn't bother training his gun on Mosen. There was the itty-bitty chance that Alaric wouldn't take kindly to it, and there was also the concern of Mosen's underlings and their potentially twitchy trigger fingers—not to mention the whole part where a bullet to the head apparently wasn't such a big deal for Mosen.

Instead, he sidled to the edge of the porch where Rachel had left her staff and bent down as best he could to snag the end of it with the fingers of his gun hand. He managed to awkwardly transfer the staff from his overly full right hand to his left, which was slung across Rachel's legs just beneath her butt.

That accomplished, he gave himself a satisfied nod and looked out to meet the gaping faces of the Reds beholding him in all his damsel-toting, cowboy-ninja-wizard glory.

"I think you're a few months early on the costume," Mosen said, turning his open back on his father.

What would Alaric do if it came to a fight? He had a feeling he was about to find out.

"Hey, there's a new sheriff in town." He glanced at Alaric. "Sorry, I've just always wanted to say that. How was your walk, cowboy?"

Alaric glared at him. "Lots to think about."

"Uh-huh, I bet. Probably lots to talk about too," he added, gesturing between the two of them with his gun hand. The movement wasn't a threatening one, but every one of the Reds gripped their guns —several of them not tranquilizers—more tightly and somehow seemed to aim harder at him. "Like how Seth's big, scary boss kicked in Jay Pryce's door earlier today."

He felt hard anger creeping onto his face.

Alaric's expression darkened as well, if such a thing were possible.

Mosen smiled at Jarek. "Your fault for involving him, Slater."

"You hurt Pryce?" Alaric said, his expression regaining some of that stoic stoniness.

"What do you care?" Mosen said. "You left those people behind, remember? And if you do care somewhere in there, then his blood's on your hands just as much as it's on Slater's." Mosen met Jarek's eyes. "And there's going to be a lot more if we don't get the nest back."

Was Mosen toying with him? Most likely, he simply figured telling Jarek didn't matter at this point, and that meant their conversation was on a clock—and probably a short one, at that.

"Ah, yes. The old end-is-nigh rave." He jostled Rachel higher on his shoulder. "Speaking of ends, what's the deal with the tranqs, Mosen? You guys going soft on us?"

Mosen's expression soured a shade. "The Overlord himself ordered that the arcanist be captured and brought to him. He made no such order for you, which brings me back to business." His smile returned in full force as he gestured toward the porch. "Take the arcanist."

The Reds started forward only to duck backward in alarm as Al brought the ship roaring down from the hilltop. Even at full power, the ship's motors weren't particularly loud, but the cacophony of blaring horns and alarm sounds that Al sent through the loudspeaker was plenty to send them scrambling for cover for a few mad moments.

Jarek was ready. As soon as the racket hit, he shuffled down the steps, raising his weapon. Gaping mouths snapped shut as the men brought their own weapons back up. He shot one down and nicked another as Al swiveled the ship around and brought the opening hatch down above him.

He glanced over his shoulder to see another Red drawing a bead on him. The man dropped dead with a neat hole in his forehead as Alaric made up his own mind.

The ship was only ten feet from the ground now. Michael appeared on the ramp and opened fire with the rifle he'd had the good sense to grab from Jarek's locker. He wasn't a crack shot, but he hit one shooter off the bat and gave the rest another reason to seek cover.

Jarek stumbled to a knee and almost dropped Rachel as a lance of fire grazed his calf, but then the ship settled down between him and the shooter. Michael slung the rifle and took Rachel from him.

He tossed her staff after them just as Mosen bellowed "Bring the ships!" and hurled Alaric at the small tool shed nearby. Alaric hit the wood with a hard, cracking thud and bounced to the ground.

Mosen paid him little attention. "Bravo team, move in! *Now!*"

Then he turned with literal red fury in his eyes and leaped toward Jarek.

A little over ten yards lay between them. Jarek could've covered the distance in Fela, but it was a leap that no human could have made from a dead start.

Mosen made it all the same.

Jarek opened fire as Mosen flew through the air. Judging from Mosen's aggravated growl, at least one of the shots found their mark. Jarek tucked and rolled to the side as Mosen crashed down where he'd just been.

He rose on a stinging leg, then ducked Mosen's savage haymaker. Sensing an impending backhand, he pushed back but staggered as his calf protested.

Pain exploded across his right cheek as Mosen's fist impacted and knocked him spinning to the ground, bell thoroughly rung. He raised the gun he'd managed to hold onto and tried to shake his vision straight as Mosen stalked toward him.

He fired once. Twice. The second shot must've found Mosen's torso, his dazed brain insisted, but it didn't stop him from sweeping in and kicking the gun from Jarek's hand.

The pain that shot through his fingers was like a splash of water in the face. His leg growled in protest, but he managed to bring it up in time to kick aside the stomp Mosen aimed at his stomach. In reply, he planted his good leg against Mosen's chest and drove it home.

Strong as Mosen was, Jarek had all the leverage at that angle. Mosen took several stumbling steps backward, just managing to keep his balance.

Jarek would've been lying if he said he'd been planning what happened next.

Al lifted the ship by a few feet and yawed it around clockwise.

Jarek gathered his strength and shouted: "Fore!"

The ship's ramp smashed into Mosen's shoulder. It wasn't moving tremendously fast, but the sheer mass of the ramp and the ship behind it was enough to send Mosen bouncing across the yard like a ragdoll, superhuman abilities or no.

A dozen different pains stabbed through Jarek as he pulled himself to his feet. "Thanks, Mr. Robot."

"Incoming ships, sir," Al said. "I suggest we leave immediately."

Across the yard, Michael was pulling Alaric to his feet. They made for the ship, Alaric stumbling along as Michael fired a few suppressing shots at the Reds who were playing against Al's ship-sized cover to line up a shot. One of them succeeded, and Michael cried out and dropped his gun.

Michael's cry seemed to snap Alaric out of his stupor. He raised his remaining revolver and gunned down the shooter. They staggered on and reached the ship's ramp at the same time as Jarek.

Mosen was stirring off to the left.

Jarek limped up the ramp, helping Alaric and Michael do the same. "Get us out of here, Al."

The ramp began to rise beneath their feet as the ship lifted off the ground. Al's voice came through the speakers: "I recommend everyone secure themselves. I anticipate mild turbulence in the immediate future."

Several bullets clanged off of the hull, and they all hit the deck as the ramp sealed shut and Al rocketed them away from Deadwood and into the empty night.

CHAPTER NINETEEN

A s peaceful as the greenery and mountain air of Deadwood
had been, Jarek couldn't say he was sad to leave the place
behind, not once that fresh mountain air had given way to
the scent of gunpowder and blood, and once that peace had—well,
that part went without saying.

They nursed their collective wounds on the return trip to Newark.
No one had been fatally injured, but that was far from saying they
were in good shape. Funny enough, the first to fall had come through
much more smoothly than the rest of them. He'd be sure to make
ample fun of Rachel later for sleeping through the entire fight, but for
now, he kind of wished he could've done the same.

He glanced through the cockpit door at her peaceful form and
smiled. She was just so cute when she was all conked out on tranqs.

Alaric and Michael sat with him in the cockpit. There wasn't much
to be done for Alaric's injuries. Given how hard he'd hit that wall,
Jarek worried about internal bleeding, but they weren't exactly
equipped to even check for that, much less do anything about it.
Luckily, Alaric was a tough old bastard.

Michael's gunshot wound, they'd done their best with. Jarek had
held him while Alaric had dug the bullet out. "Dug" was definitely an

appropriate choice of words. It had been a bit of a butcher job. Thankfully, they'd loaded the kid up with some pain meds before they'd gotten started to ease the process.

At first, he'd been worried about the potency of the drugs, as old as they were, but judging from the glazed look in Michael's eyes and the easy smile on his mouth, they'd worked just fine. Of course, the kid was probably also a lightweight, given his disdain for alcohol.

His own bright collection of battle favors didn't really merit any specific care, though there was plenty of grating pain to go around. Even by his standards, this much fighting in twenty-four hours was excessive.

"Can we go any higher?" Michael asked for the fourth time.

"It's all good, Mikey. We lost 'em, remember? No one's gonna see us up here." He finished the last of four sutures on Michael's arm, wrapped the area up tight, and began cleaning everything up.

"How are you holding up?" he added to Alaric.

For a brief moment, Alaric looked lost—utterly, hopelessly without direction. Then he seemed to remember where he was, and dark anger began to creep over his face.

"Too soon," Jarek murmured. "Fair enough."

He backed out of the cockpit, his cheeks warming as he thought about the things he'd said to Alaric earlier that day—not to mention the fact that he'd unknowingly shot the guy's son last night. And what the hell gave with that? Was Seth a Weston or a Mosen? Had he changed his name after everything that had happened?

At least Jarek hadn't accidentally killed Alaric's son. That wouldn't have made things any simpler. Not that having Mosen around made things simple—for anyone.

Was he an asshole for thinking that? Probably. Okay, definitely. Maybe.

He liked to think his heart was in the right place when it mattered, but sometimes he wished he was more adept at helping people without resorting to the gun or the sword. The internal threats—those were the tricky ones.

Alaric's situation with Seth was about as messed up as they came.

And then there was the small contingent of Reds they'd left behind in his town. He'd been waiting for Alaric to go into a fit of rage and insist they return him to his people, but he hadn't. Maybe because he realized the Reds would almost certainly be chasing after them instead of sticking around in Deadwood.

Then again, for all Jarek knew, Alaric might simply be quiet right now because he'd had a nervous breakdown or some kind of stroke. How would he know? The guy was a steel trap.

He started putting away the medical supplies Pryce had given him a few years back.

Pryce.

That poor old lovable bastard.

If it wasn't for Pryce, he wouldn't have even lived long enough to earn that ridiculous nickname. Pryce had helped Jarek a hundred times through the years, maybe more. He'd never thought twice about it.

And now—

He stifled a manic laugh. Pryce would have just said the thought rattling obscenely in his mind.

"He finally paid the Pryce for it," he murmured, and clenched his jaw against the pressure of hot tears. "Goddammit."

"I do hope he's okay," Al said quietly in his ear.

That made two of them. He'd tried Pryce's comm half a dozen times after the initial attack and another half a dozen times since they'd jetted out of Deadwood. The fact that he had yet to receive any answer didn't mean that Pryce was dead. Neither did Mosen saying that Pryce's blood was on his hands.

But those things didn't inspire confidence, either. If his experience in the post-Catastrophe world had taught him anything, it was that stories had bad endings a lot more often than good.

None of that stopped him from hoping that Pryce was still alive. He just recognized the hope for what it was.

The one (and maybe only) bright side was that they'd technically succeeded at their original mission: they'd recovered Alaric. Assuming things didn't somehow fall to shit in the next hour, and assuming

Alaric was stable and willing to get them to Hux's safe place, he might actually get Fela back.

And once he had Fela, if Pryce was alive, he'd find him. He'd cut the entire damn Red Fortress to ribbons if he had to.

With that resolution, he stepped back into the cockpit and settled into the pilot's seat.

The trip clock updated by a couple of minutes. Just under an hour left.

In the copilot's seat beside him, Alaric gazed out the windshield with faraway eyes. For a while, they sat in silence. Behind them, Michael seemed to have slipped into an opioid-enhanced doze.

To Jarek's surprise, Alaric broke the silence. "I reckon you might've had a point."

He looked over at Alaric. His expression hadn't changed.

"I've been running," Alaric said. "For five goddamn years, I've been running, and for the life of me, I don't know where I was hopin' it'd take me."

"There are worse ways you could have spent those five years, man. You were helping people."

"I was. But not the ones who really needed it."

"I'm sure that's not how the people you've kept safe see it. Matter of perspective, I guess."

Alaric turned to him, his gaze intense. "And what do you see when you look at my son from your perspective?"

Christ, how was he supposed to answer that? Somehow, "a sadistic monster" didn't really seem like the right thing to say. "What happened to him, it's not your fault, Alaric. We're dealing with shit we have no comprehension of when it comes to the raknoth."

"True enough," Alaric said. "Doesn't forgive our mistakes, though."

"If you're not happy with the direction you're running, there's no reason you can't change course."

"You get that from a fortune cookie?"

He smiled. "Just a snippet from the vault of good life advice I can't ever seem to follow myself."

"Mmm," Alaric said, possibly with the faintest trace of a smile.

"And for what it's worth, that business about shooting your son back in Newark—sorry about that."

There it was: the deepest, surliest frown he'd ever seen. Apparently, all the others had been warm-ups.

"I just, uh, didn't really see it all playing out this way. I mean"—he spread his hands—"how was I supposed to know when he's going by Mosen?"

Alaric's frown didn't soften. "Mosen was his mother's maiden name. I imagine the Overlord has him going by the name as some kind of sick joke after what he made Seth do."

Jarek ran a hand through the back of his hair, searching for some reasonable response. "Right. Makes sense. I guess. I, uh—"

Behind them, Rachel gave a hoarse groan and shifted on the cot. Bless her sleepy little heart.

"I better go check on her. Good talk." He stood and made haste toward the cabin.

"Jarek."

He froze and turned back.

Alaric gave him a deep nod. "Thank you. For what you said a minute ago."

Jarek nodded back. He went to check on Rachel feeling confused and shaken and maybe just a little bit helpful.

CHAPTER TWENTY

A hand caressed Rachel's cheek, warm and gentle in its touch if not in its texture.

"Nap time's over, sweetheart."

She blinked and squinted through bleary eyes to find Jarek Slater's stupid grin hovering over her. Why the hell did that make her want to smile back? And on top of that, why were they back in Jarek's ship? And in the air?

"What the hell happened?"

"You totally snoozed through a whole big battle," he said. "Not cool, by the way, but probably forgivable on account of all the tranquilizers and everything."

Too disoriented and apparently hungover on tranquilizers to formulate a clever comeback, she simply groaned and rolled over.

He patted her back. "There, there. We're almost back to Newark. Just wanted to make sure you're ready to move."

From the feel of it, "ready" was going to be a stretch anytime in the near future, but she pulled herself up.

The feeble glow of Newark was in sight when she sidled into the cockpit a few minutes later. The few dull patches of poorly lit browns and grays that parted the thick darkness below them looked about as shitty as she felt.

"So, uh," Jarek said, "can someone tell me where it is we're actually going?"

Alaric glanced back. "It's still the old terminal?"

Michael nodded his sleepy confirmation from the bench opposite her. Alaric dropped a nav pin on the map northeast of Newark. Almost immediately, Al began banking the ship northward and gaining altitude, skirting around Newark nice and high in the night sky.

"You okay, Spongehead?" she asked.

The wrap on Michael's arm was thorough, and he looked entirely more zonked than usual.

He shot her a happy thumbs-up.

"Mikey's feeling great," Jarek said. "No worries."

"What happened? And what the hell did you give him?"

Michael held his bandaged arm up. "I got shot, Rache."

"Annnd we gave him something for the pain before we dug the bullet out," Jarek added.

But he'd been wearing her catcher, hadn't he?

"How did—"

Her fingers brushed the small disk clipped to the front of her belt.

She looked at Michael. "Why the hell weren't you wearing the catcher?"

"Asked him the same question," Jarek said. "He had to leave you unattended to grab Alaric. He was worried you might take a stray bullet or something."

Michael bobbed his head agreeably.

"Jesus. I pass out for a couple of hours, and all hell breaks loose."

She closed her eyes and breathed out some of the tension. It was done. At least everyone was still alive.

Jarek was watching her when she opened her eyes again.

"Not to be a bother, but you guys mind strapping in for landing?"

She rolled her eyes at what she assumed was an unnecessary precaution. She should have known better, coming from Jarek.

Once their harnesses had each clicked, he brought them down fast enough that her stomach found its way into her throat. Removed from the city lights, it was hard to tell how close they were to the ground, but he waited until well after what seemed like the too-late zone to pull them out of the dive.

Her stomach lurched into her pelvis before settling back into place, and then they were skimming along over the surface of a river that was nearly too dark to make out. After a few more minutes of bobbing and weaving, they came to a hover in an enormous lot filled to the brim with rusty old shipping containers.

"Fun ride," she grumbled.

"Not the first time a lady's said that to me." Jarek extended his fist to Alaric for a bump.

Alaric gave the fist a stern frown, turned back to the windshield, and gestured to a spot where several of the dilapidated containers formed a nice alcove. "That'll do just fine."

"Thank you, Wild Bill." Jarek retracted the unbumped fist and guided the ship gently into the parking space.

No one spoke as they left the ship. Michael shuffled across the lot at the head of the pack, apparently recognizing where he was despite the drugs and the monotonous repetition of their surroundings. At least his head seemed to be marginally clearing now that he was up and moving.

After a quarter of a mile or so, he and Alaric veered toward an unassuming, rust-red shipping container. It didn't look remotely different than its neighbors, but they seemed to recognize it somehow, maybe by the serial code printed on its side.

The container's doors weren't locked, and inside, it appeared to be empty—"appeared" being the operative word, she assumed.

Her assumption turned out to be accurate.

Michael crossed to the back wall of the container, felt around for several seconds, and slid a small hidden panel aside to reveal a dimly lit keypad. Alaric pulled the container door shut behind them as Michael tapped a sequence into the pad and slid the false wall panel back in place, leaving them standing in darkness too thick to see one another.

Nothing happened.

"So, uh, granted I'm not an expert on secret hideouts," Jarek said after half a minute had stretched by, "but I thought super-secret access panels were usually supposed to open doors or, ya know, do something."

"Double verification protocol," Michael said. "There's the code, then the IR cameras, and they're probably calling up the chain right now to check about you guys."

"Isn't that triple—agh, never mind. This is why you Resistance guys never get anything done. Too busy running around playing spy-party grab-ass."

She allowed herself a small smile in the darkness. It faded a moment later when Michael's words set in and she realized the Resistance goons were probably watching.

"Jesus," Jarek said a minute later, "We should have brought drinks and made it a—"

A series of tiny pops sounded, followed by the steady hum of an electric motor. A line of light appeared across the floor and stretched into a rectangular opening as two sections of the floor slid apart to reveal a descending concrete stairwell.

"Maybe you can talk your way into a drink down there," Michael said.

"I won't hold my breath," Jarek said, as Michael started down the steps with Alaric a few steps behind. "I've heard these people aren't my biggest fans."

"Guess I buy that," she said, "given that this doesn't look like a brothel or a bar."

Jarek held up a finger as he composed his retort. She turned away to follow the others down the stairs, hiding her grin.

"Hey!" he called after her. "I never pay for the sex!"

The stairwell was uncomfortably cramped. No one would ever dream of calling her tall, but she still had to duck her head to avoid the ceiling. God knew how Jarek was doing behind her. A pang of claustrophobic anxiety clutched at her chest when the hidden door began sliding shut behind them.

The room at the bottom was considerably more open than the stairwell but far too cramped to be described as anything close to spacious or comfortable. Four men were waiting for them, all dressed casually in jeans and T-shirts and pretty much looking the part of everyday citizens, minus the guns and armored vests. Aside from the few appreciative glances they turned her way, they stared at Alaric with something like awe.

At the end of the firing line stood a beautiful woman with raven-dark hair and light brown skin that somehow glowed even under the sterile lighting. Her scarlet Henley clung to a build that looked like it had some ass-kicking potential under the hood.

Beside her, Jarek was looking at the woman as if he'd be happy to volunteer for said ass-kicking.

"So there you have it, boys," the woman said in a commanding tone, the fine line of her brow arching in an amused expression, "just in case any of you were wondering—Jarek Slater earns his lays."

Apparently, they'd been listening.

The firing squad snickered.

Jarek ran a hand through the back of his hair. "And satisfies them, for what it's worth. You know, within reason."

It really never ended. Rachel stifled a smile.

The woman inclined her head toward him, still amused. "Your reputation precedes you, Mr. Slater"—she turned to Alaric—"though not as much as Alaric Weston's precedes him."

To Rachel's surprise, the woman stepped forward to hug Alaric.

"It's good to see you again," she said quietly as she pulled away.

"You're a sight for sore eyes, Lea," Alaric said, a warm smile cracking through his usual stoic visage.

"I'll second that," Michael said as Lea turned to embrace him next.

This hug was longer and, she thought, more intimate. She couldn't quite make out what Lea murmured in Michael's ear, but she almost rolled her eyes at the awkward pat her brother laid on Lea's back before she pulled away.

Smooth move, Spongehead.

"And you must be Rachel Cross," Lea said, turning to face her. "So nice to finally meet you."

She gave Lea a polite smile, not particularly enjoying being on this side of the catch-up game.

"We should move, Lea," Michael said.

Lea nodded, looking back to him and Alaric. "The commanders will want to see you two right away. We'll probably have to wait until the morning to gather the full council. Most of the base is asleep." Lea glanced at her and Jarek. "We can show you guys to the guest quarters if you'd like to get some sleep yourselves."

Jarek shrugged. "Whatever gets this party moving, sister."

Lea turned her questioning look to Rachel. She mirrored Jarek's shrug. "I'm with stupid here."

The corner of Jarek's mouth twitched up, and a few of the men chuckled.

They set off down the lone hallway leading out of the small room. Like the room they'd just left, the hallway was composed of cinderblock walls and smoother concrete floors, giving it a cold, hard feel under the buzzing lights. The entire place was a claustrophobic's nightmare. They passed by a few rooms before coming to a slightly more open space that acted as a hub between multiple hallways and a common room of sorts.

The few Resistance members who were still awake and lounging in the small, sparsely decorated common room stared openly as they passed. Most of the stares were directed toward the legend himself, Alaric Weston, but she and Jarek got a few baffled looks as well. It didn't seem like the kind of place that saw many new faces, and between Jarek's ninja-commando aesthetic and her glyphed staff clanking along on the concrete floor, she supposed they made fairly odd strangers at that.

In the next hallway, they paused in front of an important-looking set of wooden double doors.

"I'll fetch the commanders," Lea said to Michael and Alaric. She gestured to two of their escorts. "Please take our guests to their quarters and see to it they're fed if they're hungry." She turned to them. "I'll see you two tomorrow."

"And here I was thinking I didn't have anything to look forward to," Jarek said, giving her that stupid roguish grin of his.

Lea's smile looked as if it might have come at least partially against her will, but she quickly pulled it under control and gave him a polite tilt of her head.

Rachel refrained from rolling her eyes. Jarek was one of those guys with that subtly assholish magnetism that made girls want to sleep with him somewhere on a fundamental level well below the lines of social stigma and self-respect. Worse, he knew it. For some reason, it irritated the shit out of her.

A couple of hallways and some tense silence later, their escorts deposited them in guest quarters that were as cramped as the rest of the base. At least the rooms were adorned by a few carpets and boring pictures. It almost made them seem a tad warmer than the bland halls outside.

Their escorts returned with sandwiches a few minutes later, and soon after that, Rachel sat on one twin-sized bed with a contentedly full belly while Jarek finished his sandwich on the other. She pulled out Michael's nearly complete bullet catcher to work on the final touches as they awaited news from him.

"You're claustrophobic, aren't you?" Jarek asked after a while, not looking up from the comm holo game he was occupying himself with.

"No," she said too quickly. "No, I'm fine. Why?"

"You've looked around at the walls every single time you've paused from your enchanting."

So he'd been paying attention.

"And you're creepily watching me because . . ."

"You're easy to watch."

Oh. She looked at him uncertainly.

He killed his holo and grinned at her. "Don't deflect. You can't hide your fears from me."

"I'm not claustrophobic."

Not claustrophobic enough to label herself, anyway. That was her story, and she was sticking to it.

He pulled back the blanket on his bed, his grin widening. "Let's test, then. Come crawl under this tightly tucked blanket with me."

"You know I'm not gonna do that."

And here it came . . .

"Ha!" he cried. "Undeniable proof!"

She smiled. "Because clearly it's impossible that a woman wouldn't otherwise be dying to crawl into bed with Jarek Slater to be 'satisfied within reason,' right?"

"At least implausible. And I might even be willing to consider going beyond reason for you."

She snorted. "Well, if that doesn't make a girl feel special . . ."

They sank back into a comfortable silence. When she was focused and ready, she gathered the will and the energy to empower the last glyph on the catcher. She let it flow, holding the enchantment tight in her mind until her head buzzed with the effort. Then it was done, and that was that.

Now she just had to give it to Michael and make damn sure the Spongehead never even thought about taking it off anywhere near a dangerous situation.

She opened her eyes carefully, consciously refraining from looking around at the cramped walls this time.

"So what are you gonna do if they try to get stingy about handing over your suit?" she asked.

He glanced in the direction of the council room, as if he could see right through the walls. "I'll figure something out. These boners aren't just gonna keep Fela for their own. She's—"

He paused, frowning down at his comm. ". . . mine . . ."

His expression went flat.

"What is it?"

He looked up, his face a little pale and his expression more uncertain than she'd ever seen it.

"It's Pryce."

CHAPTER TWENTY-ONE

J arek couldn't think of a time he'd been more afraid to press a button.

Part of him (and not a small part) had begun wrapping itself around the idea that Pryce was gone. It was easier that way. But now here his comm was, buzzing with the dead man's call. So maybe he was okay. Maybe he'd managed to give the Reds the slip.

While holding onto his life and his comm in the process?

Not probable. The more likely scenario was that the Reds had held Pryce to use as bait in case Jarek and the others managed to slip Mosen's team. And the Red King would know by now that they had.

Of course, there was one easy way to find out. At the end of the day, it didn't matter; if Pryce was alive, he was going after him, trap or no.

He gritted his teeth and reached for the Accept button. Rachel watched from the other bed, looking almost as tense as he felt.

The holo sprang up between them to reveal Pryce seated in a worn armchair. Jarek registered that he was looking at Pryce's home. Pryce sported a few bruises, a patch of his shirt was stained with blood, and he looked sullen as all hell, but he was alive. As far as Jarek could tell, he wasn't terribly injured.

Jarek sat stunned silent by the warm relief that poured through him, so strong for a moment that he thought it might lift him straight up from the bed and have him bouncing on his toes. Quickly enough, though, the sensation gave way to the uneasiness tugging at his guts.

He bit down the urge to start crying things like "Pryce! Are you all right?"

Something wasn't right. The way Pryce was sitting, the angle of his camera that clearly indicated his comm wasn't on his wrist, the somehow intensely neutral look on his face . . . Someone was there with him. Three guesses who.

"You look like crap, old man."

Pryce flicked an eyebrow. "You should see the other guy."

Before he'd even finished, the image in the holo whirled as someone moved Pryce's comm. The image settled on the face of a man with sandy blond hair and a strong jawline. He might've been in his late forties, but Jarek had a feeling he wasn't. He recognized the face. He'd seen it just last night. Only then, the irises hadn't been pale blue. In fact, there hadn't even been irises.

"Your Highness," he said.

"Jarek Slater." The Red King's voice was less raspy than the last time he'd heard it. "I will make this simple. You give me back the nest, and I will give you Jay Pryce, alive and unharmed."

He thought about bullshitting the raknoth, but what good ever came of that? If this was going to be a hostage situation, what he needed was to make sure they'd actually bring Pryce to whatever meeting they arranged.

"I need Pryce by my side before I give you a location."

"The exchange will happen at the location, once the presence of the nest is confirmed."

He wasn't sure he particularly cared about what happened to this nest thing everyone was raving about, but he wouldn't be able to find the damn thing either way without Alaric's help. Bursting into their little Command meeting to borrow Alaric and go turn over the potentially uber-dangerous alien toy probably wasn't going to fly.

They should have gone straight to grab Fela when they'd had the chance. Without her, he didn't stand a chance against the Red King. He was sure of that. But with Fela, and maybe with Rachel's help, they might just be able to save Pryce and eliminate one of the Resistance's most powerful enemies at the same time. Everyone could win.

All he needed was enough time to get Fela back.

"What if I don't have the location?" he said.

The raknoth's eyes pulsed with a menacing scarlet glow. "Then you must get Weston to talk, if you want to save your friend's life."

The King passed off the comm to a new cameraman and strode around to stand behind Pryce with ominous intent. Pryce tensed as the King placed a hand lightly on his head.

"Hey—"

"You have one hour." The King said. Then he struck at the side of Pryce's neck like a viper. He sank his teeth in, eyes coming alive with crimson fire as darker red pooled around his mouth and dripped down Pryce's neck.

Pryce gave a faint cry of pain and surprise but quickly grew subdued, even languid, as if the bite had some narcotic effect. The King continued lapping up his blood like a thirsty dog.

"Stop," Jarek said through gritted teeth. "Stop!"

The King took a few more slurps of blood, then parted from Pryce's neck to shoot Jarek a serious look.

"One hour, Jarek Slater."

The call ended.

Jarek held the icy hand of panic at bay long enough to set a timer on his comm. Then he squeezed his hands into fists and slammed them down on the bed.

"Dammit!"

He bounced to his feet and began pacing back and forth.

What the hell was he going to do?

The image of that sick bastard drinking Pryce's blood hovered in his mind, pushing out all attempts at productive thought.

"Focus, sir," Al said quietly in his ear. "Deep breath."

Jarek suppressed the urge to tell him to take a deep breath of his ass. Al was right. Pryce needed him.

Think.

The Resistance wouldn't care about Pryce, certainly not enough to risk losing this allegedly world-endangering artifact. Asking them to make an honest deal with the Red King was off the table.

But getting them to back his reclaiming Fela so he could go kill one of their biggest problems dead? He might sell them on that one.

He turned to Rachel. "I need Fela. And, uh . . ."

Just say the words, you pansy.

He held out a hand. "And I need help, Rachel. I can't—"

She clapped her hand to his forearm, then looked up at him expectantly. "Go on. Don't let me stop you there."

"—can't wait to see the looks on their faces when I . . ."

Her brow arched.

"Fine." He pulled her to her feet so that they were less than a foot apart. "I can't do this without you."

She looked up at him, searching his face, leaning in almost imperceptibly. His mind went momentarily blank, his chest fluttering in a way he'd nearly forgotten it could.

Then she reached up and thwapped him on the forehead with a flick of her finger.

"Ow!"

She pushed past him and grabbed her staff from where it leaned against the wall. "Let's go, dude!"

He touched his forehead. What the hell had just happened? A glance at his comm timer reminded him that the answer to that question mattered about zero percent right now.

He slung his sword over his shoulder just as Michael opened the door, looking frustrated.

They all exchanged a look and then, at almost exactly the same time, all said, "What happened?"

He pushed ahead. "Pryce is alive. The Red King has him over at the shop. Get me to Fela right now, and there might be a raknoth head in it for the Resistance."

"Oh," Michael said, his eyes wide. "Oh, Jesus—okay." He licked his lips, glancing between Jarek and Rachel and slowly nodding to himself. "Okay, well, the commanders want to move on Hux's safe right away anyways, but . . ." His mouth drew into a tight line, and he looked down. "Shit."

The word sounded foreign coming out of Michael's mouth, but it wasn't the light profanity Jarek cared about. Something was up.

"What is it?" Rachel asked.

Michael glanced at her, then, seemingly with great effort, turned his gaze to meet Jarek's eyes. "I need to show you something. Alone."

Rachel scowled at them. "Screw that."

"Now's not really the time, Mikey," he agreed. "We have less than an hour."

Michael directed a sobering look at each of them. "Please. It's important, I promise."

"I think you should see what he wants, sir," Al said quietly in his ear.

A look with Rachel told him they were equally taken aback by Michael's odd behavior. "Go find Alaric?" he asked Rachel.

After a slight hesitation, she nodded.

He turned back to Michael. "Two minutes, Mikey. Make it snappy."

They split in the hallway outside, Rachel turning back the way they'd came as Michael guided him left and then right at the end of the hall.

"So what's the deal?" Jarek asked quietly as they moved down the empty cinder-block hallway at a brisk pace.

Michael didn't meet Jarek's eye. "I might have screwed up."

An uneasy feeling tugged at his stomach. "You might have to be a bit more specific, buddy. What's going on? Out with it."

"I . . ." Michael shook his head. "Easier to just show you."

A minute later, Michael guided them into an antechamber that led to heavy vault door. The tiny room was similar to the others throughout HQ and empty but for the guard who sat behind a small desk, staring at his tablet.

The guard frowned at them with a bulldog face as they entered, then nodded at Michael. "Carver. Glad to see you made it out alive." He turned his bulldog stare to Jarek and added, "Who's he?" in a way that strongly implied an unspoken, *And what the fuck is he doing here?*

"New recruit," Michael said. "Apparently, he might be able to work with that exo we found a few weeks back."

Jarek had taken punches to the head that left him less stunned than Michael's words.

"I didn't hear about this from Command," the bulldog said. His frown deepened as he glanced down at his tablet then back up at Jarek. "And it's the middle of the night, man."

Michael shrugged. "Orders." He crossed to the keypad by the heavy door.

Could Fela really be in there? Had Michael been lying to him this entire time?

The beginnings of anger licked at the base of Jarek's stupefied mind.

"Hey, hold up a second." The bulldog stood up and moved toward Michael.

Michael spun around counterclockwise and shoved the guy into the wall. The bulldog's eyes went wide, but Michael was already pulling the stun gun from the guy's belt and turning it against him.

The bulldog made a couple of jerking grunts and slid limply down the wall. Once his bulk was resting on the concrete floor, Michael pulled the comm from his wrist and turned back to the door's access panel.

"What the fuck is going on?"

An odd combination of brewing anger and hopeful excitement swirled in his chest as Michael swiped the comm over the panel and tapped in a string of numbers.

By way of reply, Michael pressed the Enter key and stepped aside. The panel's LED flashed green, and the door unlocked with a series of heavy clicks.

Jarek stepped numbly to the door and peered through.

Fela. Finally.

He crossed the room in a stupor and put a hand on the flimsy cage that contained her—a Faraday cage, he took it. That probably explained why Al (ship Al, that is) hadn't been able to get a fix on her all this time—that and the fact that her power pack had been removed. He spotted it on the nearby table beside the scattered assortment of explosives, heavy weapons, and other rare gadgets they kept in the vault.

The dark gray exosuit was deactivated, collapsed down into compact form in the cage, just waiting for someone to come power her up. Waiting for him.

And she'd been here this entire time.

He turned slowly to face Michael. He'd risked his ass to free Michael from the Fortress. He'd nearly lost his life twice more running around the country on Michael's damn quest.

And his suit had been here within easy reach throughout all of it.

"You lied to me."

Somehow, those four words seemed to express every violent thought that was coursing through his mind.

Michael certainly cringed enough to think that was so. "Hux and I found it a few weeks ago. And once you showed up at the Fortress, I thought if I could just get you to . . . It doesn't matter. I was wrong. And now they're talking about keeping it until they can get past Al and put one of their own—our own—people in the driver's seat. I'm sorry, Jar—"

Scarlet lightning crackled through his brain. The next thing he knew, the knuckles of his right hand were pulsing with pain, and Michael was lying in an incoherent heap on the floor.

He clamped his right hand over his mouth, clenching his jaw and squeezing until the pain grew strong enough to pierce the numb haze that clogged his mind. His eyes were moist with unspilled tears. The anger came flowing back in, calmer and more controlled, but hot and bitter nonetheless.

"Sir," Al said quietly in his ear, "is it . . ."

"It's her, Al. We've got our girl back."

"Oh, dear."

Al should've been excited. Just like Jarek should've been. But he was too angry to be excited.

He'd been stupid. Worse, he'd been naive. He'd broken the goddamn golden rule: don't trust anyone but Al and Pryce. That was it. If they were a living human and their name wasn't Jay Pryce, you didn't trust them. Because if you did, bad things happened. Every. Damn. Time.

Simple enough.

You sure as hell didn't let yourself think that maybe, just maybe, these Resistance a-holes weren't so bad just because you were chumming it up with a few people close to them.

"Dammit!" He kicked at the Faraday cage.

He grabbed at the cage and gave a few yanks. Maybe it wasn't so flimsy after all. It was, however, bottomless and not fixed to the ground, probably because it had been meant to shield Fela from outside signals, not to keep her locked up. That was what the vault door had been for.

He could tip the cage, but it'd be noisy if he wasn't careful.

Fuck it. Let them try to stop him.

He bent down, grabbed the mesh, and heaved upward. The cage was heavier than it looked, but he cast it over with a wordless cry. It hit the floor in a jostling crash, freeing Fela's collapsed form.

He grabbed the power pack from the table and crouched behind the suit to pry out the manual release lever and open the housing. He slid the power pack home, closed the small hatch, and began stripping off his weapons and clothes.

"Sir!" Al cried from Fela's external speakers as she rebooted from hibernation.

Relief sped his fingers over the last fastenings of his clothes. "Hey, buddy."

"I'll begin synchronizing my data with Fela's storage momentarily," said the Al that was still aboard the ship's computer.

He stepped into the collapsed suit's open boots and quivered as Fela responded to his presence. She began folding up around him, wrapping him in her armored embrace. The sensation of the smooth, flesh-like polymer membrane closing in on his skin was like coming home after far too long on the road—familiar, comfortable, and, above all, safe.

Michael shifted on the floor, mumbled something incoherent, and then lay still again.

He buckled on his gun belt and sword. "You had your shot, Mikey."

Thanks to Fela's auditory sensors, he heard the Resistance agent step into the antechamber outside well before the man's startled intake of breath.

"What the hell's going on here?" the agent whispered outside.

"Sir," Al said, through the earpiece in his helmet this time, "what the hell *is* going on here?"

With a deliberate thought, he slid the helmet faceplate closed and brought the display to life. The feed from his comm timer ticked away in the lower left corner.

"Oh, you know, Al." He grabbed the hefty sword he used with Fela from the nearby rack and clipped the sheath to the connectors Pryce had installed on Fela's back. "Burning bridges. Saving Pryce." He clenched his fists, relishing the power at his fingertips. "Just another day at the office."

The one bright side to this betrayal was that he had plenty of time left on the Red King's one-hour deadline.

In the corner of the room, an orange alarm light flashed to life, accompanied by a quiet but irritating rhythmic buzzing tone.

Plenty of time. Sure.

CHAPTER TWENTY-TWO

Rachel was urgently explaining Pryce's predicament to Alaric outside the council room's double doors when the orange strobes and the annoying, buzzing alarm began. At the end of the hallway, a few men trotted through the common room, sidearms drawn. Further off, someone was shouting something.

She had a bad feeling whatever was going on had something to do with Jarek and Michael's mysterious disappearance.

Before she could say anything to Alaric, one of the double doors pushed open. The slightly paunchy but solid-looking man Alaric had identified as Commander John Nelken emerged. Nelken had a hard face and an ex-military air about him. He'd clearly been as pleased as a cat on bath day when she'd interrupted their meeting to speak with Alaric.

For a second, Nelken looked confused himself. Then a gunshot from the direction she'd seen those men running snapped all three of them into action. Alaric's revolver appeared in his hand, and Nelken turned to call something to his fellow commanders back in the chamber.

She set off for the common room at a jog. As she entered, shouts echoed from the hall to her left. Three more Resistance men with shotguns came storming out of a room further down the hall and barreled off in the direction of the sounds.

Before they reached the end of the hall, a man-shaped form blurred around the corner, moving far too fast to control its turn. Instead, the thing leaped up and reoriented in midair so that its feet touched down on the wall. Its legs continued pumping without missing a beat. It skittered along the wall a few steps before launching itself at the foremost of the men running toward it.

Her startled brain began fitting the pieces together. The dark gray thing she could only assume was Fela dropped three men effortlessly, almost gently, into crumpled heaps in the space of two seconds. Fela (and presumably Jarek inside) continued down the hall without a noticeable pause.

Then he saw her.

At first, she wasn't sure he'd stop at all. The thing dug in its heels and skidded to halt near the next hallway, leaving small gouges in the concrete floor.

"Jarek?"

The dark gray surfaces of the suit looked like something out of an anatomy book. Instead of the bulky, angular armor she'd been expecting, Fela was smooth and round, resembling a well-muscled man several inches taller and wider than Jarek.

In some spots, the dark gray material was bundled into fibers like those of a skinned muscle. In others, particularly at the shoulders and along the torso and thighs, a smoother, lighter-gray material emerged like armor plating.

She recognized the smaller of the two swords crisscrossed over the back of the exosuit and the gun belt strapped above its hips. That was definitely Jarek in there, which meant several things, not the least of which was that either the Resistance had been lying to Michael about Fela's whereabouts, or Michael had been lying to her and Jarek this entire time.

The thought made her feel hollow inside. She fixed her eyes on the dark slit across Fela's face plate and waited.

A voice growled out. "Did you know?"

The voice was unmistakably Jarek's, though it was a shade deeper and minutely garbled through the speakers.

"No. I had no idea, Jarek."

He seemed to consider that. Then he gave a slight nod and turned back for the exit.

"Wait!"

His armored form slowed.

More shouts were coming now from multiple directions. She wasn't even sure what she wanted to say. "What happened to needing—"

A gunshot barked to her right, painfully loud in the enclosed space. She whipped around. Alaric was yanking the shooter's gun hand down and away from Jarek, but other men and women were spilling into the common room now, most of them armed. And now that the first shot had been fired, the others didn't hesitate.

Jarek sprinted down the exit hallway, moving far faster than she'd ever seen a human move. She thought she saw multiple shots ping off Fela's back and into the surrounding walls, but he didn't seem to pay them any mind.

He disappeared around the corner at the far end of the hall, and several Resistance men and women ran to follow.

Two men to her right were alternately eyeing her and looking in the direction Jarek had disappeared. One of them stepped toward her. "You're gonna have to come w—"

"Touch me," she said, "and I'll put you through that wall."

His eyes widened and his nostrils flared, but he and his partner both took a step back, hands in plain sight.

She spun on her heels and tromped down the hall Jarek had come from.

If Fela had been here all along—if Michael had known all along—then she could maybe understand why Jarek was pissed enough to blow out of here like that. But if he'd taken it out on Michael . . . And if Michael had deliberately lied to her . . .

For now, she just needed to make sure Michael was okay.

She picked up her pace, following the trail of sullen and groaning

Resistance fighters Jarek had strewn in his wake. When she found Michael in the hallway a minute later, she breathed a sigh of relief.

He appeared unharmed aside from the swollen, reddening patch of dark skin at the outer edge of his left eye. He was alternatively blinking his eyes as if to clear his vision, but he quickly stopped when he spotted her.

She didn't need to ask. His expression told her everything.

"You knew all along."

He nodded. "I thought I could get him to join us if I showed him the good we could do. The plan was always to give Fela back. At least I thought it was. The council had other ideas."

"You lied to me," she whispered.

Because that's what it boiled down to: whatever the reasons, Michael had lied. And he'd lied to *her*.

"No," he croaked. "No, Rache, I wasn't—I didn't mean to . . ."

She could see he was only beginning to fully register what he'd done.

"I'm sorry, Rache."

She wasn't sure how to respond, so she gave a curt nod. "I'm going to help him get Pryce back."

She could feel his unspoken protest behind her, but she didn't pause to give him time to voice his opinions.

Michael, her naive, do-gooder little Spongehead, had lied to her. It didn't sound right even in her head. She didn't need the fingers of one hand to count off the number of people she really trusted in this world, and Michael was at the top of that list. Or he had been, at least.

Maybe it didn't change much, really. He was still her brother. She would still put her life on the line for him right this moment without a second thought.

But that didn't mean it didn't hurt like hell.

After her family had been taken from her, when John Carver had found her and given her a home, she'd been a broken, frightened thing. John might have found her, but Michael had saved her. To an outsider, it would have appeared that she'd been the one taking care of him. In truth, she knew it had been the other way around.

Michael had helped restore her to something resembling a whole person. And even after he'd grown up big and strong, he'd always remained her precious Spongehead, the one person she could truly trust, the linchpin that held it all together. But now that linchpin felt eroded, corrupted.

She needed to focus on something she could control right now, something she could fix. Something like making sure Pryce didn't become another casualty of this mess.

Jarek had also been lied to. She got that. But it didn't make her any less pissed that he'd attacked her brother, given the finger to teamwork, and run off by himself.

She took a roundabout way back toward the council room to avoid the growing crowd. Alaric was there among several others, including Nelken and the two commanders she'd interrupted earlier.

Alaric, Nelken, and one of the other commanders, a short, strong-looking black woman, were the only ones who didn't look as if they thought the sky might be falling.

Alaric spotted her and stepped to meet her at the mouth of the hallway, but Nelken broke away and planted himself between them. "Ms. Cross—"

She let some of her anger free, and a sudden wind swept through the tight hallway, ruffling hair and clothes, among other things— Nelken's resolve, for instance. The commander took a small step back, hands raised in peace.

"I have a friend to track down and at least one ass to kick," Rachel said quietly, "so if you'd kindly get the fuck out of my way . . ."

Nelken glanced at Alaric, who shrugged, a small smile creeping onto his face.

"Delightful," Nelken said. "Now if you don't mind stowing the attitude for one minute, maybe we can talk about our next move. Alaric's already filled me in about Pryce. I assume that's where Slater's headed?"

She stared dumbly as she tried to decide if she'd been out of line or if Nelken's response should make her even more pissed.

"I need to get over there," she finally said. "He can't take them all on and protect Pryce at the same time. I need a ship."

Alaric nodded his agreement.

Nelken scratched at his square jaw, thinking. "This might be the time to move on Hux's safe, while the Reds are busy." He glanced at her. "I can't spare our only working ship, but I can give you a vehicle and a small team."

"You're gonna help him? You're not mad?"

"Of course I am," he said, his pale eyes hardening. "We can't let Slater's actions drop. But now isn't the time to squabble. We have an opening. We should take it."

Fair enough.

A ship would've been considerably faster, and she wasn't crazy about the idea of unknown Resistance fighters watching her back. But any vehicle was better than nothing, and having a couple of gun hands along might not be the worst thing in the world.

"Okay," she said, "let's do it then."

"I'll go with her," came Michael's voice from behind.

"Me too," Lea called. She was hovering close to Michael as if she were afraid he might keel over.

Nelken's expression hardened as he focused on Michael. "You are going to have a long chat with me when this is done about how Slater miraculously stumbled upon that exo."

Michael didn't argue or defend himself. He just gave a small nod, his eyes grave. As betrayed as she felt right now, she had to give it to him: he wasn't shirking the responsibility for any of his actions.

Nelken stared at Michael until he appeared satisfied. "Very well, then." He looked at Alaric. "You're ready to move?"

Alaric fumbled a pouch out of his jacket pocket. "Reckon I better be." He shoved a little wad of green leaves into his mouth and began chewing.

Nelken nodded. "Good. The teams should all be loaded up soon."

Alaric frowned. "Still not convinced it wouldn't be better to stick with one truck."

"It's a small enough force." Nelken didn't sound absolutely

convinced himself. "Better to have backup and options if you're spotted."

Rachel leaned forward, interjecting herself. "We'd better get moving if we want to get to Pryce's in time to matter."

"Right," Nelken said. He looked at the three of them as if he'd just had a thought. "Perhaps you should take the skipper."

"It's only seated for two," Lea said.

"We're small," Rachel said. "We'll figure it out. Let's go."

"Guess we'll see you back here, then," Michael said to Alaric and Nelken.

That was assuming all of their plans went off without a hitch. Still, she didn't mind the little bit of optimism.

"You're sure you don't wanna stick with Alaric?" she said quietly to Michael as they hurried down the next hallway. "You've been pretty hell-bent on finding that nest thing."

"We can't abandon Jarek now. And Pryce might not even be in danger right now if I'd just . . . Rache, I—"

"—fucked up," she finished for him. "I'll say it for you, since you're so scared of the big words."

He nodded, his face tight. "I did. I'm sorry."

She sighed. "I know you are."

It was pretty much what she'd expected him to say, but it was still nice to hear him say it—a small confirmation that he was still her Michael, even if he'd scuffed his shiny surface.

She stepped behind him to leave room for a man and woman to pass by in the other direction. "Let's just get over there before Jarek does something crazy."

"That's a pretty tall order."

She smiled despite herself. He had a point. She just hoped Pryce was still okay.

A few minutes later, the three of them were climbing onto the narrow saddle of the skipper, which looked a bit like a motorcycle that had sprouted stubby wings. With its four little electric motors, it was more or less a tiny version of an airship—one that was much easier to fall off of, but that risk seemed well worth it right now in light of the added speed.

They straddled the skipper, Michael at the controls in front and Lea sandwiched between him and her. It was a tight fit, and Rachel had to resort to tucking her staff to her side like a lance, but it worked.

Michael brought the skipper jerkily off the ground, and she stifled a cry of dismay at the small taste of how hazardous this ride was going to be. She clutched at Lea, and Michael guided them out of the underground garage.

As they tore off toward Newark through the dark night, she had all she could do to keep from disturbing their balance while desperately hoping they weren't already too late.

CHAPTER TWENTY-THREE

"Ｆor the five-hundredth time," Jarek said, shaking his head, "drop it, Al! You weren't even here for all this shit. Unless you two finished merging . . ."

"We—umm, I did, sir. I dare say it looks like I've missed quite the adventure. But I still don't see why we couldn't apologize to the Resistance once Pryce is safe."

He rubbed at his eyes. "Jesus, it never ends. Eye on the prize, buddy. Focus up!"

They'd be to Pryce's shop in a few minutes, and his plan hadn't evolved beyond kicking the door in and beating everyone inside to bloody pulps (excluding Pryce, of course).

What made it worse was that he was about ninety-eight percent sure he was walking straight into a trap. Why else would the Red King have kept Pryce in his shop instead of dragging him back to the Red Fortress?

Sure, he probably would have preferred Jarek to have called back by the end of the allotted hour with the location of his goods, but the fact that he'd made no effort to conceal their location meant he was ready and willing to handle any half-cocked rescue attempts. Which was exactly what this was.

At least Jarek would have no shortage of people to hit. Who said he wasn't an optimist?

But Al's comments continued to nibble at him.

"So explain this to me, Al. They powered you down and locked you up, and you still wanna help them?"

"Sir, we both know that very few people think of me as anything other than software. It was an understandable action on their part. I don't like how they treated you, but they are trying to clear the way for the world to get back on its feet. There's no reason we can't be friends."

Jarek barked a short laugh. "Yeah, we've never heard that one before, right? Remember the Iron Eagles? It's not like the Resistance has a prayer of ever actually winning this war against the raknoth, anyway."

"Certainly not without you, sir."

"Flattery will get you nowhere, Mr. Robot. And besides, I'm not sure beating the raknoth even matters at this point."

"Jesus," Al said in a nearly perfect imitation of Jarek. "It never ends."

"I hate it when you do that."

He focused as they drew close enough to spot the dark outline of a medium-sized ship in the park beside Pryce's place. "Game time, Al."

Al brought the ship to a stationary hover at the northern edge of the park. "I'm picking up thirteen life forms inside, sir."

"Christ, how's that for lucky?"

"Two more at the front entrance, and at least two more still on board the ship."

One of those seventeen was presumably Pryce, which left him at a square sixteen on one.

Great.

He'd fought against worse odds with Fela and won, but one of those blips Al saw was the Red King. He was pretty sure that tipped the odds away from his favor.

Too bad Rachel wasn't here to help him do this without getting Pryce shot. But he couldn't turn back now. Even if he could, he wasn't entirely sure she'd still be with him now that he'd decked Michael and blown out of there.

It was just him and Al, just as it had always been.

He withdrew two flashbangs from his locker of goodies and tucked them into his gun belt. He eyed the Big Whacker, then decided against it. He had Fela's "small" sword strapped on already, and speed was going to be key here.

"All right. Let's see what we can do about these numbers. Get me over the sentries at the front."

"Of course, sir."

Al inched the ship forward, dropping the boarding ramp before Jarek had to ask. The two Reds posted at Pryce's front door were already raising their weapons as Jarek leaped from the boarding ramp.

He landed on the closer of the two and drove him to the ground with a disturbing combination of snaps and wet crunching sounds. A muffled cry of agony escaped from beneath the armored hand he'd clamped over the Red's mouth. He punched the poor bastard in the side of the head and sprang forward to slap aside the second Red's rifle.

Without Fela, the blow would have bought him a moment to close the distance on the guy. With Fela's added strength, the backhand broke bones, tore the rifle free of the Red's grip, and nearly sent him tumbling to the ground.

He grabbed the Red by his armored vest. Resisting the urge to throw him through the window of the building across the street, he yanked him closer instead. He brought a closed fist down on top of the man's head, aiming for a level of force that would incapacitate without killing, though it was never really a sure thing.

The Red crumpled to the curb, incapacitated to say the least.

Jarek placed his hand on the doorknob to Pryce's shop.

"Front room appears empty, sir," Al said. "Looks like a few of them are stirring in the shop."

He stepped into the front room, a pistol in his right hand and a flashbang in his left. He kept his voice low enough that it would be inaudible outside of his sealed helmet. "You ready to do our sharp-shooter thing?"

"Ready, sir."

He approached the door to the shop, pulled the pin from the flash-bang, and prepared himself for the puppet act.

Jarek was a decent shot—not the finest in the land by any means, but not bad. Al, on the other hand, was a stone-cold deadeye with unsurprisingly robotic precision. The catch was that Al wasn't capable of voluntarily causing direct bodily harm to living humans. He could, however, point guns at them, and Jarek was more than capable of pulling triggers.

Neither one of them were big fans of the loophole. The near conflict made Al uncomfortable, and Jarek usually preferred to stick to beatdowns that left his opponents breathing. When they had the choice, they usually found other ways. But sometimes they didn't.

He reached for the doorknob and prepared to chuck the flashbang into the room.

"Wait," Al said. "I think I'm seeing—"

Jarek tuned in with Fela's auditory sensors.

Murmurs. Shifting weights and shuffling boots. Quick, padding footsteps . . . headed straight for the door.

"Move!" Al cried. "Get out of the—"

He was already darting to the right when the metal door to Pryce's shop tore from its hinges with a groaning screech. Not fast enough. The door slammed straight into his left side and knocked him to the ground.

He reflexively raised his gun but lowered it with a curse as the Red King stepped through, eyes awash with red raknoth fire.

"Where is the nest?"

"Where is the Pryce?"

The raknoth scowled at him, the skin of his hands and face shifting a few shades greener. When he spoke, his voice was raspier than before. "It would appear you have no intention of holding to our bargain."

He swallowed the urge to tell him he had a bargain for his ass.

"How's this for a bargain? Give me Pryce and we walk—no fighting, no helping those rebel scum. This isn't our fight. I just wanted my exo back, and I've got it."

The Red King looked at him as if he were a particularly offensive pile of garbage. "You are a man without honor, Jarek Slater. Your choices were clear: the nest for Pryce, or death for both of—"

Jarek raised his gun and fired off four rounds in rapid succession. No reason to start acting honorably now, right? At least two or three shots must have hit, but it was hard to tell. The Red King sprang into motion, diving for him with no concern for the rounds pelting into the deepening green of his scaly hide.

Jarek swept his pistol butt at the King's head, but the raknoth lunged in and drove him flat on his back. Even with Fela's protection, the impact drove the air out of Jarek's lungs, and he immediately realized he'd underestimated the Red King's strength. He twisted out of the way of a punch that obliterated the ground where his head had been, and he slammed the butt of his gun into the Red King's head once, twice, three times.

The blows only succeeded at making the raknoth angrier. The King caught Jarek's wrist in a steel grip and drove it to the ground with one hand while he raised the other, which had sprouted short but nasty claws, to strike.

Jarek reached up to grab the raknoth's arm and dropped the flashbang just behind his head—the flashbang whose lever he'd let fly the moment the raknoth had come down on top of him.

"Say cheese, asshole."

The grenade detonated with a sonorous pop and a flash of blinding light. Thanks to Fela's lightning-fast sensory filters, the light wasn't blinding to Jarek and the sound not nearly so intense.

On top of him, the Red King roared, shaking his head in disorientation. Jarek took advantage of the opening to plant a doublehanded shove into the King's chest. The raknoth was heavy—absurdly so—but Fela was strong. The shove launched the King back into the wall with a thud and a crack.

Jarek kipped to his feet and wasted no time in closing on the thrashing raknoth. He caught the King by an arm and planted a few more pistol whips on his head. Each one of those blows would have killed a normal man twice over, but this felt more like bashing a rock instead of a skull.

Shouts came from the shop as the Reds scrambled to rally and come to their master's aid. He needed to get Pryce and get out of there.

He pivoted with a violent jerk and threw the raknoth back into the shop.

"Get ready, Al."

He chucked the second flashbang into the room beside the Red King and drew his second pistol as the raknoth leaped up to kick at the flashbang with his—not feet. Appendages. Clawed, scaly green appendages.

But the King was a hair too late. The flashbang detonated.

Jarek was already charging. He cut the Red King's roar short with a hefty chest kick that sent the raknoth sailing across the room. Then he raised his weapons and relaxed as best he could.

"Take it, Al."

Fela tracked left, taking Jarek's arms with her as Al sighted in on their first target and said, "Pull."

Jarek squeezed the triggers. Two Reds fell dead.

Al was already taking aim at the next pair.

"Pull," Al said. "Pull. Pull, pull."

Each time, Jarek squeezed the triggers, doing his best not to disturb Al's aim. Between his own movements and the staggering of the Reds, the system wasn't perfect, but in the space of four seconds, they dropped six of ten targets to the floor.

Those four seconds were all they had.

The Red King, already recovered from a kick that would have killed an elephant, barreled toward them, eyes blazing red. Al had the insight to aim a shot at one ruby eye, but the raknoth lowered his head when he saw it coming.

Jarek capitalized on the momentary break in line of sight to leap high and right. He flew over the charging raknoth and landed on a heavy wooden worktable with a deep thud. He paused long enough to snap off a shot at the one Red who hadn't managed to scramble to cover, holstered one pistol, and leaped again, this time for the tightly winding spiral staircase in the corner.

He vaulted over the metal railing, which groaned and bent beneath his grip, and landed about a third of the way up the staircase.

Below, the Red King strode toward him, no longer in any great rush by the looks of it. A second later, Jarek realized why.

He heard shuffling from above and the sound of a gun hammer being cocked. A moment later, a pair of feet came into view, followed by another. They descended the stairs until Jarek could see that the first set belonged to Pryce. Behind him came Mosen, holding a large pistol to Pryce's back.

"Hey, Slater," he said, his cold eyes gleaming. "Was hoping we'd catch you soon."

CHAPTER TWENTY-FOUR

J arek looked between Pryce and Mosen, glad for the cover of
Fela's faceplate as he gnashed his teeth in apprehensive
indecision.

"You have broken our bargain, Jarek Slater," the Red King
called from below. "Give us the location of the nest, or Jay Pryce's life
is forfeit."

Pryce visibly swallowed, watching to see what he would do.

"Okay." He consciously let go of the railing, holstered his pistol,
and raised his hands in surrender. "Okay, okay." He gave Pryce and
Mosen a little wave and added, "Hi, by the way."

Mosen gave him a predatory grin and waved his gun demon-
stratively.

Jarek swallowed. God, his mouth was dry. "Why don't you hand
me the old man, and I'll tell you guys everything I know."

He wasn't going to tell them anything (not that he even had much
to tell), but it was worth a shot. He was a man without honor, after all.

"I find that unlikely, given the circumstances," the Red King said.

"Oh, come on. What did you expect me to do? For the record,
calling someone to say you're gonna kill their friends if they don't do
what you want isn't making a freaking bargain. That's called ransom."

"I believe ransom implies a monetary payment," Pryce said. His eyes widened as he realized he'd spoken out loud.

Mosen frowned at the back of Pryce's head.

Jarek turned his palms upward. "Either way, I think we can all agree it's kind of a dick move."

A low growl rumbled from the Red King.

"Look, if you kill Pryce, you can bet your scaly ass you're not getting a peep out of me. I'll blow this suit and kill us all if I have to."

At that, the three Reds watching from below exchanged uneasy glances.

"You're so full of shit, Slater." Mosen raised his gun to the back of Pryce's head. "You have no idea where the nest is. You have nothing." He looked to the Red King, asking for permission.

The Red King held up a hand. Those glowing red eyes looked directionless without irises or pupils, but Jarek noticed slight movements of the raknoth's head from himself to Pryce and back.

"No," the King said. "If I must end Jarek Slater for breaking our bargain—"

Jarek cleared his throat.

The Red King showed him teeth that would now be more accurately described as fangs. "—then let Jay Pryce witness his foolish friend being torn to pieces. He can spread the word about what happens to even the mightiest of humans who think to stand against the raknoth."

Jarek managed to keep his voice level. "You calling me mighty?"

"The mightiest of ants is still but an insect," the King said.

"Oh, boy," he mumbled so quietly only Al could hear. "We have a philosopher on our hands."

"What did you say?" the Red King said.

Christ on a cracker, had he heard that?

"Careful, sir," Al said, his volume dialed down in Jarek's ear. "Our conversation might not be private with him around."

The raknoth didn't seem to hear that, at least. Jarek gave Al a deliberate blink of acknowledgment, glad again for the coverage of Fela's faceplate.

He glanced at Pryce one more time, vaulted the railing, and dropped to the floor below with a solid thud. With a smooth, practiced motion, he drew the large, straight blade strapped to his back and spun it through a few tight revolutions. "I said—"

He heard the clanking footsteps on the stairs just before Al cried, "Behind you!"

He hopped to the right, avoiding Mosen by less than a second. Before he could reorient himself, the Red King was on him, catching him in a tackle that carried him straight into the brick wall several yards behind.

Armor or no, slamming halfway through a brick wall was more than a little jarring. He managed to score a few hard blows to the side of the King's head with the pommel of his sword while he waited for his senses to straighten out. Just when things seemed to be settling, the world spun again, and the accelerometer of his stomach informed him he'd just been thrown across the room.

The wall he slammed into a moment later confirmed the fact.

All things considered—advanced armor to disperse the impact force, adaptable smart membrane to absorb some of that force and lengthen the deceleration phase, and years of pain threshold training —it still wasn't a fun ride. In fact, it hurt like shit, and the shower of hand tools that rained down on him only added insult to the cheap shot.

"Okay." He pulled himself to wobbly feet and readied the sword he'd only held on to thanks to Fela's tremendous grip. He swept aside a slew of fallen tools with one foot. "Now Pryce is gonna kill you guys if I don't. You have no idea how meticulous he is about this place."

The Red King watched him, eyes burning brighter than before as a slow smile stretched his lips. The structure of the raknoth's entire face seemed to be changing before his eyes. His mouth began to protrude like a small snout, and his skin grew darker, its scaly texture deepening.

"Uh, I think you've got something on your face, buddy."

The Red King tilted his head back and made an alternating growl-hiss Jarek took for laughter. Mosen looked back and forth between them, his own eyes tinged with red now.

"You are a peculiar one amongst your kind, human," the King said. "I think I would have preferred not to kill you."

Jarek stalked to the center of the room, sword at the ready and senses alert. "Hey, offer still stands."

The raknoth waved Mosen back. "I hope you will at least offer a satisfactory fight. It has been far too long."

Jarek touched the tip of his sword to his helmet in a mocking salute. The Red King's smile widened, a low growl building in his throat.

The raknoth lunged forward.

Jarek was ready. He sidestepped, whipping his blade around in one hand and then bringing it down with both on the King's outstretched upper arm. The sword jarred in his hands as if the blade had struck something like concrete or steel. Seemingly unaffected, the King pivoted to take a swipe at him.

He ducked past the blow and spun to land another sword strike against the raknoth's left trapezius. Again, the result was under-whelming. The King dropped his weight and launched himself back-ward, slamming into him back first like the world's most savage tortoise. Jarek got his hands up against the odd attack, but that didn't keep him from sliding across the floor until they slammed to a halt against Pryce's worktable.

He ducked the King's follow-up elbow strike and stabbed his sword up and forward as the raknoth completed his rotation. The sword didn't have the best stabbing tip in the world, but it was decent enough to dig into the Red King's gut by at least a couple of inches with the Fela-powered stab.

The King's eyes widened in surprise, and a small shriek escaped him as Jarek threw his strength behind the sword again. The blade sank deeper, but not as easily as it should have. It was like pushing through a thick wall of sand—super-dense, super-hard sand that also happened to be trying to kill him.

With a furious snarl, the Red King clamped a hand over one of

Jarek's and threw a low punch with the other. Jarek was dropping his elbow and shoulder to push into the blow when he realized it wasn't aimed at him. Instead, the King's fist slammed into the broad face of the sword blade just as his other hand wrenched down on Jarek's like a nuclear-powered vise grip, holding it firmly in place.

The blade snapped with a sharp crack. Jarek stared in shock at what now amounted to a short dagger. The King bared gleaming fangs in Jarek's face and clamped onto Jarek's free arm. Jarek flipped the jagged, broken blade into a reverse grip and made a stab for the raknoth, but the King turned, whipping him into a brutal throw.

The world spun in a confusing blur. Jarek had a fraction of a second to note that it was a small miracle the raknoth hadn't torn Fela's (or his own) arm off. Then something hard and unyielding slammed into his ribs on the right, breaking his momentum. He fell to the ground in a crouch next to Pryce's shelf of raw metals.

"Sir!" Al cried.

"I'm fine." He tasted blood. Hopefully, he'd just bitten his lip.

Mosen and the other Reds had gathered by the staircase and were watching him with an array of sneers. Pryce stood on the other side of the staircase now, his eyes wide and intense. Pryce took a few steps toward him, but one of the Reds cut him off.

The Red King was occupied by the worktable, laboriously pulling the broken blade from his gut. It sucked free, and he threw it aside with a roar.

Jarek swallowed and stood, still clutching the broken sword. The King started toward him with menacing purpose, only to freeze and tilt his head as if he'd seen or heard something.

"The comms, sir," Al said.

He focused. Fela's auditory sensors worked their magic, homing in on a message coming from multiple earpieces, judging from the reactions of everyone in the room.

"—ed at Port Newark. Repeat: Resistance activity sighted at Port Newark. Multiple vehicles and at least a dozen troops gathering by the warehouses. Please advise."

Had they decided to make a move for the nest so soon? If so, then

Alaric must be with them. Probably Michael too, and maybe—Jarek's stomach fell—maybe Rachel as well.

And judging from way the Red King's eyes flared, they were about to have a whole lot of Reds coming down on them.

"Try to warn them, Al," he said quietly. "Local broadcast, if you can't find a direct way."

"Of course, sir."

The fire in the Red King's eyes looked hungrier as he regarded Jarek. "Time to leave. Kill them both."

After that, things got hairy fast.

Jarek darted for Pryce, but strong, scaly green arms made a grab for him from behind. He dropped his hips back and threw a wild stab over his shoulder with the broken sword. He was rewarded with a high, ugly screech as the remnant of the blade found some soft target and the arms retreated.

Mosen had already turned his gun on Pryce.

He ripped the broken hilt free from the King and hurled it at Mosen. He was shocked to hear a pained cry, and a spot of blood appeared as the blade sank into Mosen's chest. Mosen staggered into the Reds behind him.

Jarek reached for his pistols. The Red King's arms clamped around him and squeezed until he thought his ribs or arms might break.

"No!" he cried as the next Red in line raised his rifle toward Pryce. "*No!*"

Pryce backed away, too stunned to do anything more than raise his hands.

Jarek bucked against the Red King's steel grip, stomping at the raknoth's foot-like appendages. It was no good.

He watched in sick, helpless horror as the Red drew a line on Pryce and pulled the trigger.

CHAPTER TWENTY-FIVE

The shots that rang out might as well have been aimed at Jarek for the way they stabbed into his being. He forgot the pain of the Red King's death lock. Pryce wore an expression of utter shock, his hands still raised in surrender.

Fear and helpless rage shifted to confusion.

Pryce was fine.

Three lead slugs floated in midair a foot away from his chest.

He could have laughed with relief. Then the Red King snarled something and hurled him into a shelf. This shelf didn't stop him like the other one had; it just toppled over with him.

For a handful of seconds, his existence became a jumbled mess of jolting impacts and jarring crashes. The few tiny spots on his body that weren't already in pain found their way there. There were shouts and gunshots and pounding footfalls. A loud thud punctuated the cacophony, followed by the sound of crumbling stone.

He pulled himself from the ruins of the shelves, and several things hit him at once. Pryce was okay. There was a large hole in the wall, through which he could see the retreating forms of the Reds. And Rachel was striding across the room toward him in all of her tiny arcanist glory, flanked by Michael and Lea, who both kept their weapons trained on the Reds' impromptu escape route.

"Was he missing an eye?" Michael asked Lea.

"I think so," she said.

Huh. Maybe Jarek had actually done some damage to the King with that backward stab. Talk about blind luck. He allowed himself a small grin and sank back into the scrap pile. It actually made a pretty comfortable nest. But maybe he was just tired.

"Asshole," Rachel's voice came to him. A few seconds later, her dirty-blond waves came into view at the edge of his vision. She scowled down at him. "What did you learn about running off to fight the big bad raknoth on your own?"

"I don't know what you're talking about." He tried to keep from groaning as he shifted his weight and commanded his faceplate open with a thought. "I had 'em right where I wanted 'em."

She snorted and offered her hand.

He got a hand beneath himself and stood without her aid, in part out of principle but also because his weight and Fela's combined approached four hundred pounds.

She didn't move back to give him space.

He met her gaze until Al pointedly cleared his throat.

"They're gone, Al?" he asked, still looking at Rachel.

"Affirmative, sir." Al spoke through Fela's speakers so the others could hear. "Returning to the Red Fortress, judging by their exit vector."

He looked over to Pryce. "You okay, old man?"

"Alive," Pryce said, his face a few shades paler than normal. "And enlightened."

"Hallelujah."

Michael and Lea were busy double-checking the downed Reds. Michael looked up and met his eyes with a wary expression.

"You skipped out on your big mission to the port?" Jarek asked.

"I, uh . . ." Michael scratched at his dark hair. "This was more important."

Jarek stared at him for a pensive beat, anger and irritation and gratitude all warring for dominance. "Well doesn't that just warm the c—"

"How'd you know about the port?" Rachel asked.

Shit. They didn't know.

"Reds spotted the Resistance team there. Heard it on the comms."

"*What?*" Michael said.

"You thought you guys scared them off just now?"

Rachel exchanged a tense look with Michael.

"We need to get over there," Michael said.

"Probably not a good idea," Jarek said. "You know, unless by 'good,' you mean 'suicidal.' Then it's probably a great idea. You kids have fun with that."

"Seriously?" Rachel said. "This coming from the same Jarek Slater who got himself imprisoned in the Red Fortress just to have a chat with my brother? From the same guy who didn't think twice about taking on a bunch of armed marauders to save some random-ass people in the mountains? Soldier of Charity, my ass."

He jabbed a finger at Michael violently enough that Michael twitched despite being far out of his reach. "They stole my suit. This little bastard had the nerve to let me run my ass around looking for it when he knew damn well they'd had it for weeks. And, in case anyone forgot, motherfuckers shot at me for taking it back. Like thirty minutes ago—again, in case anyone forgot."

"Come on," she said. "You weren't exactly being gentle on your way out."

"If Jarek held grudges at everyone who'd ever taken a few shots at him," Pryce said, surprising all of them, "he wouldn't have any friends at all."

Brimming anger flashed red hot. "I don't have any friends," Jarek snapped.

It wasn't just anger. It was a sense of betrayal—that old hot weight of embarrassment at having allowed himself to trust, even just a little bit. It was something he'd never planned to feel again.

"Whose side are you on anyway, ya old bastard?" he added to Pryce, feeling slightly guilty about his previous comment.

Pryce held up his hands in peace. Jarek looked back at Rachel. "Look, I appreciate you saving Pryce's bacon—"

"And yours," she said.

He turned to Michael. "There might even be a splash of gratitude in here for you too, Mikey, underneath all the voices telling me to kick your ass. But I didn't sign up for this. I held my end of the deal. I've got Fela. Pryce is safe." He splayed his hands. "Game over."

"And what about Alaric and all the other men and women at the port?" Michael said. "You're okay with them dying when you might be able to do something about it?"

"They all made their choices. People die, Mikey. I can't protect every crazy bastard out there."

"And the nest," Michael said. "You can't just be okay with the Red King getting his hands on—"

"On what? A giant egg that might as well be his favorite lawn ornament for all we know about it? Not worth dying for. Not my fight."

Michael took a step closer. "How can you—"

"Michael," Rachel said. "You two go get the skipper ready."

Michael clearly struggled with the argument brimming on his lips, but he nodded to Pryce, gestured to Lea, and left.

Pryce called his thanks after them. He gave an uncertain glance at Rachel and Jarek, then crossed to the small sea of fallen tools and began the considerable task of clearing the chaos, making an effort to look as busy as possible.

Jarek held Rachel's stern gaze for several seconds before she said, "So nothing matters, and the world is all hopeless shit. Fine. But here you are, duking it out with a small army to save one man."

"Yeah, but—"

"You talk a good game, dude, but all signs point to the terrifying fact that you might give half a fuck."

"Who said I didn't?"

There was a flicker of frustration or maybe even hurt in her eyes. "You didn't have to come here alone."

"And you don't have to go to the ports," he said, waving an armored hand at her. "It's gonna be a death trap over there, and what's the freaking point? You brought your brother home safe. You've done enough."

"That doesn't do much good to the people who are about to die out there. I don't know about you, but it seems like the past fifteen years have been a pretty good lesson that doing enough isn't really enough anymore."

"We can't trust the Resistance to be the answer," he said. "Clearly, they can't be trusted. None of them can. And we don't need them. We can find people who need help, and we can help them."

"And what the hell does it look like I'm doing right now?"

He bit back the retort on his tongue. Her eyes softened, and he realized he was reaching to sweep a rogue strand of wavy, dirty-blond hair from the side of her face. She caught his hand before it got there, a small, tired smile in her eyes.

"Don't go," he said. "The Red King is too strong."

She gently pushed his hand away. "We make our own choices, and we live with them. I don't need Jarek Slater to save me."

He searched her face. "You're . . ."

She watched him, one eyebrow slightly arched in expectation.

He didn't even know what he was trying to say. Where was this doubt coming from?

". . . just so pretty when you're serious."

Her eyes fell along with the rest of her face. *Nice one, asshole.*

It hurt to watch.

She glanced at Pryce, who was only marginally keeping up the charade of reordering his tools.

"Goodbye, Jarek."

He watched her go, clenching and unclenching his jaw, reminding himself to despise the Resistance—to remember that Michael had betrayed him and that he didn't owe Rachel or Alaric a damn thing.

Fela's auditory sensors relayed the sounds from outside as their ride powered up, lifted off, and faded away into the night. A distant clap of thunder rumbled through the silence it left behind. A few seconds later, rain began to patter down, easily audible through the impromptu doorway the Red King had gifted to Pryce's wall.

He walked over in silence to help Pryce start cleaning up.

This wasn't his fight. He wasn't sure there was even a reason it should be anyone else's. But it absolutely wasn't his.

But maybe, if he was being honest, those were his friends—the closest thing he had to friends outside of Pryce and Al, at least.

They'd set their mission aside to come help him and Pryce, hadn't they? And Rachel . . . She hadn't faltered for a second when he'd asked her for help.

And he'd just let her walk away without a peep.

Shit.

He'd meant what he said: he couldn't trust the Resistance. He'd never make that kind of mistake again.

But maybe this wasn't about trusting the Resistance. Maybe this was about trusting Rachel. Maybe it was about setting aside his grievances with the Resistance (and with organized outfits of all shapes and sizes, for that matter) to do what he could to make sure a few good people made it through the night.

"Fuck." He began to chuckle.

"Sir?"

Pryce was watching him, the concern in his eyes brightening into amusement as Jarek's chuckle strengthened.

"What a crock of shit," Jarek said, looking out through the hole the Red King had rammed through the wall. The rain was picking up now. "Of course they need Jarek Slater to save them."

The ghost of a smile touched Pryce's lips. "Feeling charitable, are we?"

Al settled the ship just outside of the Red King's improvised door in silent invitation.

Jarek shook his head and grinned despite himself as he started toward the ship. "I really need to get myself a new nickname."

CHAPTER TWENTY-SIX

The only thing worse than a tense skipper ride toward serious danger was a tense skipper ride toward serious danger in the rain. Rachel huddled down behind Lea, who huddled behind Michael, who in turn huddled over the handlebars behind the small windshield as best he could. It didn't do any of them much good. Drops of rain pelted their exposed skin like pellets, and by the time they were nearing the port, they were all worried, afraid, and soaked to the bone.

What Rachel wouldn't have given for a warm bed and a few hours of sleep right then. It was, what, three in the morning now? She'd barely had a moment to breathe since she'd stepped into that dingy pub two days ago. To say she was on her last legs was putting it mildly.

Through the darkness ahead, she could just make out the shapes of warehouses and abandoned shipping containers. She clung to Lea and leaned into the turn as Michael slowed the skipper and veered away from the main road into the graveyard of rusted metal shells. The containers loomed on either side, row after row of them, a dull monotony of unwanted scrap that faded into the darkness at the edges of the skipper's lights.

She'd half expected to arrive at the scene to find a raging battle in progress, but other than the hum of motors and the patter of rain, the night was quiet. They passed the field of shipping containers and rounded the corner into the wide lane that separated the two rows of buildings beyond.

The warehouse buildings were large and rectangular with high windows and slanted metal roofs, drab both from age and by design. Luckily, the three trucks lined up outside the third building on the left were a clear enough indicator where they could expect to find Alaric and the others. Unluckily, their presence also meant the Reds, probably only minutes behind them now, would have just as easy of a time finding them.

A few of the nine or ten Resistance troops by the trucks trained weapons in their direction as they approached, but they quickly stood down at a gesture from a stocky guy with a thick beard, apparently the first one to recognize Michael and Lea. Michael set the skipper down by the warehouse behind the line of trucks.

Their bearded friend approached with a weary look. "Daniels, Carver. We weren't expecting company."

"I hate to tell you," Michael said, "but I think we're about to get a lot more. We got a tip that the Reds spotted you here. They can't be far behind us."

The soldier looked between the three of them as if searching for some indication that they were playing a sick joke. "Shit." He jutted his chin toward the corner of the adjacent building. "You better go tell the warehouse crew to hurry it up, then."

Michael nodded, and they made for the warehouse as the bearded soldier began rallying the troops.

The door at the corner of the warehouse hung ajar, providing a spooky glimpse into the nearly complete darkness inside. Rachel exchanged a short look with Michael and Lea, then tapped on her comm light and stepped into the darkness.

The door creaked a faint greeting, sending a little jolt of anxious energy through her chest. She reminded herself of the clearly more pressing matter of the approaching Reds and set off through the dark, following the flickers of light she spotted within.

The warehouse was surprisingly intact inside. She hadn't exactly toured many warehouses in her life, but this one looked exactly like she assumed they all must: crates and boxes in abundant supply, some arranged in an orderly fashion on large metal shelves, others stacked neatly on top of white plastic pallets. The most obvious sign of the place's age was the layer of dust that covered pretty much everything, thick enough that it was readily visible under the shine of her light.

Rain on the building's metal roof masked the sound of their footsteps, and their lights gave life to an entire city of dancing shadows. Despite everything, she had to suppress a smile when Michael jumped at one of the flickering apparitions. Then she jumped herself as lightning flashed through the grimy windows. Thunder followed, close and powerful.

They reached a row of storage bays on the south wall around the midpoint of the warehouse. Each bay was guarded by a dull brown bay door and an access panel. The second door from the left had been hauled open. Light and voices poured from inside.

An odd sensation tingled at the edge of her mind, vaguely resembling a telepathic presence. It grew with each step until the small storage space came into view.

The room looked like a safe house, complete with a cot, rations, weapons, and other supplies. In the back corner, Alaric and two Resistance men were at work maneuvering something large and gray onto a red dolly.

There it was—the mysterious nest everyone was ready to kill each other over (though it wasn't as if the Reds and the Resistance had needed a reason to do that before). The egg-like device was mostly smooth but for a round panel at the top and a small base that let it stand on a level surface. She was sure this was the source of the odd telepathic presence. She was also sure she didn't like it.

Alaric turned at their entrance, his hand drifting toward the revolver at his hip in favor of the rifle slung across his back. He relaxed when his eyes found them.

At least until Michael blurted, "We need to get the nest out of here. Now."

Alaric went alert, searching their faces. "Reds?"

"Sounds like they saw you on the way over," Lea said. "We need to get this out of here now."

Michael was already beside the odd device, reaching to help. He bent down to grab the nest's base and pressed his palm to its smooth surface along the way. As soon as he touched it, Michael gave a tiny shudder, and the vague telepathic presence stirred.

Rachel sprang forward and tugged him back. "What the shit was that?" Her voice sounded tight.

He glanced back at her with a deep frown furrowed into his brow. Before he could say anything, the rhythmic clacking of rapidly approaching boots drew their attention to the bay door. A young man appeared there, panting and red in the face, and Rachel knew they were already too late.

"They're here," the runner said between breaths. "Three big trucks of 'em."

Gunshots from the front of the warehouse confirmed his warning, not quite as loud as the thunderclap had been, but loud enough.

Everyone looked to Alaric for direction. Nobody seemed to remember he'd left the Resistance; he was still Commander Weston to them.

"Let's go," he said. He pointed to the two men with the dolly. "You two bring the nest up front. We'll keep 'em busy. You"—he pointed to the red-faced guy who'd brought the message—"get word back to HQ. Tell them to send the ship. No point trying to keep a low profile now."

Then Alaric was moving out of the room at a jog. She fell in beside him, and Michael and Lea followed.

Three trucks of Reds. She wasn't sure how big the trucks were, but that didn't sound so bad. Not yet. Five or ten minutes from now, when the rest of them started showing up, it would probably be a different story. They needed to be out of here by then, although she wasn't entirely sure how the Resistance could hope to shake pursuit in those clunky trucks of theirs. That was probably why Alaric had called for a ship.

Too bad Jarek hadn't brought his. She silently cursed him for being a small-minded child. But that didn't matter now. She would do what she could to get Michael and the others out of this safely. That was all she could do.

The sound of fighting picked up as they approached the front of the warehouse. What had begun as a few tentative shots in the dark night had built to a steady stream of automatic weapons trading choirs of man-made thunder back and forth in the rain.

The Resistance troops had moved the trucks to form a line of rudimentary cover near the warehouse door. Twenty-five yards to the right, the Reds were slowly advancing in three big, dark trucks—the same blocky transports she'd seen in front of the Red Fortress. The trucks looked as if they could carry at least ten men each, and there were at least a dozen men already on the pavement, firing at the Resistance line.

"The drivers!" someone cried. "Hit the drivers!"

Several shots slammed into the enemy windshields and confirmed that they were bulletproof.

Alaric moved to the center of the Resistance line without hesitation.

"Keep her close to you," Rachel yelled to Michael, tilting her head toward Lea.

Michael nodded, his hand drifting to the bullet catcher she'd made damn sure was clipped to his belt. He moved to the right side of the line with Lea. Rachel slid in next to Alaric to put him in her sphere of protection.

The fighting was furious. Thunder rumbled. Guns roared. Hundreds of bullets slammed into the trucks and the pavement and the warehouse behind them. Between the racket, the rain, and the headlights beaming straight into their faces, she could barely tell what was going on. If not for the floodlights the Resistance troops had thrown on top of the trucks facing the enemy line, she would've been blind.

Every bullet made her cringe. She'd found out in Deadwood just how lousy cars were as cover, and the Resistance truck line was no different. The people directly around her and Michael might've been safe enough thanks to the catchers, but the others weren't. Two men in their line had already slumped down against the trucks, clutching at wounds.

She had to do something.

It took clear, careful focus to shape the barrier so that it would protect the men and women behind the trucks while leaving the way clear for them to return fire. Once she'd conjured the construct, it became immediately apparent how hard it was going to be to maintain.

Bullet after bullet smacked into her defenses, each one hitting like a heavy punch. Energy crackled through her body as she channeled from batteries to barrier. After the first few dozen bullets, she knew she couldn't keep it up until the Resistance ship arrived.

But she didn't have a choice.

She clenched her teeth. If she failed, people died—simple as that. She could do it. She had to.

"Grenades!" someone cried.

Her will nearly broke outright at the pair of dull thunks from the truck bed to her right. She snapped her eyes shut and sank deeper into her extended senses, reaching out to find the deadly little spheres that were about to blow half their line to paste.

Splitting her mind so many ways was nearly insurmountable, but somehow she held the barrier in place, locked onto the grenades, and hurled them back toward the Reds.

She opened her eyes just in time to see the grenades detonate in front of the enemy line and knock a couple of Reds from their feet. A hot rush of air surged against the barrier. Then it was gone.

A fierce cheer went up from the Resistance line.

"Well done," Alaric said next to her.

Had it been? Then maybe fate could be kind and get that damn ship there before she had to do it again.

Even if there had been somewhere left to go, she doubted their trucks would run, given the pounding they were taking. And given the pounding she and her barrier were taking, there wouldn't be much left for the ship to collect if it didn't get here in the next few minutes.

A soldier from the warehouse rushed over to Alaric. The nest was ready at the warehouse entrance, and the ship would be there in less than ten minutes.

Cold dread wrapped its arms around her chest. Five minutes would be bad enough. Ten would be damn near impossible.

But a ship was coming. And they were holding. All she had to do was keep holding.

She growled wordlessly as three more pairs of headlights appeared at the far end of the row of warehouses.

"Shit," said Alaric next to her.

"Incoming ship!" someone cried to their left.

That was it. If that was the Red King—hell, if it was even his maid —they were screwed.

The ship soared in over the left row of warehouses and slowed over the Reds. She squinted against the floodlights blazing down on their engagement and waited to glimpse their condemnation.

Some thirty feet above them, Jarek's armored figure sprang into the open air. Rachel tensed as he came to a brutally fast landing, but he turned his momentum into a ballistic roll and sprang to his feet without missing a beat.

He moved into the ranks of the Reds with ruthless efficiency, slamming men into the trucks and batting others down with their own weapons. He kicked one Red hard enough that the guy took down two of his allies like a human missile.

Rachel looked down the Resistance line. Every face—some confused, some awed, some frightened—was turned to Jarek as he dismantled what remained of the first batch of Red forces.

She released her barrier and slumped against the truck, exhausted. From the looks of it, he hardly needed her help. Most of the Reds she could see were already on the ground, unconscious, dead, or too injured to fight. Jarek had scooped up an assault rifle and was mingling bullets with fists and kicks now that the remaining men were scattering.

But when she spotted one of the Reds yanking the pin from a hand grenade, she jolted into action. She extended a hand and focused, catching the explosive only a few feet from the soldier's hand. He stared slack-jawed at the hovering grenade for a full second before diving away, arms covering his head.

The grenade detonated with a vicious boom, slamming his body against the pavement. She felt the shock wave as a warm gust of air on her rain-soaked face.

Jarek came flying over the truck in an impossible leap that ended with a hard kick to one Red's sternum. He threw the Red's partner into the side of the nearest truck hard enough to visibly rock it.

To the left, another Red was rounding the closest truck, his rifle leveled at the distracted Resistance line.

Alaric wasn't so distracted. His rifle barked, and the Red collapsed to the pavement.

Automatic fire roared out from the other side of the Red's truck. Rachel jumped as several slugs slammed to a halt on the field of her catcher, bringing a sudden chill made all the worse by the rain soaking through her very being. Before she could force her weary mind to respond, the Resistance line had gunned the shooter down.

And then silence—or at least what seemed like silence after the raging firefight.

Thick rain fell to the pavement. Archaic gasoline truck engines rumbled in the Reds' now-empty trucks.

The peace was only momentary. Gunfire erupted from further down the warehouse row as the incoming Reds opened up on Jarek's ship, which Al had been using to run interference. The ship veered up and around, heading back toward them.

"You guys can say it," Jarek called, his voice amplified through Fela's speakers. "You're happy as shit to see us right now."

Everyone stared dumbly except for maybe Alaric, who didn't deign to dignify that with a response. Al brought the ship to hover over

Jarek, and Pryce appeared on the open ramp, lugging that ridiculously large sword Jarek kept on board.

"Incoming," he called, tossing it down.

Jarek caught the monstrous weapon with one hand. Even with Fela's help, it couldn't have been easy, but he absorbed the sword's momentum smoothly and strapped the sheath to Fela's back. "Let's move, people! Get to the ship! We've got an angry green monster on the way."

Al swung the ship around and settled it behind the Resistance line with a slight metallic groan.

Jarek easily hurdled the truck line to land behind Rachel and Alaric.

"I know you're happy to see me," he said, clearly to her.

Of course she was glad to see him. But she wasn't about to say it. She rolled her eyes at Fela's faceplate and the big, stupid grin she knew lay underneath. They had about thirty seconds before the Reds would be on them in force again, and she didn't want to inflate his head so much that he floated away and left them to get out of there on their own.

His faceplate slid open to reveal him eyeing her with curiosity. "How many bullets did you just stop, Goldilocks?"

She must look as bad as she felt. She shrugged.

"HQ says five minutes on that ship," someone called.

He cocked his head. "No working ships, huh, Mikey?"

Michael gave a helpless shrug. "That part was true yesterday."

"We can't fit everyone in your ship with the device," Alaric said. "Gonna have to hold them until—"

A metallic thud sounded from the top of the warehouse. All eyes cut upward just as a ship soared past, blinding them with powerful floodlights. There was a second dark blur of motion above them, and then the cab of the lead Resistance truck imploded. A figure sliced down directly into the groaning metal and shattering glass, unaffected by the violence of the impact.

A figure with a single fiery-red eye.

CHAPTER TWENTY-SEVEN

J arek had to give it to Alaric, the old cowboy was as fast as he was unshakable. While the rest of the Resistance line was busy jumping out of their skins or falling to their asses in surprise, Alaric raised his rifle in a smooth motion and unloaded the remainder of his mag on the Red King.

The carbine packed enough of a punch that the King couldn't ignore it outright. He roared and lashed out from the twisted ruin of the truck cab. Alaric threw himself back fast enough that the swipe only caught the tip of his rifle.

Jarek darted forward as Alaric stumbled back. The bullets might not have seriously damaged the raknoth, but they'd rattled him enough that he couldn't avoid Jarek's flying kick.

The kick drove the King from his perch down to the pavement on the other side of the truck, where he rolled to his feet to face them. Overhead, his ship descended and rotated to reveal several Reds aiming assault rifles at them from the open hatch in the ship's breast.

"Hold fire!" the Red King bellowed.

That was unexpected. Jarek kept his rifle trained loosely on the King.

The raknoth looked less beastly now than he had at Pryce's, nearly human again but for the glowing red eye. That eye seemed to be directed past him.

He followed the raknoth's gaze to what could only be the nest, floating out of the warehouse propelled by Rachel's raised hand.

What the hell was she—

Oh.

He turned back to the King with his best nonchalant grin.

"The nest," the Red King said, his expression betraying his tension. "Walk away now, and we will give you the night before resuming our quarrel."

Jarek shot Rachel a quick wink. "Is it just me, boys, or does it feel like ol' One-Eye's scared his baby might get caught in the crossfire? What would happen, Red? Would we get to see this doomsday you keep telling us about?"

"Jarek Slater." The Red King growled the name as if it were a curse. "You do not comprehend the destruction you toy with."

He spread his hands. "That's kinda the point. You wouldn't ask the fat kid to keep an eye on your cupcakes, would you?"

"What?"

"You know, the—ah, never mind. Not the point."

"I tire of this game, Jarek Slater. What is your point?"

The point was that they needed to buy time until the Resistance ship showed up. The only problem was it was hard to say which side benefited more from the standstill. They needed the Resistance ship to get everyone out, but they also had to still be alive when it showed up for that to matter. Every second they stood here was another second more of the Red army could show up.

"Scanners detect incoming, sir," Al said in his ear, right on cue. "A ship and two more trucks, likely from the Red Fortress."

He cursed himself for having even thought it. So maybe stalling wasn't the way to go.

"The point is that it doesn't seem like such a hot idea to hand over a weapon of mass destruction to the guys that blew the freaking world up with weapons of mass destruction."

The three truckloads of fresh Reds were now squared up behind the King. Past the armed men hovering above, the lights of a second ship appeared in the distance.

The Red King sniffed. At first, Jarek thought it was a conversational gesture, but then the raknoth sniffed again, investigating some scent.

"Fetch Jay Pryce from that ship," the King said. "Kill these imbeciles, and—"

"Hey!" Jarek shouted, determined to keep the Red King's attention. He got it.

The King went from perfect ease one second to a hurtling, raknoth-shaped missile the next. Jarek leaped backward and brought the butt of his commandeered rifle down on the King's back as the raknoth caught him in a tackle around the waist. It didn't stop the King from driving him to the ground several yards behind the Resistance line.

The breath left his lungs as he hit the pavement with who knew how many hundreds of pounds of angry raknoth on top of him.

The King loosed a ferocious roar in his face. Al closed Jarek's faceplate for him as he responded with a fist in the raknoth's darkening face.

The King shook it off, clamped a hand over Jarek's faceplate, and muscled his head to the side, raising his other hand to strike.

An invisible truckload of force slammed into the King, knocking him off of Jarek. Jarek kipped to his feet, not sparing the second to thank Rachel for the save. He leveled his rifle at the raknoth and emptied the magazine.

The bark of the rifle was like a match to a keg of gunpowder. Both sides of the tense standoff opened fire in a rumbling cacophony that split the rainy night sky.

"Fools!" the Red King cried, catching his balance and starting forward. "Watch the nest!"

If the Red gunfire died down, it was hard to tell beneath the fury the Resistance line was laying down. A second Red ship was sweeping in now. The Red King's ship spewed out a shower of sparks and lurched drunkenly.

Jarek caught a glimpse of Rachel lowering her staff, her face white as a sheet, and then he squared off with the approaching raknoth.

The King had eyes (or eye, rather) only for the nest, but that didn't stop him from taking a swipe at Jarek as he charged past. Jarek caught the blow on his empty rifle and delivered a few choice elbow strikes before darting back. The King eagerly followed, and he slammed the rifle into the raknoth's head like a baseball bat.

The blow jarred the King, but not enough to stop him. He caught Jarek around the waist and drove in, forcing Jarek to furiously backpedal toward the Resistance line just to keep his feet. In a few steps, they'd slam straight into the trucks, probably killing whoever happened to be in their way. He couldn't get the leverage to break their momentum.

So instead, he let himself topple backward. At the last moment, he wrapped the Red King in a bear hug and jumped up and back as hard as he could.

They took off like a misshapen cannonball, arcing over the Resistance truck line toward the Red armada.

"Roll, sir, roll!" Al barked.

He didn't hesitate. He grabbed fistfuls of the Red King's stupid long coat and twisted his weight around their shared axis.

They spun through the air, rotating just enough that the King was leading when they slammed into the hood of one of the Reds' big transport trucks.

The edge of the hood caught the raknoth's back with a force and angle that would've severed a human spinal cord three times over. Jarek wasn't even sure the bastard had a spinal cord to sever, but the King didn't seem to be in too bad of shape as they tumbled to the pavement.

A ground-shaking crash jerked their attention to the left. The Red King's ship had gone down, its engines spitting sparks and black smoke. Another point for Rachel.

Jarek rolled over his left shoulder and onto his feet. The King rose and followed, now in full scaly-green-monster mode.

They circled like boxers until the King tired of the caution. Jarek dodged one swipe, dipped another, and stepped forward to block a third while driving a punch into the King's scaly mug.

The King caught Jarek's wrist and dragged him along as he stumbled back. What began as a stumble turned into an attack as the raknoth yanked him by one wrist into a brutal clothesline.

The stars cleared from his vision enough just in time for him to parry a vicious stomp aside with his elbow. Panic swelled in his chest. He needed space. He needed to get his damn sword out.

He twisted around on the pavement and planted a hard kick into the King's hip. The raknoth roared and staggered back several steps.

More importantly, the reactionary force sent Jarek sliding several yards across the rain-soaked pavement.

At the end of the slide, he kipped to his feet and drew the Big Whacker.

The sword the King had snapped in two at Pryce's hadn't exactly been a wispy foil, but it paled in comparison to the Big Whacker. The Whacker was like an ax blade that just kept going. The thing weighed about twenty freaking pounds. Without Fela, it was useless for anything faster-paced than chopping firewood.

But with Fela, the Whacker was really good at hacking big things to tiny pieces.

Jarek swung the behemoth blade through a couple of revolutions and held it at the ready as the Red King stalked toward him, rumbling a low growl. The raknoth's features had grown completely reptilian. His hair had disappeared beneath scaly hide, and his mouth had elongated into something more like a snout.

Jarek realized the fighting had quieted around them. The second Red ship was hanging back after Rachel's attack on the first, hovering over the trucks waiting in line to deliver their troops. The Resistance and Red troops were still exchanging fire here and there, but nothing like before.

Maybe they were scared of catching him and their King in the crossfire. More likely, they were waiting to see how the heavyweight rumble panned out.

"I believe the Resistance ship is nearly here, sir," Al said quietly in his ear. "I recommend we leave with all haste."

"No shit," he murmured. "Just gonna whack the one-eyed monster first."

"Charming, sir. I'll tell Pryce to get the others moving."

"Wonderful."

All he had to do now was kill the Red King or hold him and his army off while the ragtag, wounded Resistance team got their shit together and ran for it. Piece of cake.

The King eyed Jarek's blade, fangs bared in what might've been a predatory smile. "Did you not learn your lesson last time, Jarek Slater?"

He shrugged. "Slow learner, I guess."

The King's smile faltered. He jerked his head up, catching a scent or a sound.

"Here they come, sir," Al said.

"Time to shake it, people!" Jarek yelled.

He plunged toward the Red King, sweeping his sword in a horizontal cut. The raknoth ducked the blow, and Jarek sidestepped his counter. Behind him, a few hopeful shouts went up from the Resistance line as the Resistance ship came soaring over the warehouses.

He didn't have time to celebrate. He ducked a particularly brutal haymaker and rolled past the follow-up swipe. He felt the King lunge after him, and he planted the Whacker so he could pivot into an upward diagonal cut from the roll.

It wasn't the strongest of strikes, but the blade met the King's incoming swipe and tore through the clawed digits of his left hand.

The cold fear in his chest gave way to primal joy as the King staggered back with a furious roar. Was that surprise on the raknoth's reptilian features? Horror? It sure as hell wasn't calm confidence anymore.

Jarek bellowed a wordless challenge and pressed the advantage, whirling the heavy blade in a great arc and stomping after the King to leverage his next swing down from high left.

The King sidestepped the strike and pedaled backward to avoid the horizontal follow up.

Jarek lunged after the raknoth, burning with predatory fire. He brought the Whacker down in a heavy, overhand sweep.

The King didn't have the time or footing to evade the blow. He raised his right arm in a futile attempt to bat the heavy blade aside and screeched as the Whacker tore through his forearm just past the elbow.

Jarek lowered his shoulder and plowed into the stunned raknoth, knocking him to the ground.

"Sir!" Al was saying. "Sir!"

The urgency in Al's voice pulled him down from his combat high. "What?"

"Multiple ships incoming from the east! Sir, I think—behind you!"

He spun to see half a dozen Reds moving in toward their fallen master.

They opened fire. He flinched at the number of bullets slamming off of Fela's armor and swung his sword once, twice.

Two Reds fell dead to the pavement, one cleaved clean in two above the hips. The sight gave the others pause, and he was pressing the attack when an unseen force bowled them backward.

Rachel and Alaric stood side by side atop one of the wrecked trucks. Alaric was firing at the enemy line while Rachel wreaked her own havoc, shoving soldiers back here and detonating grenades there. The pair of them were steaming, their breaths condensing in the freezing aura as Rachel's catcher kept far too many bullets at bay.

Behind the truck, a couple of Resistance troops held the line with them. The rest had loaded the numerous wounded aboard the Resistance ship. Michael was frantically hauling the nest that way with the help of two others.

"Get them out of here!" Jarek cried at Alaric.

Bullets pelted off his armor. He ignored them and raised his sword. He wasn't sure how one went about properly killing a raknoth, but removing the King's head seemed like a good place to—

"Incoming drone!" Al cried.

"Wha—"

"Assault drone, sir," Al said. "We need to leave!"

"Well shit, Al!"

The Red King huffed a growl-hiss of laughter and began crawling to his feet. "Congratulations, Jarek Slater. You have incurred the wrath of the Overlord himself."

Jarek's insides turned to ice. The Overlord's army dwarfed the Red King's. If the Overlord was coming . . .

It didn't matter. They were leaving. Preferably before the drone arrived, because—

The sound of rushing air from Fela's auditory sensors informed him it was already too late.

"It's coming in for a pass," Al said.

The sleek shape banked over the right row of warehouses and dipped to fly low over the Reds.

"I recommend you take cover, sir."

"Helpful!" Jarek cried. He sheathed his sword and yanked the King up from the ground.

The drone opened fire.

The thing's rotary cannon sounded like an enormously loud chainsaw. It hit with devastating effect.

The King bucked against him, far from subdued and still plenty strong despite the missing arm and mangled hand. Jarek managed to pull the raknoth in front of him before the drone's fire washed over them.

A rapid series of jerks ripped through the King as the bullets tore into him. More than one found its way through the raknoth to slam into Jarek's armor, but the King's body slowed the projectiles enough that Fela held.

For the first pass, at least. The thing would be back.

The King slumped in his arms. Behind the trucks, two more Resistance soldiers had fallen, and several new holes dotted both ships. Alaric clutched at a shuddering Rachel, frost and ice visible in their hair and on the truck around them.

"The nest!" Michael cried from over by the Resistance ship. "The nest is hit!"

Time slowed.

Was this it? All of that work and fighting, all to go up in flames together?

He stood tense, not breathing.

Nothing happened.

"Move your asses!" Alaric snapped.

Reality snapped back around him. The remaining troops ran over to fetch the new wounded (or dead) and help Michael finish loading the device.

"Fools," the Red King hissed weakly against his chest. "This planet will burn, thanks to you and your friends."

"This planet *did* burn thanks to you and yours," Jarek said.

"Three more ships arriving, sir," Al said. "The Overlord, I assume."

It was well beyond time to get the hell out of here. Just one head to remove first.

He moved to toss the raknoth to the pavement. "See you in hell, Stumpy."

"Wait!" Al said.

"What?"

"I suggest we take him."

The drone streaked back the way it had come, preparing to come back for another pass. They needed to be gone. Now.

"Take a raknoth prisoner? Now? Did you short-circuit, Al?"

"Oh please, sir. You develop an aversion to outlandish ideas now, of all times? We need to know what he knows about the nest and everything else. He's not going anywhere fast."

Al had a point. The drone had torn the King to confetti. His struggles were woefully slow and weak. The fact he was even still alive, much less conscious, was actually pretty creepy. And Al was right: the King would have all kinds of juicy information.

There wasn't time to think about this.

"Come on, Stumpy." He threw the mostly limp raknoth over his shoulder. Even missing an arm, the raknoth somehow had all the weight of a medium-sized bear.

"What the hell?" Rachel cried as he approached their truck.

"Prisoner," he said with a grunt. "Get to the ship, and don't worry about it. We need to get the hell out of here."

No one argued with that. Pryce and the two Resistance soldiers still holding the line helped Rachel and Alaric down from the truck. They limped toward the ship. Jarek hurdled the truck behind them and nearly lost his footing on the mess of slushy ice. Ahead, the Resistance ship was already lifting off.

With no one left to hold the line, the Reds pressed after them without fear. Jarek tried to keep himself between the Reds and the rest of his people. Bullets slammed into his back and the ship hull. One shot found its way through to a soldier just as the group reached the boarding ramp.

"Go!" Jarek shouted. He scooped the guy up by the back of his armored vest and pounded up the ramp behind the others.

"Drone incoming, sir," Al said through the cabin's speakers. "If Rachel could—"

"Get us in the air, Al," Rachel said, pushing back toward the ramp. "I've got it."

"You heard the lady!" He set the wounded soldier on the cot and tossed the Red King roughly to the other side of the cabin as the ship lifted off. "Tie him up," he said to Pryce, but Alaric was already there with rope from Jarek's locker.

"And put this on him," Rachel added, throwing Alaric the pendant she'd been wearing around her neck.

She joined Jarek at the open hatch as the drone opened up with its buzzing rotary cannon. She slammed her staff down to the ramp, and bullets large enough to rip through a raknoth cracked and zinged off a wall of thin air a few yards in front of them.

The drone roared past.

She sank to her knees and moaned. "Not a smart plan."

He'd never seen her so pale.

"It's circling to our nine," Al said.

"We need to take that thing out or we're cooked up here." Jarek opened his faceplate and sank down next to Rachel.

She met his eyes, every part of her looking utterly drained.

"I can't," she whispered, her head sagging. "I'm so tired, Jarek, and that thing's so fast. I don't know if I could even hit it with anything."

"Hey." He slipped a hand over her cheek. "I believe in you, Goldilocks."

She searched his face with tired eyes.

"Plus," he said, "if you don't do it, you guys are all gonna die horrible deaths."

"*You* guys?"

"Hey, we're flying over water." He patted his armored chest. "I would definitely survive the fall in this baby."

"Asshole." A faint smile touched her lips.

The night sky lit with a crackle of lightning and boom of thunder.

He frowned into the rainy night. "Too bad the lightning doesn't have our backs."

Rachel's hand came down on his forearm. She was staring at him as if he'd just said the most brilliant thing she'd ever heard.

"Here it comes," Al said.

Rachel pulled herself to her feet by her staff. "Turn us, Al."

Jarek closed his faceplate and stood with her, supporting her around the waist. Al banked to the right. On his in-helmet display, the drone cruised toward them in the darkness.

Rachel's eyes drifted closed, her face a still mask of focus. The air around her tingled with electric charge.

The drone's first shots traced toward the ship. She tensed beneath his arm, and his helmet display distorted with odd colors and bursts of static. His stomach pulled up into his chest.

She let out a wordless yell.

A brilliant flash of lightning lanced from the sky and tagged the drone. The thunderclap shook his bones as the drone transformed into a tumbling ball of flames and plummeted into the bay.

Then the night was quiet again.

He slid his faceplate open, some of the tightness easing out of his chest.

She'd just called lightning down from the freaking sky. What did you say to people who could do that?

"See? I knew you had it—oop!"

He pulled her to him as she went slack, then gathered her up in his arms. "Rachel?"

She was out like a light.

Silence held the cabin as he peered down at Rachel, either asleep or unconscious, then back at the pale faces of the others.

Finally, he smiled and made a little flourish. "Ta-da!"

CHAPTER TWENTY-EIGHT

After the madness of battle, where every second could mean the difference between life and death, a few minutes of peace went a long way.

Though it felt as if he'd been drifting through his trance for close to an hour, Jarek wasn't particularly surprised to see that only five minutes had passed since their escape as Pryce settled down in the copilot's chair next to him.

"Well . . ." Pryce said.

"Well."

"Guess you crazy kids won the day."

Jarek glanced back at Rachel's peacefully sleeping form with a tired smile. "Guess we did." He cocked his head. "Pretty handily too. I mean, I don't wanna just casually toss the word 'superheroes' around, but . . ."

Pryce gave a light chuckle. "I'm glad you got Fela back."

He nodded and waited for Pryce to say whatever was clearly lingering on his tongue.

"Guess I'm glad you stuck your neck out to save my crazy old ass too."

Jarek frowned. "It's not like you got pulled into this mess by random chance. You were in trouble because I brought it to your door. Of course I was gonna come for you."

"Oh, yeah," Pryce said with a small smile. "Totally agree. You screwed me over big time. Even so, my cockles are telling me it's a thanks I owe you."

"Ick. Tell your cockles to keep their distance, old man."

Pryce wiggled his eyebrows, then glanced back to the cabin. "Still can't believe you captured a real live raknoth."

He eyed Pryce. "You're just getting excited thinking about all the stuff you could learn from him, aren't you?"

Pryce gave a guilty smile. "It's also pretty damn impressive, though. I believe you have the honor of being the first to pull it off."

"I almost didn't. Motherfucker's strong. And fast. Oh, which reminds me—Al, I totally thought up a name for that move where you yaw the ship around and nail the baddies."

"The Yawt Club, sir?"

"I . . . wha . . ." His mouth worked soundlessly for a few seconds before he sighed and threw a scowl nowhere in particular. "Dammit! Every time, Al!" He turned to Pryce. "This is why the machines are beating us."

He waited a few seconds for Al's nonchalant declaration of his superior robot brain, but it didn't come.

"Al?"

"Sorry, sir. The other ship, they're trying to hail us, but it's . . ."

He traded a glance with Pryce, then sat up. "Patch it through up here."

The speakers came alive with a few bursts of static. "—reading this? That nest thing isn't d—"

"Al?"

"Working on it."

"—place to land. Probably shouldn't take this thing back to HQ until—"

A solid column of pure white radiance lanced into the sky from the other ship's location half a mile ahead, thick and bright enough to be seen for miles, probably tens of miles. As abruptly as it had begun, it ended. From start to finish, the entire light show had lasted maybe three seconds, and it hadn't made a single sound.

"Michael!" Rachel cried out on the bench behind them.

He spun. She'd gone bolt upright and was staring at him with frantic eyes.

He turned his own wide eyes to Pryce, who mirrored the expression.

Alaric and their other two passengers crammed up into the cockpit to have a look, but it was over—gone without a trace.

Back in the cabin, the Red King began to laugh his growl-hiss of a laugh.

"What the hell was that?" Jarek finally said. He glanced at the console displays. The Resistance ship looked a little unstable, but it was still flying. "Get them back on the radio, Al."

"Trying, sir."

"—that?"

"Hello?" Jarek said.

"Yeah, we got you now," the radio voice said. "Don't know what the hell that was, but, uh, we might be . . . I think we're okay over here."

"No damage?" Jarek said. "No one's hurt? The damn roof's not blown off?"

"Roof's still here. This is—"

Rachel leaned in over his shoulder. "Michael Carver. Is Michael Carver okay?"

"Guys, is Carver all right back there?"

A pause. A voice in the background. "Oh. Uh, sounds like he got knocked out in the blast, but he's breathing. They're taking care of him."

More raknoth laughter from the cabin.

In the cockpit, no one said a word. Jarek tried to swallow against a dry mouth as he stood. Fela's sensors informed him that Rachel's grip on his shoulder was inordinately tight.

"It's okay." He gently pried her hand free from his shoulder. "Michael's okay. We're gonna figure this out. C'mon."

She was tough; she'd shown him that enough times by now, but they'd been through too much in the past two days. She had to be even more exhausted than he was. They needed rest. Days of it. But first, he knew, Rachel needed to know that Michael was all right, and they all needed to know what the hell had just happened.

Something told him that flash of light hadn't been good news. Luckily, they had a scaly green bundle of answers sitting in the back cabin.

The King was still hiss-laughing to himself back there.

Jarek had once come across the smoking ruins of a homestead and found the sole survivor laughing deliriously kneeling among the remains of his family and the marauders who'd killed them only to fall to the man's maddened fury. That laugh had haunted him, and it was all too similar to the laugh now drifting up from the cabin. It made him feel hollow inside.

Clearly, the raknoth knew something. But what the hell would have him laughing like that?

He strode back to the cabin to find out.

The Red King looked up with his single glowing red orb of an eye. His skin was still covered in green scales. At the sight of Jarek, he ceased his eerie laughter and bared his fangs in an almost manic grin.

It only deepened the unease spreading through Jarek.

"What the hell was that?" he demanded.

The raknoth's grin widened, and his eye pulsed brighter. "The call."

He laughed again, and cold, primitive dread settled in Jarek's stomach. He felt the others hovering behind him, all silently wondering the same thing he was.

"The call for what?"

The King plopped his head against the wall and drew out the moment, still grinning.

Jarek was too tired to mince words. Too tired to deal with whatever was bad enough to have a blood-sucking monster laughing like this. But they needed to know.

He stepped closer and was about to ask more forcefully when the Red King stirred and fixed him with a cold, hard stare. The raknoth's voice rumbled low in his throat.

"Retribution."

END BOOK ONE

AUTHOR'S NOTE
(UPDATED SEPTEMBER 6TH, 2020)

What would YOU do if, tomorrow, all of our world leaders sprouted red eyes and started launching nukes without warning?

That, Dear Reader, was pretty much the question I was asking myself as I sat down to start writing The Harvesters Series. Or so I tell myself in hindsight.

In truth, this series really began more as a protracted byproduct of my procrastination than anything else.

See, before that big glitzy apocalypse question really grabbed me, I was already elbows deep working on another book—the first book I'd ever written, in fact. A lengthy tome that was in fact starting to look like the beginning of an epic sci-fi trilogy. But there was a problem.

I had this cool, action-packed alien invasion story going down on this world called Enochia.

I had this neat-o idea about how these events were all tenuously connected back to this ancient world called Earth.

I even knew the broad strokes of what had happened back on poor ol' Earth.

(SPOILER ALERT: It involved world leaders one day sprouting red eyes and launching many, many nukes without warning.)

What I *didn't* have was a totally firm grasp on WHY Earth had been devastated, or WHAT happened next. And boy, did I need to know the answers to those questions.

In fact, I needed to know SO MUCH that, much like a man trying to change a light bulb in a house of loose shelves and squeaky drawers, I chucked the tome of my Enochian work-in-progress aside to go focus on these new, *totally* important sidetracks.

(In my defense, they were oh-so-shiny and exciting.)

I meant to spend an afternoon at the drawing board doing some worldbuilding to satisfy my curiosity.

I ended up writing the four-book Harvesters series (plus two prequel novellas and multiple short stories) instead.

And while it all started with a simple questions (*what would YOU do when the nukes started flying and all the rules went out the window?*), I was pleasantly surprised to find a much more interesting story quickly taking shape before my eyes.

A story about two outcasts finding each other in a world gone horribly sideways. (And, yes, ALSO a story with LOTS of action, bloodthirsty aliens, and explosively snark-tastic shenanigans, too. But mostly the "outcasts" thing.)

And it didn't end there, either.

Because the more I watched Rachel and Jarek come to life struggling against the raknoth and their bleak post-apocalyptic settings in these books, the more I needed to know WHY they were the people they so clearly *were* under the surface.

Why was Jarek so bitter about the world when he so clearly wanted to do good?

Why was Rachel so closed off when her powers allowed her to see the world with a depth that few of us could shake a wizard's staff at?

Sure, I had workable ideas. Broad strokes. Loose, hand-wavy things.

I knew the general flavor of the story pie. I even had a decent idea of what most of the ingredients were. But I didn't have the full recipe.

We'd come full circle. Turtles all the way down.

Again, I found myself needing to know.

So I rolled up my sleeves and went to work, reverse engineering exactly how one ends up with one wise-cracking, sword-slinging, exo-suit-wearing Jarek Slater, and a chop-busting, magic-slinging Rachel Cross to match.

I had a blast finding my answers via the prequel novellas, *Cursed Blood* and *Soldier of Charity*. More importantly, I think you will too.

(And better yet, you can grab 'em both for free.)

All you have to do is go to *lukermitchell.com/red-gambit-signup* to join my mailing list and download your free copies of *Cursed Blood* and *Soldier of Charity* today!

In addition to occasional behind-the-scenes notes like the one above (which was actually adapted from one of my Sunday newsletters), as a member of the list, you'll also get access to free books from all of my other fictional worlds—as well as discounts and short stories you won't find anywhere else.

(Rachel's origin story *Cursed Blood*, for instance, is only available in the box set or to my mailing list readers.)

Sign up at the above link to grab both Harvesters novellas free today, and enjoy!

And if newsletters and email shenanigans aren't your bag, no worries. You can always visit *lukermitchell.com/books* to find the complete list of my published works—and to grab *Hell to Pay* (Book 2) and continue the series today!

Whichever way you go from here, I just want you to know that I really do appreciate you coming along for this ride. I sure hope you've enjoyed it, and here's hoping you enjoy the next one even more! Thanks so much for reading. We'll see you on the other side.

Cheers,
Luke Mitchell

ACKNOWLEDGMENTS

Every time I've been asked what I was going to write for the dedication section of this book (and this has happened a surprising number of times), I've given what could arguably be considered a very selfish answer: I never intended on writing a dedication, because I didn't write this book for someone else. I wrote it for me. I wrote it because I've found a great passion for writing, and I love it so much that I thought I just might try to make a career of it.

So there you have it. This book is dedicated to me—selfish prick that I am!

Joking (or maybe not joking?) aside, what I do have are acknowledgments, and those are quite plentiful!

Firstly, I'd like to thank my steadfast love and light, Marina. She's been described as many things. Genius. Doctor. Beautiful person, inside and out. To me, she is my Puffin, and with her wings at my back, all things are possible. Except maybe actual flight. We're working on it.

My mom, bless her yarn-filled heart, also gets her fair share of credit where dealing with my ever-brooding crap is concerned. And, I suppose, for birthing me at the start of all of this. Good on you, ma. Suffice it to say, you're the best.

To the friends who managed to contain their laughter when I told them I'd dropped out of my fully-funded PhD studies in neuroscience to write science fiction without an iota of certainty I could succeed, thank you as well. Your company on those rare occasions I venture out of my writing cave has been paramount to maintaining what sanity I have left.

To my vigilant editor, Lisa, I thank you a million times for your good judgment and gentle yet unwavering guidance. Without you, this would have been a much different and almost certainly inferior story. On a similar note, a big thank you to the loyal members of my small but fierce ARC team, whose support has been crucial in polishing and launching this book (not to mention in assuring me that this story isn't half bad).

I'd be remiss if I didn't say thanks to my good friend Simon, who kindly took my sad attempt at formatting a paperback and whipped it into lovely shape for those five readers who were insistent on holding a physical copy of this book in their very own hands.

Lastly, I give my thanks to you, the reader who elected to pick my book up from the pile of millions. If I were to decide to follow conventions and actually dedicate this book to anyone, it would be to you. I'm not going to say this book wouldn't have been possible without you. Strictly speaking, I probably would have written it either way. BUT, if not for you and readers like you, no one would have given a crap, and that's a pretty monumental 'but.' Every time you read one of my books, you're helping me to continue writing them, and boy does that make me happy. So thank you for that. Truly.

May your favorite characters always live and your most fantastical adventures never tarnish.

Happy reading,
Luke Mitchell

ABOUT THE AUTHOR

Not a llama. Mostly human.

Luke is a storyteller whose dreams include learning the ways of the Force, becoming a sentient robot, and maybe even one day growing up. Also, lots of zombies... Don't ask.

Oh, and that "growing up" bit? That was a lie.

After studying engineering science at Penn State and neuroengineering at Drexel, Luke finally decided to throw in the towel on building a working Iron Man suit and opted instead to simply make things up and write them down. Boy, is he having more fun now.

When he's not holed up in his writing cave trying to string words together, he can often be found powerlifting, video-gaming, reading, and/or drinking the darkest, most roasty beers he can get his mitts on. Sometimes all at once.

But you know what? That's enough about Luke. He's really not that interesting. Still, if you'd like to say hi to him for whatever reason, he'd probably be glad to hear from you!

Go to **lukermitchell.com/red-gambit-signup** to join the mailing list and grab your free copies of *Soldier of Charity* and the list-exclusive *Cursed Blood*!

Additionally (as you wish)…

Follow me on BookBub for new release alerts
bookbub.com/authors/luke-r-mitchell

Browse the rest of my published titles
lukermitchell.com/books

Join the Patreon team for digital copies of ALL of my work (past, present, and future) — and much more!
patreon.com/lukermitchell

Thank you for reading!

CPSIA information can be obtained
at www.ICGtesting.com
Printed in the USA
LVHW040255230623
750517LV00004B/500